Ghosts of the Missing

ALSO BY

KATHLEEN DONOHOE

Ashes of Fiery Weather

GHOSTS OF THE MISSING

KATHLEEN DONOHOE

Mariner Books
Houghton Mifflin Harcourt
Boston New York 2020

hmhbooks.com

Library of Congress Cataloging-in-Publication Data
Names: Donohoe, Kathleen, author.
Title: Ghosts of the missing / Kathleen Donohoe.
Description: Boston : Houghton Mifflin Harcourt, 2020.
Identifiers: LCCN 2019023912 (print) | LCCN 2019023913 (ebook) |
ISBN 9780544557178 (trade paperback) | ISBN 9780544557185 (ebook)
Subjects: LCSH: Missing children—Fiction. |
GSAFD: Suspense fiction. | Mystery fiction.
Classification: LCC PS3604.O5646 G48 2020 (print) |
LCC PS3604.O5646 (ebook) | DDC 813/.6—dc23
LC record available at https://lccn.loc.gov/2019023912
LC ebook record available at https://lccn.loc.gov/2019023913

Book design by Emily Snyder

Printed in the United States of America
DOC 10 9 8 7 6 5 4 3 2 1

To Travis and Liam
And for Jennifer

Ghosts of the Missing

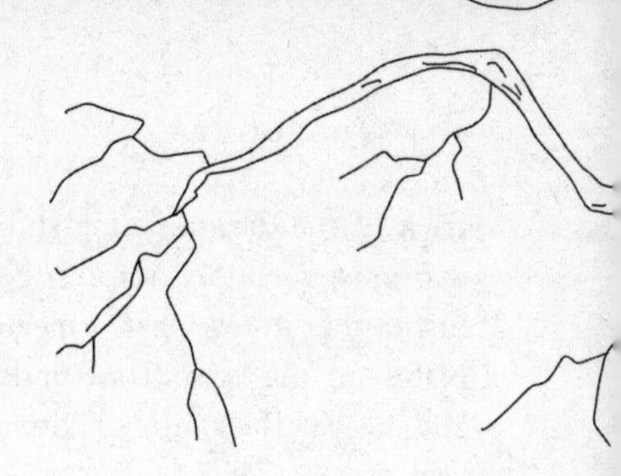

PROLOGUE

The woman was no one, until the bell began to ring.

The boy first saw her at the mountain ash, picking the berries, he believed, that were red and ripe in midautumn, too bitter for any creature but a bird. He was eleven then, and she was grown, near twenty at least. By her clothes and her red hair, unbraided, Cassius Moye placed her as an Irish girl, a servant. Within ten steps, he had forgotten her.

Yet when he passed near the tree again, hurrying to leave the woods before full dark, he heard a bell ringing. Looking up, he saw only a gathering of October stars. The sound persisted. Had he been younger, he might have run. Older, he'd have scoffed. But as it was, he listened carefully, aware that this was a story he would tell forever. As he neared the mountain ash, the sound grew stronger. It was coming from the tree, but he could see no other source.

The next morning at breakfast, Cassius told his mother. His father was already gone to work at Moye Foundry and Ironworks, the business he'd begun with his wife's inheritance, and which had become as prosperous as he'd promised her. Cassius knew his father would not tolerate the story, but he was disappointed when his mother dismissed it as a trick of the darkness. He should not be in the woods at all, and most certainly not at night. Though neither the boy nor his mother knew what it meant, the girl carefully setting the plates on the breakfront understood what Cassius had seen and heard. Back in the kitchen, she repeated what he had said.

One year later, on the twenty-seventh of October 1855, in the big houses along the Hudson River, Irish girls slipped down the narrow staircases that took them from their attic rooms to the plain servants' doors that freed them in the gardens. They met at the front gate of Moye House, and when complete, the gathering walked into the woods. Each held a lit candle in one hand and a small bell in the other, a thumb on the clapper to keep it silent.

The oldest of the servant girls was twenty-two and the youngest no more than twelve. For their first years in America, all they remembered of home was hunger like a claw and their escape on the sea. Often they dreamed that there had been no ship, that they'd crawled across the rough waves of the Atlantic. Cassius's story made them remember Ireland, the feast day of Saint Maren, and how they had petitioned the saint with their prayers when they were children.

After entering the woods, they called up a song in Irish, the first language, the one they rarely spoke. They tied the bells to the branches of the mountain ash, which they called the *crainn níos gasta*, the quicken tree. Four days later, the girls returned. Untied the ribbon. Caught the bell in one hand. In Ireland, the bell had been meant to carry a prayer to the saint. In America, it was a wish.

The woman the boy had seen walked with them. They knew it, though none of them saw her, or knew who she was, or who among them she belonged to. They only sensed the extra footfall, the voice that was not a voice but an echo.

To this day, the woman and the bell haunt the woods. On nights when the wind is not too rough, the chime of the bell can be heard. In bell-speak, it is saying, Who looks for you?

1

ADAIR

March 2010

The children are untethered.

Their parents glide over the frozen surface of Prospect Park Lake, holding kite strings taut from the wind or simple magic. They are writing the names of the children into the ice with the blades of their skates. But the boys and girls, six in all, are drifting up into the storm, their arms outstretched. The sky awaits.

A summer ago, I was sketching this scene on a bench in Prospect Park, the third day of a heat wave that made descending into the subway a trip to a circle of hell. Always, I liked to draw out of the current season, but this, visiting winter in August, had been a deliberate diversion.

A woman parked her stroller and sat beside me as her daughter took off on a scooter. We recognized each other at the same time, and when she smiled and said hello, I returned her greeting through a grimace. A year ago, I had temped at Emily's office.

When I was introduced to her, she said, "Nice to meet you, Adair."

Not "Claire" or "Blair" or "I'm sorry, what?"

Indeed, the whole three months I'd been there, she'd greeted me every morning as she passed by the front desk, where I sat waiting for the phone to ring. When she went out to lunch, she'd ask if I wanted anything. I always declined, not wanting to burden her with an extra cup of coffee, though it was hard to cross the long hours of the afternoon on only the weak coffee in the office kitchen.

This friendliness, intermittent as it was, meant we couldn't politely ignore each other, not while sitting on the same bench. As though it were a chore on a list, Emily initiated small talk.

"You know, I wasn't sure that was you for a minute. I didn't remember your hair as red. Well, reddish, I should say." She smiled. "Did you get highlights? I like it."

I answered slowly, out of practice. It was Sunday afternoon and I hadn't spoken to another person since Friday afternoon when I left work.

"It's brown, really. The red only shows in the sun," I said, reaching up self-consciously to touch the ends. It was getting long again, nearly to my shoulders.

The baby, Hazel, was about to turn one, she told me. Soon she would go back to work full time, and God, was she looking forward to it. I recalled the office with its hospital-green walls and the droning meetings I transcribed, where every voice sounded like a housefly butting against a windowpane.

"That's great," I said.

Emily laughed, and before she could continue her obligatory update, she caught sight of the sketchpad in my lap.

"That's very good," she said.

Her obvious surprise qualified as a backhanded compliment. You can draw? You're an artist? The girl who answered our phones? The girl who spent an entire eight-hour workday shredding our old files? But I was used to the amazement when my temporary coworkers saw me in a new context. It was as if they'd learned the Xerox machine had a lovely singing voice.

"Really, Adair. These are fantastic. Can I—?"

I hesitated before handing my book to her. She studied the sketch and asked if I drew portraits of children. Say yes, she added, because then she would pay me to draw her oldest.

Yes, I answered.

She smiled. Come up with a price, she told me. Then double it.

I saw her only twice more, when I drew her daughter and when I delivered the final portrait. But she emailed me frequently, mostly introductions to this mom or that one, all of whom hired me.

Once Emily was back at work, she had no time for side projects like mentoring talented but rudderless young women she came across in city parks. Her emails grew so brief they were the snail mail equivalent of a postcard ("great!"), and I chided myself for believing that she'd become a friend.

But my business had gotten its start. After a week of trying to think of a clever name, I went with the simple Portraits by Adair. They became a must-have in the neighborhood. A Maclaren stroller. A McCrohan portrait. My surname, easy to spell but tricky out loud, had finally proved an asset. (Crow-what? Hand?)

Then, a year after our meeting in the park, Emily emailed and asked me to draw Hazel, who was now two. Emily and her husband lived in Cobble Hill, four stops on the F train from me. It was nearly four o'clock in the afternoon when I arrived at the door beneath the stoop, as instructed. I rang the doorbell.

Emily answered as I was about to pull my glove off and knock. Her hair was a lighter shade of blond than I remembered, and it was pulled back in a messy bun that on Emily looked stylish. She was tall, too, and I straightened my shoulders as I went into the hallway.

She leaned in as if to hug me, but I put my hand out before she could. Unfazed, she took my hand and squeezed it gently.

"Thank you for coming on short notice. I figured I'd better let you draw Hazel while you still can."

Emily led me into the living room. Hazel was in an armchair, an iPad in her lap. She didn't look up as we came in. When I took a seat on the black couch, Emily offered me tea or coffee and then hesitated.

"I have wine as well?"

When I said wine would be great, she looked so happy that I was glad I hadn't opted for caffeine.

Before departing for the kitchen, she knelt in front of Hazel and gathered the toddler's feet in her hands. "Hazel, love? Adair is here to draw your picture. Remember, like we talked about?"

The little girl glanced up briefly. Emily squeezed her feet and stood up.

"We don't usually allow screen time during the day," she said, "but James had her today and they were at the park for two hours, so she's tired. Willow's on a playdate."

I wanted to tell Emily that I didn't care if Hazel watched cartoons for twelve hours straight, but instead I said, "It's better if she ignores me anyway."

"Hazel is excellent at ignoring adults," Emily said, apparently cheered by the realization that she was not going to have to coax her child into responsiveness. "I told the pediatrician I was worried about her hearing and he laughed at me."

Drawing Willow had set the template for how I worked. I always asked to sketch in person, but not so the children could pose for me. I liked to see what toys they chose and how they looked when they changed expression and what made them do so. This helped me decide where to settle a child. A train or a castle? In the sky or at sea or in space or in the woods or a garden?

Sometimes parents wanted one picture of all their children together, and I obliged, but I did prefer to draw them alone. Collective dreams were more difficult to capture.

On one of my earliest jobs, a four-year-old boy asked me to draw his imaginary friend beside him. No, his mother said wearily. Only you, Max.

When she left the room for a moment, I asked Max what his friend looked like. He whispered the answer, a child who'd always have secrets. When you get the picture back, I told him, look at the moon. I made a shadow of the craters, as though the old man, slightly bent, were standing just out of sight.

"Hazel, do you have any imaginary friends?"

Hazel glanced at me with her lips pursed, shook her head and turned back to the screen. She was more solid than Willow and brown-haired. Had their parents somehow foreseen this, or had the girls simply become their names? I would not have guessed the two were sisters.

Emily came back with a bottle of wine, already opened, and two glasses. She poured, then handed me a glass and set the bottle on the coffee table. It was, I noticed, already half empty. Emily took the iPad and I waited for Hazel to protest, but she stood up, resigned, and meandered over to a basket of toys.

I set the glass down and opened my sketchpad, angling it slightly for privacy. I didn't voluntarily show parents the sketches when I was done, but if asked, I'd acquiesce. The page did unsettle some, since it wasn't a capture of a whole child but drawings of eyes, a hand, a foot, a nose, a smile. The rough drafts of children.

"Why am I drawing her while I can?" I asked. "Are you moving?"

"Maybe. It's not definite yet."

I wasn't surprised. Two kids in an apartment. They were probably *overdue* to move to Long Island or Westchester.

Emily asked how long I'd lived in Brooklyn, and I told her absently that I'd moved here right after college, almost four years ago. I'd had a roommate until recently but now I lived alone, and it was better.

Lots of the mothers talked to me as I worked, either because they felt they had to be good hostesses or because they were uneasy with silence. Maybe it was because they'd spent the day with toddlers and were happy to talk to anyone who could answer in full sentences. When I'd drawn Willow, Emily had sat at her laptop for most of the session, glancing up occasionally to watch.

"How the hell can you afford your own place? No offense," Emily said, "but is it a walk-in closet in somebody's house?"

I smiled. "My landlady's owned her house since the fifties, and she could get a lot more than what she's charging me."

I deliberately let her stand as an elderly widow (she was) who either didn't realize she could easily charge $2,000 a month for the four rooms on the top floor of her brownstone, or refused to, on moral grounds.

I was quite practiced in this sleight of hand, where I left out the parts of the story that would lead to questions. Like that it was my uncle who knew Sarah, and it was he who had called her to see if she would rent to me when I suddenly found myself with no roommate and not nearly enough money to live on my own.

Sarah was a poet who had taught school for twenty-five years, writing when she could find the time. Long ago, she'd decided tenants were too much trouble, but for me she made an exception, as a favor to my uncle but also to support an artist in a city that had turned from haven to burden.

"You studied art in school, right?" Emily asked. "I think I remember you telling me this."

"I did. Art with a minor in art history. I thought maybe I'd work in a museum. I mean, I still might," I said, though it had been almost two years since I'd sent out a résumé.

"An art major," Emily said, amused. "How did your parents feel about it? Willow keeps saying she wants to be an actress, and James keeps telling her that's fine as long as she learns to code."

My pencil faltered on the page but I didn't look up. "My mother was a photographer and my father was an artist too, so—" I stopped, as ever unsure how to describe two careers that had never been realized.

"So you come by it naturally. Well, neither of us has an artistic bone in our body, so I don't know where Willow gets it. I mean, if she has it. She hasn't tried acting yet. We were going to start lessons or one of those theater summer camps, to see if she likes it, but money's going to be tight for a while."

"Because of moving?" I asked.

Emily lifted her wine glass in a toast. "James and I are separating."

"I'm sorry," I said after a startled minute. I looked at Hazel, but she didn't appear to be listening.

Emily shrugged, avoiding my eyes. "James can't pay half the rent here and on a place of his own. We've been talking about it for a month—we're being very civil—but it's about logistics. Nobody tells you that organizing a divorce is like planning a wedding. You know how weddings are supposed to be about beginning a life together but they're really about where you stick the cousins you never see?" Emily said. "It's also plain embarrassing. None of the books say that either. I haven't told any of my friends yet."

I understood then. The wine was prodding her to rehearse the news, and I was the audience.

"I'm sorry," I said again.

Emily sighed. "Are your parents still together?"

I nodded, cursing myself for mentioning *photographer, artist.* This had made them real.

"How long have they been married? Mine celebrated their thirty-ninth few months ago."

For a moment, I panicked. Did everybody have this information at hand?

"They got married, I think, almost two years before I was born," I said.

"James says the girls will be fine. Every kid goes through some childhood trauma. If it's something as normal as divorce, you're lucky. He might be right. For me, it was my brother when he was in high school. Drugs, stealing. He's fine now, but I do have something. You must have something. Everybody does, right?"

She said it absently, not really a question, but I felt claustrophobic. It was like my first weeks of college, with my newly made friends sharing confidences, and me avoiding the personal by directing a question back to them.

The word "orphan" confused people, as if modern medicine had made it an anachronism. I'd have used it, though, if the story I had to tell began with my mother struggling in the ocean, my father swimming out to save her, one riptide taking them both. A fire, and both of them lost while I was saved. Me lifted out of our car, my parents still inside. This last one was born of a dream or a memory, I wasn't sure which, of a time when we were going someplace but in the end did not.

Even two different fatal illnesses would have been easier to grasp. Leukemia and a brain tumor. But I said nothing, unwilling to tell the truth and draw an arrow straight to me.

"A girl in my town went missing when I was twelve," I said.

Emily sat up straighter. "Jesus, really? You've told me where you're from—"

"Culleton, New York. It's about two hours from here. I wasn't born there, but I moved there," I said, as though my parents had chosen it for the cobblestone streets in the historic district or for its literary fame as the birthplace of a famous writer. Forget that I had an ancestor from Ireland there before the place was even named. That we—she—were woven into its myths.

Hazel glanced at me as she rooted through the toy basket, checking to see if I was still watching. She set some Legos on the floor and began snapping them together, up and up but not in a straight line. A builder, then. I went back to sketching.

"Right, right," Emily said. "There's a writers' residence there. A mom in Willow's class was talking about applying."

I'd always known it was possible in writer-choked Brooklyn that somebody would hear my last name and say, Any relation to Michan McCrohan, the poet?

Long before it was Moye House Writers' Colony, it was where Cassius Moye, the writer, was born and lived his whole life, except for the years he'd gone to fight the Civil War.

When I was sixteen, I'd drawn a charcoal of him sitting at his desk, just to break him out of the solemn stare in the daguerreotype that was always published with articles about him. That photograph had been taken shortly before he joined the Union army, a rich man who could have bought his way out of the fight but instead chose to go.

In my sketch, he is neither the young man heading off to war nor the broken man who returned home. This was intentional too. I wanted to take him out of his time. It was possible to be born at precisely the wrong moment. I knew what it was to be caught up in a tide that would take you simply because you were there, then.

In my rendering, Cassius is slouched in his chair, his hands folded on his stomach, his legs outstretched as he gazed out the window, smiling slightly. The picture is framed and hangs on the wall of the study where Cassius wrote.

"When did this happen? How old was she?"

Maybe Emily was glad to change the subject, or maybe she was interested in true crime. My hand ached from gripping the pencil.

"Fifteen years ago, in 1995," I said. "She was almost thirteen."

Almost. A climbing word. A word like hand, outstretched.

"Your age, then," Emily said with something like wonder. "Did you know her?"

"Culleton's not that big," I said, reaching for the wine with my right hand, the pencil dangling from my left. "We were in the same school. The Catholic school."

On my first day at St. Maren's, my uncle had said to me, "Keep your head down and learn what you can, Adair." Michan, tall and sober, his beard a brighter red than his hair. Michan, who patiently corrected those who mispronounced his name. It's Mike-an. Michael, but with an *n*. The mothers dropping off their children turned as he passed by, touching their waists.

I wiped a clammy hand on my jeans.

"That's awful. Do they know what happened? Is it one of those cases where they know who did it and have no evidence?" she asked.

I shook my head. "Her mother said she took both her and her other daughter, who was a baby, into town to go to the Halloween parade. But nobody saw her. Nobody saw her since the day before. There were a lot of strangers in town, though."

Emily's back was to the hallway, but from my vantage point I could see the darkened staircase that led up to the parlor floor. One blue-jeaned leg appeared and then another.

I recalled the age progressions. Rowan Kinnane at fifteen, at twenty-five. Incarnations of the dark-haired, blue-eyed girl who'd been photographed on her front porch on Easter Sunday, 1995. The collar of her green dress was crooked, the pearl button pressed against her throat. She was not wearing her glasses.

The picture appeared on the Missing posters that were stapled to every telephone pole in Culleton throughout that autumn and winter. Yet by the time she vanished in October, she'd grown her bangs out. She'd never worn a dress unless she had to. The wrong girl was being advertised. Each time I passed a poster, I'd touch the photograph as if to sweep her bangs aside with the tip of my finger. Even when her image turned gray and indistinct, worn away by weather, I'd try to fix it.

The Rowan who knelt on Emily's step and peered at me from between the railings of the banister was the twelve-year-old who looked as she had when I last saw her, two days before she disappeared. Her hair was pulled back in two barrettes. She straightened her glasses, the ones with the square frames that our classmates had teased her about.

You don't haunt other people's houses, I thought.

She grinned in the way that had driven her mother a little bit mad.

You don't haunt houses. You haunt people.

I looked away. The wine glass felt heavy in my hand. I cupped the bottom.

"And they never found her. I can't even imagine," Emily said. "Did it ever happen again?"

I drew a rudimentary tree beneath Hazel's hand.

"She was the only one," I said.

How much simpler it would be if another local girl had stepped into the same abyss. Then another and another. The abductor could be decisively declared a stranger, a random child-hunter.

"There were searches, a lot of searches, but no, they never found a thing," I said and then repeated it. "Not a thing."

In the woods behind Moye House there is a chapel. Once, it was the only Catholic church in the area, built to serve the Irish who came to work on the railroad and in the foundry. By the end of the nineteenth century, it had been replaced by a much grander church and the chapel bell was saved for Christmas Eve. But it rang on the morning of the first full day Rowan was gone, in the hope that if she was only lost in the woods or on the mountain, she might hear it and know which way to walk.

If I opened my bedroom window on those first two days, I could hear the volunteers in the woods calling her name so persistently that it seemed impossible she would not answer, if only for some peace.

Hazel stood up and said she wanted to go to her room. We followed her, and as if the change of scenery signaled the end of the subject, Emily moved on.

When I left, it was getting dark and the air smelled of snow. The second glass of wine had made my head fuzzy, but then all I'd eaten that day was a can of Campbell's tomato soup. I didn't cook at all anymore and barely bothered with groceries.

I got off the subway and began to walk the two blocks to my apartment. When the priest approached, his cassock swinging about his ankles, I moved to let him pass on the narrow sidewalk, quick-stepping onto an erupted slab of concrete beside the curb. The damage had been done by the roots of a tree that was long gone, felled by a storm years ago. The priest was almost upon me, and I bowed my head slightly and smoothed a hand over my skirt with a reflexive respect I didn't feel yet couldn't help.

As he was about to reach me, there was a ripple in the air, some slight disturbance, and he became a woman wearing a belted black coat, her hair pale and not cut short, as I'd originally thought, but skimmed back from her face.

She passed me by. I turned around to stare after her, trying to turn her back into a priest, but my vision stayed corrected. After she disappeared around the corner, I continued walking, faster than before, heedless of the icy sidewalk. Whenever this happened, the confusion was intense.

The patient yellow Labrador sitting beside a parking meter is a woman in white who has knelt to fix the buckle on her shoe. The hipster carrying an instrument is a businessman holding a briefcase. A couple walking with a child are only passing each other on the sidewalk, nothing at all between them but her shopping bag.

If there is a word for this phenomenon of turning one thing into another, of mis-seeing, I've never found it. Perhaps it doesn't happen to anybody else. Maybe it's just me. Me and my untrustworthy eyes, green as a cat's.

* * *

It wasn't the cold that woke me.

In Moye House, where I finished growing up, winter leaked around the window frames and the high ceilings drew warmth up, away from us, as we huddled in our beds or walked any one of the hallways or sat at the island in the kitchen, hands wrapped around a warm mug. Old houses are thoughtless, the way the beautiful can be.

But because of Moye House, I had practice for this apartment. Sarah had moved into the brownstone as a bride, and in widowhood shifted her life to the parlor floor, the center of the house. Nights, she turned the thermostat way down, but I was too indebted to complain.

My bed was a nest of quilts and blankets. I'd go shopping for clothes and instead of new jeans or fresh skirts for work, I'd bring home reversible comforters and patchwork quilts. It wasn't the cold. I knew how to be cold. What I didn't know, not really, was how to be warm.

It may have been a siren, already gone in the distance before I opened my eyes. A shout on the street. A dog barking. Or this: if you cannot sleep, it means you are lost in someone else's dream.

The proverb does not say whether lost means a reverie, or if it's lost as in cannot be found, but I imagined a search party calling my name across a dreamscape that veered between the familiar and the foreign. The October woods of Culleton, New York, raining orange and burgundy, and those same woods with licks of flame on the ends of the branches instead of leaves.

I sat up in bed, struggling briefly against the weight of the blankets. The clock said 2:07. I'd stayed up late working on Hazel's sketch, which I liked to do while a visit was still fresh. But now, knowing I'd never get back to sleep, I went to the bookcase in the corner of my room and slipped a sketchbook out from between the novels.

Plenty of other sketchbooks were scattered around my apartment, splayed open on the coffee table, sunk in the folds of the couch. I couldn't stand a cluttered sketchbook, so I went through them quickly. When they were about half full with experiments, false starts and, yes, pieces I was actually satisfied with, I started a new one.

This one with the red cover I tucked away like a child hiding a diary, though there was no one to search for it. I fetched a box of good pencils from my desk. They had been a gift from my uncle on my twenty-fifth birthday. He sent them with a note:

Adair,

Happy quarter century.

Michan

He often phrased my age in words, the way a mother might say her toddler was twenty-seven months instead of two years old. Maybe it was because he was a writer. But unlike the mothers, he wasn't trying to slow time. He liked to give my age more weight.

I set my desk chair in front of the window and began to draw with Repose Gray, a shade with silver overtones, as if I were drawing the scene outside the window. The deserted street had the look of a Hopper painting, heavy with the sense that someone lonely has just left the canvas.

I thought of all the things I could have told Emily, like pointing out the coincidence of a child gone missing in a town famous for a story called "The Lost Girl." Cassius Moye had written many other stories as well as a novel and a play, but it was "The Lost Girl" that he was remembered for.

I could have told Emily that the missing girl had not been particularly prized in town before she vanished.

Rowan Kinnane would not have been the beauty of her generation. Neither was she an athlete or a scholar, on course to be valedictorian of her high school class. She could not sing. When questioned by reporters, those who'd known Rowan described her as quiet, a loner, shy, and awkward. Words for pity.

The parade was not for Halloween but Quicken Day, which existed no place else but Culleton. Rowan had been scheduled to dress in a costume and march, as she'd done for the past seven years. Given her age, it would likely have been the last time. Teenagers never bothered with it.

There was a "homemade costumes" rule that had long been ignored or met with half measures. A crown of cardboard and glue and glitter worn with an older sister's slightly too big princess dress. A sheet cut in half and hemmed into a cape to pair with a store-bought superhero outfit.

But Rowan's mother was the exception. Some wondered if Evelyn was cheating. She didn't look the part of seamstress. She had a full-time job. She probably hadn't learned to sew as a girl. She hadn't had the right kind of mother for it.

Once, Rowan came as Rosie the Riveter. When asked by the reporter for the *Culleton Beacon* how she felt about dressing up as such a good role model for girls, Rowan answered, "She wasn't an actual person."

Rowan hunched her shoulders and was clumsy with the accessories. She kept her eyes on the ground as she walked, the daughter of a beauty with no such promise. She missed it, people said, as though her mother's looks were a train that pulled away without her.

Evelyn.

Evelyn, who said that she drove into town with both Rowan and the baby, Libby, Rowan's half sister, who was eighteen months old. Her husband, Rowan's stepfather, was out of town. The parade was to begin at two o'clock. They got a late start, she admitted, because Rowan had refused to put on her costume. She would go to the party at Moye House afterward, but she would not march. Evelyn gave in, yes, angry but afraid they would miss the parade altogether. She went outside first and got the baby in her car seat. Rowan followed shortly after, climbing into the front seat.

Evelyn parked her car in the back of the municipal lot that served downtown Culleton's main shopping district, a three-block stretch of stores, restaurants and an assortment of other businesses. As she got out of the car, Rowan opened the passenger door and jumped out. As Evelyn began unbuckling Libby from her car seat, Rowan took off across the parking lot. She was wearing jeans and a long-sleeved red shirt with a denim jacket over it. Evelyn claimed Rowan was wearing sneakers, blue with a white stripe, but they would later be found placed neatly by the back door of the house. Her brown hair was pulled back with two mismatched barrettes, holding back her bangs. She was wearing her glasses, of course.

Evelyn called Rowan's name. She said she did. But without looking back, Rowan ducked into the alley between the pharmacy and the bookstore. The alley led directly onto Vine Street, where the children were chaotically gathering for the parade.

Evelyn walked in the parade with Libby, pushing her in

the stroller, and after, she continued on to Moye House. The party was held on the back lawn, an expanse of grass that ended at the steps leading to the thirty-acre grounds, the rose, wildflower and moon gardens, each delineated by a network of flagstone paths and tall hedges. That evening, the temperature was supposed to drop precipitously, but the afternoon was a fall day made to order, making the forecast difficult to fathom.

Only at 6 p.m., as the party broke up, did Evelyn start asking several people if they'd seen Rowan. Nobody had. She drove home, expecting to find Rowan in the living room, slouched in front of the television. But the windows were dark.

Yet Evelyn did not call the police. Instead, she arranged for Libby's regular babysitter to come over, and once the sixteen-year-old arrived, Evelyn left in her car. She peered through the locked gate at the Maple Street playground. She went next to the movie theater. The teenage boy selling tickets shrugged. Evelyn did not demand to see a manager or ask that the theater be searched. She crossed the street and returned to her car and sat for a long time, at least ten minutes according to the ticket seller, before she pulled away.

Next Evelyn parked on Vine Street. First she knocked on the door of the bookstore, even though it was closed. She ducked into Doyle's Pub next door. The crowd was shoulder-to-shoulder, everyone talking through a fog of cigarette smoke. Evelyn elbowed her way through and left by the side door. She didn't ask anyone if they'd seen Rowan.

By 8 p.m., Libby was asleep and the babysitter was watching television in the living room. Evelyn opened the front door and dropped her purse in the hallway. She ran to the kitchen, where she picked up the phone and called the police. It had been six hours, Evelyn said, since she'd last seen her daughter.

Over the first week, the facts were gathered by the police and reported by the press, which had descended on Culleton by midafternoon of October 29, when hours of daylight had failed to find Rowan Kinnane.

On Friday, October 27, the mailman saw Rowan arrive home from school, alone. She had checked the mailbox, peering inside and then putting her hand in and feeling around. He remembered that because he'd thought it was funny. The mailbox was not very deep. It did not swallow letters.

At around 8:30 Friday night, Leo Phelan said, Evelyn called him because the smoke detector in the upstairs hallway was chirping. The house Evelyn rented belonged to Leo's grandmother, long in a nursing home. From the time Evelyn first moved in, a single parent to seven-year-old Rowan, Leo had been the one to come by and shovel the snow or mow the lawn.

After Evelyn had married, her new husband moved in, and by the fall of 1995, they'd bought a new house and planned to move as soon as the renovations were finished.

That night, with Evelyn's husband out of town, it was nineteen-year-old Leo who fetched a ladder from the garage and changed the smoke alarm battery so that it wouldn't keep the baby awake. Rowan, Leo said, had watched him from the doorway of her bedroom.

The lone sighting on Saturday was a classmate who thought she saw Rowan in Byrd's New & Used Books shortly before the parade began. Rowan had not been in costume, and she was carrying a red envelope in her hand. But the boy who lived across the street said he'd watched Evelyn leave for the parade, and only the baby was with her.

No other customers at Byrd's Books saw Rowan go in or leave. Though the post office was on the same block, it closed at noon on Saturdays, including the lobby. The bookstore sighting was dismissed. And so only her mother's word put Rowan in town.

At the beginning of week three, Evelyn, who had talked to the press several times, had been slated to give another interview, but she abruptly canceled it when a story aired claiming that "police sources" had revealed that under questioning, Leo Phelan admitted he had stayed at Evelyn's for a while after fixing her smoke detector. Maybe an hour. No more than two. They were talking, he said. They were friends. She'd been trying to persuade him to go to college. If he was perfectly happy working at Degare Mountain State Park as a groundskeeper, and taking tourists on hikes through the woods, fine, she'd said, but he'd never get promoted without a degree. He'd laughed and said he'd never take a job where he had to wear a tie and sit at a desk all day. That was it, the whole conversation.

Stories in the press, stitched together with "alleged" and "reliable sources," began to tell of a strained mother-daughter relationship, of a girl unhappy with her stepfather and the slew of new rules he'd implemented. Rowan, long the only child of a single mother, had been pushed to the outskirts of a reconfigured family.

Had I recited all of this to Emily, she would have listened avidly. What happened next?, I pictured her saying.

Nothing. After the first volunteer-driven searches, there were three professional searches of Degare Mountain. After the final push, Thanksgiving week, park rangers kept Rowan's Missing poster up in the visitors' center, beside a sign that asked hikers to report any items of clothing they found on the trails. Lost jackets, socks and even shoes were hardly unusual, but if anything looked like it might belong to a twelve-year-old, it should be picked up. Culleton's first snow, a gentle coating in December, brought with it the end of anticipation. Anticipation of Rowan being found, alive or dead.

Regular stories in the press ceased. Brief updates were tucked into the dead space right before the Letters to the Editor page. Around the anniversary of the disappearance, stories were more detailed, but only because they repeated all the facts and theories, often with little differentiation between the two.

As the mystery aged, speculation still allowed for the possibility that Rowan was alive, but this was primarily for sport. Answers were spun out of every possibility without the weight of evidence. Her name itself came to mean the act of vanishing.

Only one thing was generally agreed upon: that by the time the volunteers mobilized in the wintry light of the following sunrise, fueled by donated coffee, they never had any chance of success. Even as the bells of Rosary Chapel rang the Angelus, both as prayer and signal by which the real lost girl might find her way home, it was too late. Rowan Kinnane was already buried in the grave that nobody has yet found.

I drew one curved line, then another, so I had the outline of a bell. The streetlight gave off a poor glow and my hand cast an interfering shadow over the page, things that bothered me when I was trying. But as it was, I didn't tilt the sketchpad. I let the shadow follow.

For nearly fifteen years I'd been drawing versions of this scene. My right hand was my body, moving with assurance as if through a dance it knew well. Not once did I have to flip the pencil upside down to erase, to turn back. When I finished, I tossed the pencil across the room and didn't listen for its landing. The sketch was rough with ragged edges, but nobody but me would see it. Two girls, alone in the woods, wearing masks, fox and hare.

I slipped the sketchbook back into the bookcase. There was a knot in the palm of my hand and my fingers ached. The tip of my nose was cold. I crawled back into bed and was falling asleep, a feeling like teetering on the edge of a cliff, when I felt a grin against my ear.

Over the years, I'd trained myself not to think about her. A deliberate pushing away, the opposite of prayer. Yet when I mentioned her to Emily, used her to deflect attention from my own story, I'd summoned Rowan from wherever she'd gone.

2

CASSIUS MOYE

He saw the Irish girl the morning of the winter fire.

Cold light was beginning to edge over Degare Mountain. He was alone in the front yard of his family's home, a boy of twelve whistling softly for his dog, Archie, who had woken him before dawn looking to go out. Cassius obliged, in keeping with the pledge of responsibility he'd made to his parents when they'd let him keep the terrier, whom he'd found starved and shivering in the woods a year ago.

It was the dead week between Christmas and the new year. Too bitter for snow, their groundskeeper had been grumbling since the holiday. With a growl, Archie ran off, probably on the scent of some small animal who didn't get to sleep away the weather. Cassius pitched his whistle higher, impatient. His toes and his fingertips were numb.

A girl appeared, running from the direction of the house, her skirt hitched in two fists nearly to her knees. Out of plain confusion, Cassius put out an arm as if to snag her by the waist. But she dashed by him and had cleared the front gate and reached the road before Cassius gave chase. He assumed she'd come out of the wild settlement on the banks of the Hudson River, a few miles away. This was where the Irish lived, not only the foundrymen who worked for William Moye, his father, but also those who'd come upstate to dig canals or lay the railroad. The foundry workers were mostly decent men, William Moye often said. Ironwork—bell-casting especially—was a skill that had to be learned, and anyone who didn't wasn't employed for long. Trust was important, and that was the reason the brothers and cousins of employees were brought on to apprentice before outsiders. It was the others who caused trouble.

But the gentlemen who owned the area's estates and the businessmen from the nearby city of Onohedo saw no distinction. They wrote letters to the newspapers decrying the "shantytown" disfiguring the countryside, with its makeshift houses where who knew how many families crowded inside. There were also two boardinghouses where the unmarried men lived, drinking nightly in the first-floor saloons.

The letter writers didn't use the name the Irish had given the settlement, Cullytown. Likely they didn't know it. Cassius had heard it from the groundskeeper, an Irishman himself but one who'd been in America since he was a child. It came from the word for "sleep" in their own language. So, Sleeptown, because it wasn't a place to live but a place to shut their eyes for the hours between shifts. A thief prowling the area would have come from there.

The girl's clothes were dark, and given the lead she had, Cassius could easily have lost her in the predawn dimness. But her pale hair, falling loose down her back, kept her clearly in his sight.

As they neared the foundry, and as Cassius was beginning to truly fall back, the foundry's fire bell rang. Cassius felt it like a punch. This was his father's greatest fear. Fire could take all he'd built in the space of an hour.

The girl stopped and leaned over, her hands on her knees. As he caught up to her, she straightened, turned around. A look of grief.

They were near the entrance to the foundry compound. The fire watch were shouting; men were running farther up the road. The girl continued, walking now. She said nothing as Cassius fell in step with her, both of them breathing harsh bursts of frost. They took the curve in the road, followed the shouts of the men and the smell of smoke.

It was the new church, the Catholic church. Cassius stopped to admire the beauty of the fire. Every window lit with leaping gold, and the steeple was burnished in orange, silhouetted against the sky.

In the spring, before the church was completed, a fire had broken out, but since it began in the late afternoon, it was caught early and the damage was minimal. "Officials Know Nothing of Fire's Cause," the newspaper headline read. Construction continued. And on Christmas Eve, Cassius and his father had stepped outside at midnight to hear the bell ring as the church celebrated its first Mass.

God help us, William Moye said ruefully. William had stayed up in case there was trouble, and Cassius had asked if he could as well. If there was an attack, it would likely be on the church again, or in the shantytown, but as William told Cassius, Moye House itself might be targeted too.

Before, the nearest Catholic church was downriver from the foundry, too far to travel in a single Sunday, so once a month the missionary priest tasked with visiting the small parishes scattered up and down the Hudson came to say Mass. He had approached William Moye about contributing to a church for the foundrymen and their families. More and more Irish were arriving every day, and that meant more churches being built all over the country. Those churches would need bells for their steeples, for the altar. Hand bells for schools and convents.

William agreed. Cassius knew that his father had been motivated by business sense and not kindness. For years, the foundrymen had been asking him to provide decent housing they could afford to rent. A church was a less expensive proposition, William explained to his son. Once built, responsibility for its upkeep would shift to the Catholic diocese of New York. The foundry and its politics would all come to Cassius one day, and William found a lesson to impart about it in nearly everything.

The arsonists, whoever they were, took a lesson from the spring fire and they'd done a more thorough job in December. Darkness gave the flames headway. The church was full of pews, greenery for the season and altar cloths, and the river was frozen, which delayed fighting the flames that much longer.

The sky had turned from purple to gray before the fire was out. All but one wall had collapsed. The bell was scorched black from smoke and flames. Ruined, someone said. Women were crying and a few were praying.

Cassius's throat was raw from the smoke. In the chaos, he'd lost the girl and, alone, he went home.

A week passed. The year 1856 began with a storm fierce enough to halt any plans the Irishmen may have had to avenge the burning of St. Maren's. The snow that fell for a full day and night also trapped Cassius indoors, except for short excursions outside with Archie.

Early in the afternoon, Cassius joined his mother, Maddy,

in her reading parlor, a small, warm room at the front of the house. His father was then meeting with the missionary priest, who asked for a new church to be built on the ruins of the old.

His father did not want further unrest, so he offered instead to clear land in the woods just outside his own property and there he'd build, not a church, but a chapel.

As Cassius came in, his mother asked him to pull the bell for the kitchen. He obliged and sat down heavily in the chair opposite her desk, where she sat writing a letter to her sister.

Maddy set down her pen at the soft knock on the door.

"Come in, Katie."

The girl entered the room. Cassius stared. She wore a white apron over her dress and her hair was hidden beneath a white cap, but it was her. For days after the fire, Cassius had waited for the housekeeper to call out that the good spoons were missing, but she had not, leaving him more confused than ever.

He had tried to describe the girl in his journal, but with each attempt, his memory failed to bring her near enough to see her properly. He'd begun to believe she might have been a waking dream or a ghost, like the redheaded girl in the woods.

But here she was again.

He'd whistled and she ran to him. Now he'd rung a bell and she'd appeared. He was, for a moment, in awe of his power. Then his mother asked the girl to bring her a cup of tea.

"Cassius?" his mother asked. Did he want anything, she meant. He shook his head.

The girl bobbed her head and stepped back in the hall without looking at him.

"She is quicker than a cat," his mother said.

Though speed should be something admirable in a servant, Cassius caught something in his mother's tone. Unease?

"How long has she been here?"

His mother set down her pen. "I've no idea. Mrs. Walsh brings those girls on."

Mrs. Walsh was the housekeeper, head of all the staff.

"Where does she find them?" Cassius asked.

"Find them?" Maddy was amused. "They're hardly rare as gems, Cassius."

The girl entered without knocking, and Maddy nodded at the small table in front of the fire. The girl set the teacup and saucer down, again without looking at him.

Cassius realized then that though she was a wonder to him, he hardly was to her. She had no doubt been in his bedroom, dusting, washing the windows and making his bed. Every morning she may have been the one to come in while he was still sleeping and lay the fire to warm his room.

Who are you? he wanted to ask. How did you know about the fire? Because she had. He had been outside first. The fire bell wasn't ringing. No smoke was rising above the trees. He had smelled only the cold.

After Cassius returned to school, days would pass without him thinking of her, and then he'd see her at work in the house or from a window, lugging a bucket from the water pump in the yard, the strain in her shoulders evident even from a distance. He would turn to see her disappearing around a corner or cresting the stairs. She was a puzzle he returned to when he had time.

His father required him in the foundry office for two hours each day, to learn the recordkeeping and accounts. But the columns of figures were like knives pointed at him. Cassius dreamed of the wider world. He wanted to go to sea and climb mountains beyond Degare, which was vast and challenging, but he'd looked at it every day of his life.

In his free time, he took books from the shelves of their

own library and brought them up to the loft to read. The loft, which overlooked the library, was an alcove, like a box seat in a theater. He could go up there and sink back into the shadows, to be invisible to anyone in the room below.

Cassius took Archie with him on a walk one drizzly Saturday afternoon. The light rain didn't bother him or the dog, who trotted happily beside him.

At Maplecrest, a house owned by a family named Croft, who came only in the summer, Cassius pushed open the gate. He headed around the side of the house to the servants' entrance, a plain wooden door that creaked when he opened it. The first time Cassius had let himself into an empty house, he'd gotten in through a window and had come away with bruised shins. This had prompted him to try the doors first, and to his surprise he'd found that most of the houses had at least one left unlocked.

Whenever he entered a summer house, he marveled at how each room stirred as he passed through it, as though waking from a long sleep. The Crofts' library was smaller than the Moyes', a one-story room, furnished sparingly. There was a desk by the window and a sofa in front of the fireplace. Archie jumped up on the middle cushion and put his head on his paws, settling in for a nap as Cassius browsed the bookshelves. There were many books about travel, which made this collection among the best to pilfer. He always wished to find a way to ask Mr. Croft if he'd done much traveling when he was young. It was hard to imagine the heavy, silent man as an adventurer. Quite probably he lived through reading, something he, Cassius, promised himself he would never do.

He spied a book bound in brown leather, with gold lettering on the spine: *Journey to Alaska: A True Account.*

As Cassius took the book from the shelf, Archie growled.

In his mind, he'd rehearsed the scene where he got caught and then had to tell his father, but he'd imagined it only for the sake of protecting himself from it actually happening.

The Irish girl stood in the doorway. She wore an apron over her gray dress but no cap, and in her hand she held a cloth.

"What are you doing here?" Cassius asked.

She said, with a smile that came and went so fast Cassius would never be quite sure he saw it, "This is how we meet."

The next Saturday, Cassius was at the desk in his father's study, on the second floor of the house, trying to finish a history essay for school, when he saw her going into the woods.

Saturday afternoons, once a month, she cleaned the Crofts' house. Mrs. Croft had asked Cassius's mother for the loan of a girl to run a cloth over the woodwork, because she hated to think of how thick the dust would be when they returned in May.

It had been a week since she'd caught him stealing from the library. He'd asked her not to tell, and she'd tilted her head and said she'd never thought of it, but anyway, nobody would believe her over him.

Abashed after that, he had said little as they walked home together. Did she call it home too? He couldn't bring himself to ask. She was silent, waiting for him not only to say something but to say something specific, he sensed. And because he was afraid of guessing wrong, he retreated into the capsizing shyness that plagued him so at school. He'd hoped for another chance.

Now, Cassius pulled on his shoes, grabbed his coat and went outside. Archie, who had been napping on his bed, followed along. The October afternoon was overcast, which made the foliage seem brighter, like a house at dusk in lamplight.

"Katie," he called, and when she appeared not to hear him, he raised his voice. "Katie!"

But she kept walking. He slowed down so that he was trailing behind her. She stopped at the quicken tree, a few feet away from the foundation of the soon-to-be chapel.

Cassius stood near her, oddly nervous.

"Will people come all the way out to the woods to go to church?" he asked, glad to have thought of something to say.

"It isn't far," she said without looking at him. She rubbed a leaf between two fingers. "This is why they're putting the church here."

It took him a moment to decipher her accent, and then another to figure out what the words meant.

"The tree?" he said, confused.

She nodded. "Do you know what it is?"

Cassius shook his head.

"A quicken tree. A rowan tree. There's one where we lived back in Ireland."

"We?"

"Most of us are from the same place." She turned to look directly at him, and that was when he saw that her eyes were green, dark as moss. He had never seen eyes that color before, and now he understood that this was why he had been unable to describe her. He'd had her wrong.

"What's your real name?"

Belatedly, he realized that Katie was what his mother called all the Irish girls who worked for her.

The corners of her mouth lifted. "Helen," she said.

She began to walk around the tree and Cassius followed.

She picked up fallen berries and put them in her pocket, then held one up for him to see.

"Birds love rowan berries," she said. "This tree is on its own, but there are more up the mountain. A bird dropped a berry and here it grew."

He stepped closer to the tree, interested. "Are they poisonous for us?"

"They're bitter."

"If you're not going to eat them, what are you collecting them for?"

"You can't eat them raw, but you can cook them. Mrs. Walsh gets headaches, and I said I would make a tea for her. She told me to leave off the old nonsense, but it works. She'll see. It's a powerful tree in Ireland. Here you would call it magic."

"I saw a girl here once with red hair," he said, and added hesitantly, "I think she was a ghost."

But Helen didn't laugh. She sat down beneath the tree and gestured for him to do the same.

For over one hundred years, her family, the Dunleavys, had been the keepers of the bell of Saint Maren. In the days when the Catholic religion was outlawed, nuns and priests under siege sought to save the relics of their monasteries and convents from being destroyed. They buried them in graveyards, sank them in riverbeds or gave them to a local family for safekeeping.

The bell was one such relic, the Dunleavys chosen because women in the family were known to have the cure, the ability to heal. For this they were respected, and they were trusted, already the keepers of secrets.

The family hid the bell, and the knowledge of the hiding place was passed from mother to eldest daughter. Every year on the feast day of Saint Maren, the family hung the bell from a branch of the quicken tree, and the women and children prayed to the saint for their intentions. After four days, they hid the bell away again. Then one year a daughter of the family disappeared and the bell along with her. She had run away and sold it for the price of ship's passage, it was said.

But her family believed the daughter had been taken by the *sí*, the fairies.

The night before, they had heard the cry of a fox outside their home. At first light the next morning, the woman of the house had found a hare on the doorstep. Saint Maren, it was said, had a pet of each: the fox warned the saint of danger and the hare carried messages from one world to the next. The mother told her children to stay inside, but the one daughter refused. Neighbors saw her at the quicken tree that day. The quicken tree is a fairy tree, the entrance into the fairies' world. She got too close. Yet no changeling was sent in her place, and this meant she would be returned.

But from then on, this line of the family was cursed. Girls born to the family lived, but the boys died in infancy or not long after. The name of the town where they lived came to be called *baile na n-iníonacha*—Ballyineen, or Daughtertown.

"The woman in the woods is—her?" Cassius asked. "The one who took the bell?" He had heard his mother speak disdainfully of the superstitious Irish. Nonsense, she would say.

"She is a thief or she is what was stolen," Helen said. "Believe what you will, but either way, she's the girl who was lost."

"But why is she here if this happened in Ireland?"

"I'm all that's left of the family. She goes with me."

* * *

After that, Cassius saw Helen most Saturdays. He watched from his bedroom window and when he saw her crossing the back garden, he went after her.

Helen always took off her shoes and left them by the quicken tree. Cassius did the same. Barefoot, they walked through the woods, the leaves crackling under their bare feet. In the beginning, he would step on a stone or a sharp stick and stifle a cry, but soon the pain didn't bother him.

Helen carried a cloth bag over her wrist and collected plants and roots and wildflowers. Some days she was silent, almost unaware of his presence. Cassius walked beside her or wandered ahead, then circled back to find her. Archie stayed with her. Other days she told him stories. She told him how, in everything you sew, you leave a bit of your soul. It was important to leave a hidden mistake so that your soul can escape. She showed him her shawl, how in the back, near the hem, there was a break in the pattern. The way out.

Days when she dusted the bookshelves at the Crofts' house, he asked her questions. She was sixteen, she said, born in winter.

Cassius waited all week for these Saturdays, and halfway through November, he told Helen he was sorry to think that soon snow would fall and they would no longer walk in the woods.

Helen laughed. "And why not?"

"It'll be cold."

"So it will."

She walked farther and Cassius followed. They came to a fallen tree and Helen sat on its trunk.

"There's a soldier in the woods," Helen said.

"A soldier?"

"He's lost," Helen said, "since your war." She turned and

looked over her shoulder; Cassius followed her gaze. He saw nothing but trees.

"What war?" Cassius asked.

Helen looked sideways at him. "Your American war."

"The American Revolution?"

Helen nodded. The soldier had not deserted, as his family had been told. He'd gotten lost in the woods. Sometimes he appeared and would follow them, hoping they'd lead him out.

"You see him?" Cassius asked.

"He was very young," Helen said. "Not much older than I am."

"What was his name?"

She tilted her head and was silent for a long moment. Cassius heard nothing but the rustle and hum of the woods.

"He doesn't say it," Helen said. "You'd think your name would be something you wouldn't forget, but it's been a long time."

The wood of a quicken tree keeps the dead from wandering. In Ireland, she explained, graveyards were often set beside them.

"If we knew where to find his bones, we could lay sticks of the rowan tree beside them. But they'll never be found. It's been too long."

Helen spoiled him for the speech of those who saw only the living. Cassius wrote about their walks in his journal and recorded the things she said. But he felt, in reading over his words, that he could never quite capture what it was like to be beside her.

Once the chapel was completed, a missionary priest added it to his circuit, arriving on the third Sunday of every month. Alongside the railroad men and foundry workers came the women and girls who worked in the big houses. May through

August saw the area's population double as the owners of the summer homes arrived. The priest said two Masses because of the influx, and even then, given the size of the chapel, only those who arrived early got a place inside. The rest listened outside, through the open doorway, along with the men.

The Angelus was only rung on Sundays when the priest came. When Cassius heard the bell ring, he would run to his father's upstairs study to watch the Irish disappear into the woods, a somber parade that belied their reputation. The Irish went to the chapel on the priestless Sundays as well. They were saying the rosary, Helen told him. In fact, they'd named it Rosary Chapel.

When it came time for college, Cassius moved to Manhattan to study business. His mother worried that he might feel lost in such a big city, but he did not. The room he lived in, the sidewalks, the buildings, were all narrow and crowded and perfect. He took his course work like medicine, the price for being there.

For the first two and a half years of the Civil War, Cassius avidly read the newspapers. He was home for the summer in July of 1863, unhappily committed to working in the foundry office, when the government instituted conscription. All men of eligible age must serve.

Cassius defended the principle behind the fight, though not the destruction and certainly not the killing.

At supper one night, when it appeared that the worst was over, he argued with his father and his cousin Augustus, who was visiting, that though he could not condone the riots, and certainly not the killing, it wasn't fair to exempt the wealthy from the war. It was not right that a rich man could pay $300 to send a substitute in his place.

"Join up if you feel that way," Augustus said.

"If I were a poor man, I would see it as an opportunity, and one I'm not going to be offered twice," William said.

"Worth getting killed or maimed over?" Cassius said.

"Yes," his father answered, and Augustus laughed.

Cassius did what he'd always been careful not to. Helen was setting down the plates. He looked at her. She averted her eyes. But later, when he left the parlor where his father and Augustus settled to talk about the business, Helen was waiting in the hallway.

Cassius stopped when he saw her. He said her name, once.

"Before you go to bed, bring him outside, around to our door, off the kitchen," she whispered.

"Who?" Cassius said.

"Him. Your cousin." Helen turned and disappeared into the dining room.

That night, Cassius told Augustus he had something to discuss with him. Augustus, intrigued, followed him out the rear door. Helen was waiting, backlit by a candle in the kitchen.

Augustus looked Helen over, from her face to her feet, and then turned to Cassius.

She is yours and you are sharing her?

Though he didn't say the words out loud, Cassius answered as if he had. "Don't you know me better than that?"

"I do," he said wryly.

Helen spoke then. "You're going to purchase a substitute to fight in the war?"

"How did you know that?" Augustus demanded.

Helen ignored this and said she had someone for him. A good man who would fight well. He, Augustus, could pay this man directly. Save the broker's fee.

Augustus laughed. Cassius stared at her. Who is he? he wanted to ask. But the arrangements were made and Helen had shut the door.

Cassius didn't move immediately. He kept his eyes on the window on the second-floor landing of the servants' stairs. A flicker of light. Then Helen's shadow, and then Helen, holding a candle, climbing up to her room on the fourth floor.

When the window was dark again, Cassius turned to go.

"Be careful," Augustus said.

"She's a friend," Cassius said.

"That's worse."

The next Saturday, Cassius found her sitting beneath the quicken tree, barefoot.

He sat down next to her but left his shoes on.

"Are you going to marry your soldier? Is he a foundryman?" he asked, trying not to sound accusatory. She had never mentioned him.

She twirled a leaf with her thumb and forefinger.

"Yes and yes," Helen said. "If he lives, we'll have the money to start a life."

"Doing what?" he asked, wide-eyed.

"What did you think, Cassius? I'd stay forever in your house, polishing your boots?"

Cassius smiled sadly. That was indeed what he'd thought.

"You told me you'd never marry. Your family is cursed."

"The daughters will live." Helen hugged her knees. "Leave yourself. You'll die if you go work for your father."

Helen's words, her warning, were in his mind the day Cassius enlisted to fight for the Union. He wrote to a college friend, a woman who was a poet and abolitionist, part of the group he had fallen in with at school, that the cause was noble, and in any case, his death would be worth the escape from a life bent over a ledger book. He wrote to her what he would have said to Helen. She had gone, and no one at Moye House knew where.

When the war ended, Cassius returned home. After two years as a prisoner of war, he weighed not much more than he did as a boy of fourteen, and with the bloody lung, as the soldiers had called it. The doctor summoned by his mother from Manhattan properly called it tuberculosis. Though he eventually recovered, his health remained fragile enough to keep him tethered to the family home. The loss of a leg or an arm would have been preferable. Those war injuries at least had more nobility to them.

When his father died, Cassius managed to stand by the grave at the service, leaning on a cane, and though his mother linked her arm through his, he felt her recrimination. You did this. You needed to prove—what? They'd endured two years of worry, believing their only son had died and been buried unnamed. He bowed his head but was not sorry. Though Cassius was unable to travel, the war had given him enough to write about. He wrote in the study upstairs, the one that had been his father's, from which he'd watched the Irish disappear into the woods.

Augustus stepped into the foundry, taking over the position that Cassius had been groomed for. Cassius lived off a percentage of the income, the owner in name only. He and his cousin made this arrangement and let it be. It was no use dwelling on the accident of birth that had seen them born to the wrong fathers.

This, Cassius wrote in a letter to the poet, his college friend. She had been in love with him before the war. To save her embarrassment, he had pretended not to notice. When she came to visit him in the autumn of 1867, she brought her husband with her, a writer, another of that group. The man had been an abolitionist too, arguing the cause in both the college and city newspapers. The pen was the only weapon he'd ever picked up.

Cassius overlooked their pity and hid his bitterness. The two became his only regular visitors. He loaned them the money to start their own press, and when it became modestly successful, they persuaded Cassius to let them publish a collection of his short stories. Why write and put the pages away in a drawer? Though they commissioned a sketch from the daguerreotype of Cassius in uniform, he would become known for the one story that didn't feature a single soldier.

The book was called *The Lost Girl and Other Stories*, and after the title story was reprinted in a popular magazine, the book began to receive attention. By the second year after its publication, those who'd read it were coming to visit the place where the story was set. Many were on weekend trips to other towns in the Hudson Valley, and they decided to take the side trip to what were still the northern outskirts of the city of Onohedo.

They came to Onohedo on the railroad and hired carriages to take them to Moye House. They timed their visits to coincide with the date named in the opening scene, October 27. Yet when they asked for directions to the real tree and for the name of the real girl, they were told that while there was a mountain ash that grew in the woods not far from Moye House, the story itself was invented.

No girl of sixteen had gone picking berries in the woods and vanished. There was no weeks-long search, no quiet giving up. Her mother did not ask for her daughter to be buried beside her if her bones were ever found. No woman appeared twenty years later claiming to be the lost girl, dividing her sisters between a miracle and a lie.

Cassius, surprised by the need people had to see the "real"

place, asserted again and again that though not directly a war story, "The Lost Girl" was inspired by all the men who wondered if they might die and be buried nameless, leaving their families in an agony of limbo. Though his health did not allow him to be part of New York City's literary life, after "The Lost Girl," the community came to him.

The poet and her husband brought company first for weekends and then for longer stays, encouraging them to hone their craft in this mountainside retreat. Many would say they got their best work done at Moye House.

At the end of the autumn of 1876, it was not another writer or an admirer of his book who came to see Cassius, but a woman who would not give her name to the girl who answered the door. Cassius had been sick for a week with a cough that took him back to nights in prison when that was all he heard from the men around him.

But he'd improved. His chest ached but he could take a deep breath. He was not writing at the time, was in between stories, and he expected no company until the weekend. He nodded his permission. A reader, he assumed.

Cassius heard the maid's footsteps on the bare floor of the hall but none behind her, and that was when he knew whom he would see behind her. Helen stepped into the room and waited. Cassius told the girl to go without a glance, and she looked from him to Helen before scurrying off.

He was sitting in front of the fireplace, a quilt over his legs, and was aware of how it gave him the appearance of an old man. Helen came into the room and sat in the chair opposite his, disorienting him for a moment. But of course, she was no longer a servant here.

She showed him the photograph in a locket she wore around her neck. Her son.

"He died?" Cassius asked.

He had, and her husband too, Helen told him. There were two girls as well, and no pension, since her husband had not been killed in the war. His death had come after, unrelated.

"What do you want from me?" Cassius asked.

To live here, Helen replied in a voice that was calm and sure.

"To work—"

But Helen said she would not be a servant again. She could live in the chapel, empty now that a proper church had been built not far from the one that burned all those years ago.

"Let me stay there for a time. I won't bother you or anyone."

Cassius nodded and said she and her daughters could stay as long as they liked.

The three of them took in sewing to support themselves. The wives of the foundrymen began to visit Helen when their children were sick, or when they were themselves. Helen was believed to be a healer.

This information was given to Cassius by his cook, who came to him because she was afraid Helen Dunleavy would poison somebody. Cassius suggested to Helen that she limit her advice to the foundry wives and the servant girls, and not the city people who came to see the mountain ash he had made famous. (The chapel, very near the tree, often startled the story tourists when they came upon it.)

What Cassius also mentioned in his journal was that Helen offered more than folk cures for headaches and fevers. She gave to the living the names of the dead. For those who wanted to know, she offered a vision of what was to come, with a warning that the future is a book whose poems keep rearranging.

3

ADAIR

October 1994

Moye House vanishes in the rain. The writers who come to stay get lost if they arrive out of a storm. The driveway curves like a question mark. Yet even those not relying on maps, those who stop in Culleton to ask for directions, inevitably drive by and keep going until they accept that they've gone too far and must turn back.

Those who missed Moye House on the first pass would find it on the second and come inside confused, insisting that the house had not been there fifteen minutes earlier.

Michan glanced at me in the rearview mirror to register my reaction as he told me this. A stormy sky had chased us all the way from Long Island, but only when we entered the Hudson Valley proper had it begun to rain.

Years later, thinking of that car ride to Moye House, about to be my new home, I'd recall the sound of the windshield wipers moving back and forth, steady and quiet, like a heartbeat. The last time I had been to Culleton it was summertime, I was four years old, and my father was still alive.

Now I was eleven and my mother had been gone a year. Since her death, I'd been living with my grandmother, but two months past the anniversary, as though she'd been marking time, she'd made a case for her own frailty. Her heart, she said. Her hip. It was time for her to move in with her other daughter.

My aunt, my mother's only sister, explained that she could not take me in. She might have claimed that she and her husband couldn't afford both the aging mother and the niece (in spite of the house in Connecticut with the freshwater pool). But she elected to be honest.

I have to think of my own kids, she'd said.

Leaning my head against the car window, I peered outside and saw the world suspended inside a raindrop.

"We won't see it, then," I said.

"I'm part of the place," Michan said. "It doesn't play tricks on me, and it won't play tricks on you."

My uncle slowed for a curve on a leaf-littered road. He was reassuring me that Moye House was now my home too. But "home" for me was only a spelling word to be used in a made-up sentence: We are going home.

Always, at my grandmother's I'd felt like a guest. I tap-tapped on the door of the bedroom where I slept. I set my dishes gently in the sink. Even when my mother was still alive, this was so.

"In books it's always the bachelor uncles who take in orphans," I said.

"We're a dependable lot," Michan said agreeably. "But bachelor? Don't write me off yet."

"Your birthday's in the summer," I said.

"August fifteenth."

This meant he was twenty-seven years old the day he arrived at my grandmother's to assume guardianship. Michan lived on the third floor of Moye House and earned his keep as a handyman, moving about the estate changing lightbulbs, hammering nails that had poked their heads above creaking floorboards, painting rooms, doing whatever was asked. Evenings, he became a resident, writing at a desk by a window that overlooked the moon garden. He was my father's only brother.

My mother used to remind me of his birthday, and together we'd choose a card and mail it to him. She always insisted I get one that said "Uncle" on it. Maybe she knew that her sister and mother would, in the end, not be able to cope, and she wanted Michan to have a drawerful of Hallmarks needling his conscience.

Janus, my mother's best friend in this world, came daily to the hospital to sit at her bedside. The dying often needed permission to leave, he said. Over and over, he had seen it. He advised my grandmother and aunt to tell her to go. Tell her that Adair would be taken care of. But they would not do it, and so he did.

He explained this to me the broiling July afternoon of the funeral, as the mourners milled around the house with paper plates of potato salad and roast beef sandwiches, as though we were all at a picnic that had been gracelessly moved indoors. I retreated to the family room, tossing aside a Raggedy Ann doll to perch on a chair in the corner, where I felt invisible beneath the photo of my mother in a cap and gown. But he found me, Janus did. He told me that he was the one who'd sprung my mother from this life. He promised that he would do the same for me someday.

As if triggered by the thought of the hospital, I began to cough, a lingering symptom of this past summer's long bout of bronchitis. Lungs can feel weak, like legs. I was a veteran of rattling respiratory infections. My doctor spoke of scarring, and I imagined, with each cough, fault lines appearing in my lungs and spreading like cracks across glass.

"I don't care much about my birthday," Michan said, and then added, "We can celebrate yours, if you want."

"Do you know when it is?" I asked.

Michan glanced at me, not using the rearview mirror. "December 19. You were five days overdue. Cathal said they were the longest five days of his life."

I closed my eyes.

When I woke, the front seat was empty and the car doors were closed. My first frantic thought was that Michan had parked the car on the side of the road and walked away.

I shoved open my door and got out to find myself in a small parking lot where there were several other cars. The rain had stopped, but the trees were dripping.

Michan was sitting nearby on a large tree stump, smoking a cigarette. He said nothing when I spotted him. We stared at each other.

His face was altered, as faces are by tears. I averted my gaze and walked over. He shifted to make room for me and I sat beside him. He dropped the cigarette and ground it out.

"Where are we?" I asked.

"Where we were going," he said.

"Moye House?" I glanced around, but there was nothing besides this parking lot, surrounded by trees. In the background, the shadow of a mountain drawn against the sky.

"Are we waiting for it to come back from wherever it goes in the rain?" I asked.

He half smiled. "The house is where it's been since 1840. I think it's 1840. Around then. A parking lot is necessary in the twentieth century, but it wasn't in the nineteenth. It was built here, out of sight of the house."

Michan stood, picked up his cigarette butt and shoved it in the pocket of his jacket.

"No littering," he said. "It's a five-minute walk. I can drive up and let you out, but then you'll have to wait there while I park the car."

"I can walk," I said.

He nodded, and I could tell he approved. I'd already vowed not to be trouble.

From the back seat, I took my schoolbag while Michan got my suitcase out of the trunk. It was the kind on wheels. He snapped the handle up and began walking, pulling it behind him. I followed him up a pitched, narrow path.

In the aftermath of rain, Moye House glimmered, making the fine lines of the stones appear like gray and blue threads, as though the house had not been built but sewn. Two linden trees flanked the stairs that led up to the front door, which was inset so deeply that the shadows often tricked newcomers into thinking there was no door at all.

When the house came into view, Michan kept trudging along, head down, but I paused. In books, old mansions heal the displaced children who are banished to them. Wardrobes are portals to other universes. Treasure maps are discovered in attics. A child exactly the right age to be a playmate emerges from the woodwork. For whatever the children have lost, the house gives something back.

Here was the house where I would live until I joined its ghosts.

Quiet hours ended at five o'clock. Michan and I entered the front hall at just past. A set of stairs curved to the second floor. Voices floated from the room on the right.

"Front parlor," Michan said.

Writers often gathered there before the communal dinner

to talk, and then after dinner, to talk and drink. Michan put a hand on my shoulder, clearly planning to usher me past the open door without stopping. But someone called his name, and he cursed softly and went back to pause at the threshold. From behind him, I peeked into the room.

Two women were sitting on opposite ends of a couch, and a man was settled in the armchair across from them. A third woman was standing. She had a white binder tucked under her arm.

She spoke. "Michan! I was wondering if you had a chance—"

Then she noticed me hovering beside him. She smiled. Later, I decided it was because she was used to being stared at, a woman so pretty that she seemed out of place in everyday life.

"This is Adair," Michan said.

"Welcome, Adair. For some crazy reason, I thought you were coming tomorrow," she said. "It can wait, Michan."

"Evelyn runs the residency office," Michan said. "Nothing would get done without her."

Evelyn rolled her eyes as she strode toward us. "I'm not going to deny that."

As she passed by, she touched my shoulder.

Michan gestured to the three people sitting, calling them "the residents." All of them greeted me with cheery hellos. One of the women laughed and said, "She looks just like you. She could be your daughter."

Then a violent blush flooded her cheeks. The other woman writer, slim with short gray hair, stood up, her hand extended. Reluctantly, I stepped into the room and accepted the handshake. She held on longer than she needed to, not letting go until I tugged deliberately.

Years later, she published an essay about meeting me in

which she claimed that she alone greeted me and offered a touch. She either hadn't seen Evelyn do so or dismissed it.

Michan guided me back into the hallway. Through an open door across the hall, I spied a bookshelf and went over and looked inside the room. The two tall windows were shrouded by sheer curtains. Floor-to-ceiling bookshelves lined the walls. Above one set of shelves, to the right, there was a small balcony with a railing made of the same dark wood.

I loved it immediately. Up there you could pretend you were on a ship. You could pretend you were royalty, or Juliet, bad end and all.

"The library," Michan said.

"No kidding," I said, and he laughed.

A woman called his name again, not Evelyn.

"That's Jorie," Michan said. "Do you remember her at all?"

Jorie Pearse had founded the writers' retreat here, in its current form. I had a flash of silver hair and a sharp, striking face. But no more.

"A little," I said.

"Wait here for me? I'll be right back." Michan turned toward the parlor.

At first I simply breathed, and then my thinking shifted. Perhaps this was not exile after all.

In a corner of the library was a glass-encased table that held photographs of Moye Foundry and one group photo of the workforce. I went over to a rolltop desk in another corner. But it was not a real desk. Beneath a sheet of glass lay a sheet of paper filled with the spidery handwriting of a century ago, which always puzzled me. Were they taught differently? Was it all in the pen?

According to a small placard, this was a letter from Cassius Moye, inviting writer friends in Manhattan to stay "in the country" with him for a time. Through the glass, I touched the words, and then turned my attention to a sculpture that stood between the two tall windows.

It was of a girl about my age. According to the inscription on the pedestal, the statue was a rendition of the girl in the classic short story "The Lost Girl" by Cassius Moye.

The Lost Girl's skirt swirled around her ankles, as though the wind were blowing. One braid was over her shoulder and the other down her back. She was walking. I put a hand on her bare foot, with the unaccountable urge to tell her to turn back. Uneasy, I turned away and crossed the room to the fireplace. Peering inside, I wondered if it worked.

When I saw, or sensed, movement behind me, I straightened. The corner of your eye is a place you can go, if you choose. Enter as quietly as you can to see what has drawn near you. To see if you should run. It came again, slight as a curtain stirring. I saw a flash of green but no more, so I turned my head a fraction. A dark-haired girl was standing beside the desk where I had been a moment ago.

A ghost, visible at this hour when the light was leaving the room? A character in the green book she held in her hand, a girl in words escaped from its pages? The Lost Girl made real and freed from her perch?

I blinked. Yet she was dressed, as I was, in jeans and sneakers. Her long hair was not in braids but held back by two barrettes. The sculpture was in place.

She walked toward me, straightening her glasses. From the hallway, a woman called, "Rowing! Rowing!"

Evelyn, I thought, and I imagined the hallway as a river.

The girl tossed something toward the couch and then ran straight at the wall of books. She veered to a library ladder I hadn't noticed before. Swiftly, she climbed up and vaulted over the railing of the balcony, just as Evelyn put her head in the library.

"Rowan?" she said. And then saw me. "I'm looking for my daughter. Your age? Brown hair?"

With effort, I did not glance up at the loft. I shook my head.

Evelyn sighed hard. "If you see her, tell her I'm looking for her." She glided off to continue her search.

I looked up. Rowan (if I'd heard correctly) was staring down at me in a way that reminded me of myself, studying someone or something so that I might draw it. It's a gaze that first takes apart, separating into lines and shapes and colors, and then reassembles to restore the whole.

"We're cousins," she said.

"I don't have any cousins here," I said.

My cousins were my aunt's children, far away in Connecticut, afraid of me.

"We're fourth cousins," she insisted.

Once upon a time, she told me, there was a woman named Helen who worked as a maid here in Moye House. She was our four-times great-grandmother. Helen was the one who'd come over from Ireland.

"How do you know that?" I asked.

"I just do." She shrugged.

I thought I understood. This was the girl in your class the teacher calls on after three kids have already given the wrong answer and she needs to move on.

"You don't look like you're dying," Rowan said.

"Well, I am," I answered, affronted.

"Nah." She grinned.

From the hallway, her mother called again. Rowan leaped back.

As I waited for her to finish hiding and come down the ladder, I went over to see what she'd tossed away. She'd meant it for me. I knew that much.

All the Woodland Creatures by Winifred Coen, illustrated by Edward Adair.

I looked up, but the girl, Rowan, did not come back in sight. Aggravated by a game I didn't understand, and perhaps emboldened by confusion, I set the book down on the table in front of the fireplace and went up the ladder. Carefully, I climbed over the railing to find an alcove, a reading nook. There was a loveseat and a small table and lamp. But Rowan was not there.

Later, I'd learn about the narrow door in the paneling and the steep stairs behind it that led to the third-floor hallway. I'd learn that dashing away from her mother and hiding was a favorite trick of hers.

I perched on the loveseat, mystified but also strangely excited at this step outside the bounds of the ordinary world. That was the first time Rowan vanished on me. The second time, Rowan did not come back. And I have grown up, waiting for her.

4
EDWARD ADAIR

In the fall of 1878, Edward Adair came to stay at Moye House. An illustrator, he'd been assigned a children's book whose story takes place in and around a forest, and the author insisted Edward join her upstate as she completed the final edits of the book. For Edward, who was twenty-six, a weekend in the country with a companion twenty years his senior did not appeal to him, but he was new to the publishing firm and understood that the assignment was not one he could refuse.

On his second morning upstate, Edward went into the woods alone, the only one of the current guests at Moye House willing to go for a walk on such a wet and chilly morning. He followed the directions to the mountain ash, given by a bored housekeeper. He had read "The Lost Girl" only the evening before and had not met the author yet. He understood that he might not. Cassius Moye didn't always appear for his guests. It depended on his health.

Edward found the tree and did a rudimentary sketch, more out of habit than anything else. Then he headed to the chapel, which interested him far more. He'd heard about the family who had taken up residence in it, a woman and her two daughters, and he thought it was like letting squirrels burrow in your attic. Edward wondered if Mr. Moye knew that if he ever wanted to evict them, he could write a letter to some bishop or other in New York. The building was still a consecrated church. Edward had been raised Catholic. He knew.

The door was open. Cautiously, Edward moved closer until he peered in and saw a woman seated at a table in the middle of the room. She beckoned him in and asked him to close the door.

The room was lit with fractured blue and green light from the stained-glass window. Besides the table where the widow sat, there were two neatly made beds, one in each corner. A single pew was pushed against one wall. The rest had been scavenged years ago, the woman told him. She said her name was Helen, and as he sat at the table with her, he noted that she was quite a bit older than she'd appeared from a distance.

Edward felt a curious excitement. He tried, and failed, to keep his eyes from her daughters. Edward couldn't decide if they were twins. One moment, he'd be certain that theirs was only a sisterly resemblance, reinforced by closeness of age and by the fact that they both wore their black hair in a single braid. The next, one or the other would look directly at him and he would decide, no, they were interchangeable.

They retreated to one of the beds. One picked up a book. The other sat with her hands in her lap. Helen didn't ask to look at his palm or to hold his watch. She stared over his shoulder as she spoke of family members of his who had died, including the grandmother he had never met. Sometimes she gave a name or part of a name. She described sketches of his that had never made it out of his notebook, and the woman he planned to marry.

"You won't," Helen told him. "She'll be the one to go, and you'll be glad."

As Edward fumbled with his wallet, Helen put up a hand

and told him she didn't accept payment. Edward put a bill on the table, declaring that writers sold books, artists sold canvases. What she did was also a gift, and it was not wrong to make a living from it. Helen nodded but neither touched the money nor pressed him to take it back.

Outside, he had not gotten far when he heard his name called.

"Mr. Adair!"

One of the daughters walked toward him, holding his sketchbook. He took it and thanked her. Without answering, she turned to go.

"Wait!" he called to her, stepping closer. "Do you do what your mother does?"

"There are enough people in the world," the girl said. "I don't need to talk to those who've already left it."

"But you can?" Edward asked.

"Don't come back," she said.

"What? Why?"

"We're cursed," she said.

"What you can do isn't a curse."

She stepped closer, into a slant of light from the recently emerged sun. It turned her blue eyes paler, almost made them vanish.

"Imagine that your daughters will live but your sons will die," she said. "Would you want to know?"

"No," Edward said, confused. "If nothing could change it."

"Go," she said.

Edward watched her walk away, her head lowered. He noticed that her feet were bare.

He told no one at Moye House about his experience, but when they gathered in the front parlor in the evening for drinks, he mentioned the chapel, casually, to see if any of the others had been there. But the only talk it generated had to do with Cassius, and how kind he was to house that Irish family.

Back in Manhattan, Edward resumed his life and work, his thoughts returning so often to that morning that it assumed the quality of a dream. More than once he was tempted to take the train back upstate, to go to the chapel and see if the door would be open for him.

But he waited.

When Edward did finally return, he found a growing town where there had been only a boardinghouse, a saloon and little else. Cassius Moye, he learned, had done what his father had always refused to do: he had housing built that the foundry employees could afford to rent. The narrow, one- or two-bedroom homes went up on the site of the old shantytown.

A church, dedicated to the men of Moye Foundry who had died in the Civil War, had been built near the place where the first one had burned a generation ago. The actual footprint was the side yard of the church, and there, in a grotto, was the scorched bell where the statue of Mary might have gone. The bell said nothing; it couldn't.

Edward found a main street with several new businesses, including a much larger general store and a post office. The boardinghouse had become a hotel, catering mostly to the Lost Girl tourists.

St. Maren's was still called the new church in 1880, when Edward Adair married Lucy Dunleavy, the younger of Helen's daughters, though by only minutes. Their three children, two boys and a girl, were baptized there. Not until the death of his second son did Edward understand that his sister-in-law, Clara, had not been speaking of herself—*Would you want to know?*—but of him. Both your sons will die. *Yours,* Edward.

On the day the baby was buried, Edward told her, "I should have said that I wanted to know."

"My mother understood what not to tell," Clara said. "I didn't. You never should have heard it."

Helen had died by then. Edward tried to forgive both her and Clara for not warning him, and he told himself that he would not have been able to do without Lucy. No, instead, he would have tried to change the future. Their first boy had died at three years old in a fall that should not have killed him. A tumble, a bump on the head, a quick kiss, but hours later he was gone. The baby died one day after his difficult birth.

Clara married the man who'd built the housing for the foundry workers. Which had been more important to the development of the town, the new homes or the new church? Edward thought the church, no matter what, would have drawn the foundry workers to settle near it. His brother-in-law declared it was the housing. Without homes, there would have been no church built. They enjoyed arguing about it, a riddle to pass the time, two men from Manhattan who had never thought they'd live in the country.

Clara and her husband had a family that was the inverse of Edward's own, two girls and a boy. When his own daughter began to speak of fortune-telling, some game she'd learned from her cousins involving the mountain ash from the Moye story, Edward forbade her from playing with them. He'd been drinking, and though he regretted it later, he never took the words back. After that, the cousins grew up in the town together, but apart. As time passed, the reason why became less important and, by the next generation, was lost altogether.

In 1884, Culleton was incorporated as a town, officially separating it from Onohedo.

Cassius Moye died a few months later, at the age of forty-one.

A year after his death, the poet and her husband, to whom he had left his house and property, held a celebration of his life and work, not on the anniversary of his death or on his birthday, but the day "The Lost Girl" began.

It became an annual tradition. On October 27, writers gathered at Moye House to read the story aloud and discuss it. Was the woman the missing child? Was there a man in the woods with the children or not? The woman was not the missing girl, but believed she was. The woman was a liar, preying on a grieving family. The return was a dream of the younger sister. It was a manifestation of guilt by the older one. A lesson in faith. A warning that there is a difference between what you can see and what you can know. A play based on the story had a successful run, and the subsequent publicity made the celebration almost as famous as the story itself.

In 1887, the citizens of Culleton held their own celebration in honor of the story that had drawn Helen Dunleavy back to Moye House after the Civil War. Because the story she told inspired what Cassius wrote, though he'd never say so, Helen was able to ask for his help. Not because he owed her a debt; Helen was always clear about that. "The Lost Girl" meant that he would remember her if she returned, and so she had.

During the day there was a picnic with games and competitions. In the evening the men went out to one of the two saloons and the married women congregated in their kitchens. A dance was held in the basement of the church for the younger set, those already done with school but not yet married.

The holiday was said to be the Irish answer to the literary tribute held at Moye House, and evidence of this was what it came to be called: Quicken Day.

5

ADAIR

2010

Spring arrived in the weeks after I drew Hazel's portrait. At my current temp job, I sat near a window. The view was a brick wall, but the sweet air coming in made it easy to pretend that an urban meadow lay behind it.

I'd been hired for a project, and as often happened, I could have finished it in a few days. But after two years of temping, I was an expert in making the job fit the time I'd been hired for—a full week in this case. I got my health insurance through the temp agency, and you had to work consistently to stay covered.

The woman I was sharing the small back office with had been at the company for fifteen years. She was there when I arrived at nine in the morning and there when I left at five. Did her coworkers know she was still working here? Or, if I mentioned her name, would they look confused and say that she'd retired years ago? She and I sat at desks across the room from each other and rarely spoke.

By Friday afternoon, I had finished and was browsing the internet, no longer even pretending to work. At a quarter of five, I decided to check my portraitsbyadair email one last time before seeing the manager for the good-bye-good-luck scene, which I always dreaded because it was awkward pretending that I was sorry to go, that I'd enjoyed my time here.

Dear Ms. McCrohan,

I hope this finds you well. I am writing because I will be staying at Moye House for a residency this October. I'd love to talk with you about your experiences growing up there. If you're interested in speaking with me, I would be pleased to meet for a coffee or a pint sometime soon.

All best,
Ciaran Riordan

This email had a different tone from others I'd received. It did not gush about Michan, praising him or calling out some particular poem as an inspiration.

Michan would have no idea who Ciaran Riordan was. Applicants might like to picture Michan reading their personal statements and reviewing their writing samples, but he was not involved at that level at all. Residents were chosen by a rotating committee that was appointed by the board. I closed my email and shut down the computer, too eager to be gone to even consider the invitation.

I entered the brownstone through the door at the top of the stoop and was beginning to climb the stairs to my apartment when I saw an envelope on the hall table. Leaning over the banister, I read my name on it. Slowly, I turned around and went back. My purse slipped off my shoulder as I picked it up. The note inside was brief:

The brownstone was going on the market. I was welcome to stay until it was sold, and for that time I would live rent-free.

I understood why Sarah, the landlady, had not told me in

person. At Moye House she'd kept to herself, with little interest in socializing with the other writers. After so many years of teaching school, she'd told Michan, she was tired of explaining things. And though the offer to live rent-free was generous, Sarah knew she would not be stuck with me for very long. The brownstone across the street had sold in a week. She might as well have added, P.S.: Start packing.

I hoisted my bag onto my shoulder. Envelope in hand, I headed back up the stairs. Halfway up, where the light from the downstairs hallway vanished, I sat down on the step.

I arrived at Emily's door with Hazel's finished portrait under my arm and then followed Emily into the living room and sat as she went into the kitchen.

She reappeared moments later with a bottle of wine and two glasses. The girls, she said, were both with James, at his new apartment. A one-bedroom. They were going to sleep on the pull-out couch, which at first might seem like an adventure, but by the next visit would spell trouble.

After she'd admired the portrait, she set it down on the coffee table and settled in the chair opposite the couch.

"Friday night! Are you going out later?" Emily asked.

I tucked my hair behind my ears. "I don't see much point."

She laughed. "The point is to meet someone, marry him, have his kids and then split up right when you've achieved some measure of financial security."

"As appealing as that sounds . . . ," I said. "But I won't be in Brooklyn much longer."

Then I explained that I'd been evicted.

Emily was silent for a moment. "I think Vincent from IT said that one of his roommates might be leaving. They have a three-bedroom, so you'd be sharing the common areas. I'm sure they'll want to keep it girl-girl-guy. I can ask him for you."

I shrugged. "Thanks, but I'm done with roommates."

"Well, even a studio around here is going to cost an arm, a leg and all expendable organs. You might get something in Queens," Emily said, but she sounded doubtful and also like she'd suggested I move to Siberia.

I laughed until I started coughing, a deep hack that even to my own ears sounded as if all my bones were rattling.

Emily winced. "That sounds awful, Adair. Have you been to a doctor?"

I shook my head and she frowned. "Go to one of those walk-in clinics. They'll give you a prescription."

Something loosened in my chest, but only metaphorically. Breathing hurt, as though my lungs were made of lead.

"It's only bronchitis," I said.

"Whatever it is, first get some good drugs. Then get in touch with Vincent from IT. At least look at the place."

I had evasion down to an art, but the wine collided with the fever I'd been running for days and I could come up with nothing but the truth. Her advice, the motherliness of it, had the effect of a key in a lock. Hoarsely, I began to talk.

"Do you remember that I told you my last roommate moved out? It's because she didn't want to live with me anymore."

Emily paused, wine glass midway to her lips. After she sipped, she said, "I can't see you blasting loud music in the middle of the night. So let me guess. Her boyfriend made a pass at you, and she blamed you instead of him."

"There was a kind of fight," I said.

I related the whole scene, starting with the night out, a typical Saturday at a local bar. Me, getting out of bed bleary-eyed at 7 a.m. to swallow a pill and leaving the prescription bottle on the bathroom sink, something I'd never once done before in the year and a half I'd been living in that apartment. Medicine did not go in the medicine cabinet. Medicine went in the corner of my sock drawer beneath my black tights.

My roommate had never heard of the drug, so she'd Googled it.

When I woke for the second time, close to noon, and went into the kitchen to make coffee, she was leaning against the sink, her arms crossed hard over her chest. She asked why I was taking this drug. She pronounced it wrong. Was I addicted? I'd nearly laughed, since it wasn't a painkiller.

Emily had lost her look of amusement. She'd been enjoying the distraction my visit allowed. Roommate drama, career uncertainty. Nostalgia for a life where nothing was settled yet. But I'd turned a strange page, and now she was in a story she couldn't follow.

"And what was it for?" she asked uneasily.

"She asked why I was taking a drug for people with AIDS."

"What?" Emily said, leaning forward as though she'd misheard.

"AIDS," I repeated for Emily, the way I'd repeated it that day, louder but with no inflection, no wound.

Then, because I was hungover and badly in need of caffeine, and there was no effective lie anyway, I'd told my roommate, this friend, that I did not have AIDS but I was HIV positive.

"Adair!" Emily said. "Good God, that wasn't very nice."

I cupped my wine glass like a chalice. Why would I have the drug otherwise? But I understood Emily's assumption that it had to be a bizarre lie.

AIDS had fallen out of the headlines long ago, when it became a *chronic but manageable disease.* Like diabetes, they said.

Far fewer people watched the sequel to the crisis, where those of us who were supposed to die instead went on living and living and living.

"In bars sometimes when guys hit on me, I tell them my name is Beatrice Rappaccini." I smiled. "But nobody gets it. A couple have told me I sure don't look Italian, but nobody's ever said, Do you mean you're poisonous?"

Emily sat back. The lines around her eyes seemed to deepen and she pursed her lips. She scanned me up and down, as if the virus were some kind of microbial troll wandering the landscape of my body. See it scaling my rib cage. Prodding my appendix curiously. Picking its way around the sharp bend of my elbow. Napping in my soft tissues. Traveling my blood like a river.

Emily rubbed her forehead. "I don't know much about it. I mean, I remember the stories on the news. It seemed like it was all you heard back then."

Back then. The eighties, she meant. The nineties.

"It's not like that anymore, if you need meds and you take them."

"Oh," she said.

With that flat *oh*, I felt the weight of guilt. All Emily had had on her agenda this evening was to drink her way to a buzz. *Oh, this is too much for a Friday night.*

So I didn't tell Emily of the following weeks when I'd come home from work to find the bathroom reeking of bleach. The smell of chlorine permeated the whole apartment. I started leaving my bedroom window open. After a month of chemicals and long silences, my roommate, whose name was the only one on the lease, told me I had to move. She said, "My parents think you should. And it's not *that*. It's that you lied."

Of course I had not lied. I'd simply said nothing.

Emily looked at me keenly. "And if you don't take the—the meds?"

I half smiled. "You get bronchitis in the middle of summer?"

Emily leaned forward, and for a moment I thought she was going to put her hand on my forehead, but she was only shifting in her seat.

"Look, Adair, you don't have a real job right now," she said. "You don't know where you'll be living by the end of this month. Go home. Hang out at your parents' until you figure it out."

I got that people my own age might assume I'd had wild college years or just terrible luck. But I'd expected Emily would guess.

"My parents are dead," I said gently, as though she'd known them and I was breaking the news.

She recoiled, not from the virus (or the thought of it), but from the scope of the tragedy. "Who raised you?"

"My uncle," I said. "My father's brother lived."

Emily spread her hands wide. Her relief was as sour as the wine on her breath. Perhaps she thought I was scheming to join her family, angling for a place at her dinner table beside her daughters.

"Go home to him, then. Take some time. Things have a way of working themselves out." Emily stood up. "But, listen, I promised I'd get some work done while I have the place to myself. If you change your mind about seeing Vincent's place, let me know."

Back home, I got into bed without bothering to get undressed. I lay on my side, because on my back, it felt like I might suffocate.

If only the future were like a tricky knot that unwound itself upon approach. Surely to see what was coming was a gift, even if it was hints, small reassurances or quick warnings.

But what was it to see the past? To touch memories not your own? Emily, on the day she met James, walking her dog in Central Park. James bending to pet the mutt, exchanging pleased smiles. My father as a boy of nine, in bed at night biting his pillow to keep from crying out with the pain as blood pooled in his joints. My mother turning away the day he explained that what he had—hemophilia—could be managed but never cured. In every case, you already know how the story ends.

6
ELSPETH & BEVIN

On October 27, 1911, the girls of Culleton gathered at dusk wearing wild-animal masks and homemade wings. They wove through the village's narrow streets. They sang:

There was a lady from the mountain
Who she is I do not know
All she wants is gold and silver
All she needs is a nice young man.

The girls, who were neither children nor grown, had a different custom that never appeared in the stories of Quicken Day that were printed yearly in Culleton's newspaper and those of surrounding towns, a perennial local-interest story. Even the women who once had participated themselves didn't give it much thought, until the year of the incident that would give it a name and notoriety.

The autumn evening had a timbre as sharp as glass, an instrument itself that carried the notes of the song for miles. The girls stopped at the rectory, which stood on the corner where Wick and Vine Streets crossed. The younger of the two priests who lived there appeared in the window of the upper parlor to listen, a cumbersome silhouette drawn against the closed curtain. The older priest remained in his bedroom on the far side of the house. Once, he'd had ambition, great hope for his career in the church, but at nearly sixty years old, he would never rise higher than monsignor. Gifted priests were not wasted on small parishes two hours from New York City. He had committed some sin, that much was clear, and the parish guessed it had to do with arrogance, not passion.

The older priest's disinterest protected the girls. Had he known the actual purpose of the march, he would have forbidden it and the girls' mothers would have made them obey, though they would have been sorry to.

As for the younger priest, there were many things he pretended not to see, and this had earned him the trust of his parishioners. Pausing to sing at the rectory, he knew, was deceit disguised as respect.

Most of the girls did indeed end the evening in front of the rectory, as they'd been instructed by their parents to be home before full dark. But nine girls between the ages of thirteen and fifteen followed the road out of town, walking more than a mile before they saw the windows of Moye House. They passed by the main gate and then followed the Chapel Road into the woods. The leaves crackled beneath their feet. The moon was halved in a field of stars. They passed the hibernating Rosary Chapel, not stopping until they reached the mountain ash. In October, its ripe berries gleamed red.

The oldest girl laid an ivy wreath beneath the tree in memory of Helen Dunleavy, the Irishwoman who had seen the dead and healed the living. Each girl walked around the tree once and then stopped, closed her eyes and asked a question. After each of the girls had taken a turn, they took bells from their pockets. The bells, small, sweet-toned, were topped by a circle exactly the right size to pull a ribbon through, and each of the girls had done so. They tied the bells to the branches of the tree.

In nine days, the questions they asked would be answered in a dream. They all knew women—mothers and aunts and grandmothers—who swore they'd seen the house that they would one day live in, the names of their future husbands, the faces of their children.

On November 5, they would return and collect the bells, putting them safely away.

Ritual done, the girls turned and left, chatting and laughing, the pretense of solemnity over. Many carried their masks tucked beneath their arms.

Elspeth lingered to let them pull ahead so that she could enjoy a quiet walk out of the woods. She had never bothered with the bells before, and she had gone only out of curiosity. Bevin walked in the opposite direction, over to the tree. She reached up and shook a low-hanging branch, and Elspeth turned.

The others had ignored both of them all evening, as they did in school, except perhaps to briefly wonder why they had even come. Though Bevin had not considered it, Elspeth realized that here in the woods, on this night at least, they should have been revered. They were both Helen's great-granddaughters.

Though distant cousins, Elspeth and Bevin had barely ever spoken. Elspeth was fourteen, younger by a year than her classmates because she had been pushed ahead a grade at her mother's insistence. The nuns who taught at the school agreed only because it meant they would be rid of Elspeth sooner. She wasn't strident in class, but consistently correct.

Bevin, though, was frequently reprimanded for gazing out the window.

"I would say she was lost in her own thoughts," one of the nuns once said of Bevin, "but I doubt she has any."

Bevin, how are the clouds today? her grandfather Edward sometimes teased.

Bevin had never gone into the woods on this night before either, warned away by her mother, who said it was courting trouble. She had not asked permission to go on this night but had simply followed the others, deciding it would be worth the punishment. Her question: if I have sons, will they die like my brother?

Bevin plucked a berry off the tree. She turned to Elspeth, holding the berry between her thumb and forefinger.

"My grandmother used to say there's nothing as red as a quicken berry."

Blood, Elspeth thought, but she only shrugged.

"I wouldn't eat that if I were you," Elspeth said.

"Granny used to make a tea out of them," Bevin said. "She was Lucy."

She gave the name, aware, of course, that Elspeth's grandmother was Clara, Lucy's twin sister.

But Elspeth ignored the reminder of who they were to each other.

"They're not poisonous if they're cooked. But raw, I think they are."

Bevin's hand fluttered and the berry reappeared in her palm. "I wasn't going to eat it anyway." She put the berry in her coat pocket. "Witches are afraid of quicken trees."

Elspeth was about to say there was no such thing as witches in 1911, but she suspected Bevin wanted to argue in favor of this, so she started walking instead. Bevin followed.

The others had to be well out of the woods already. Bevin began to sing softly. Her voice had a throatiness to it that was absent when she spoke. She was often asked to sing at funerals and weddings.

A bell began to ring, a bell with a far more resonant tone than the little bells left on the tree. Both girls stopped walking.

"What is that?" Elspeth asked.

"The chapel?" Bevin said uncertainly.

Elspeth shook her head. The chapel bell rang only on Christmas morning. The doors were kept locked, and though it was possible someone had broken in and climbed up to the bell gable, this ringing was much too faint.

Then they heard a voice calling, woman or girl, they couldn't tell. Neither could they make out what she was saying.

"That's Mabel Gerity," Elspeth said.

Mabel was a patient tormentor. Hanging back after the others had gone so she could creep up behind them and scare them was the sort of thing she would do.

Then the wind changed direction, and it turned from brisk to biting cold. Snow began to fall. Elspeth saw the flakes alight on Bevin's dark hair, and she felt them on her own forehead and cheeks. Mabel could not have made the season change.

"Someone's coming," Bevin said.

"Yes," Elspeth whispered.

Bevin turned to the left and Elspeth to the right. Their shoulders touched.

They heard, then, dozens of footsteps. Both Elspeth and Bevin later said that they waited for a line of people to appear, moving steadily through the woods. But the two girls saw nothing but the trees, unmoving. That the sound was disconnected from its source, Bevin would say, was more frightening than if a corps of ghosts had appeared. The bell never stopped ringing.

The footsteps vanished as abruptly as they had begun. The

snowflakes turned back to falling leaves. Bevin moved first. She turned left, then right, then all the way around until she was facing Elspeth.

"Who were they?" Bevin whispered.

She expected Elspeth to snap at her, but Elspeth simply said, "I don't know."

And with this, Bevin knew it had been real.

Elspeth, for her part, would admit that her instinctive response to Bevin's question was indeed aggravation. How was she supposed to know? But she was exhausted, as if they'd both been running for miles.

Though the temperature was now back to autumn, Elspeth was shivering.

They put their masks back on. Bevin and Elspeth, fox and hare, about to be forever linked in Culleton's history.

Together they walked out of the woods, their shoulders touching. They passed Moye House, the gold from its windows the only light in either direction.

Only when they reached town did they remove the masks. There, in front of the rectory, they stared at each other briefly before turning away and heading toward their homes.

Alone, Bevin might not have been believed. It was Elspeth's reluctant corroboration that gave the tale its weight. Elspeth would have kept it to herself, a secret to revisit, to ponder, but Bevin took to the attention.

The story spread, and many believed it, because the two who told it were descended from a woman who had herself seen ghosts. Others declared what the girls had inherited was a penchant for lying. A short article about the incident appeared in the newspaper, its tone amused and gently mocking.

Other girls began to claim that, even if they hadn't seen or heard anything themselves, they'd sensed something strange in the woods. They had been scared too, and they'd hurried home, nearly running by the end.

They didn't, Elspeth said scornfully.

You don't know that, Bevin answered.

On November 5, Elspeth and Bevin went together to collect the bells from the quicken tree. For almost an hour, they waited for the others at the end of Chapel Road.

Elspeth suddenly began to walk, and Bevin followed. They reached the tree and silently began to untie the bells from the branches.

"There's no way of knowing who these belong to, is there?" Elspeth asked.

Bevin shook her head. They both put the bells they took down in their pockets.

Elspeth soon refused to speak of that night at all, but Bevin brought the ghost seekers into the woods to show them the place where the two of them had been standing.

The older priest, angry at the attention brought to the parish, forbade the procession the next year. Several girls went anyway, slipping out of their houses while their parents slept and creeping into the woods with Bevin leading the way. There were no bells, no singing and no Elspeth with her frown and credibility. The woods remained silent.

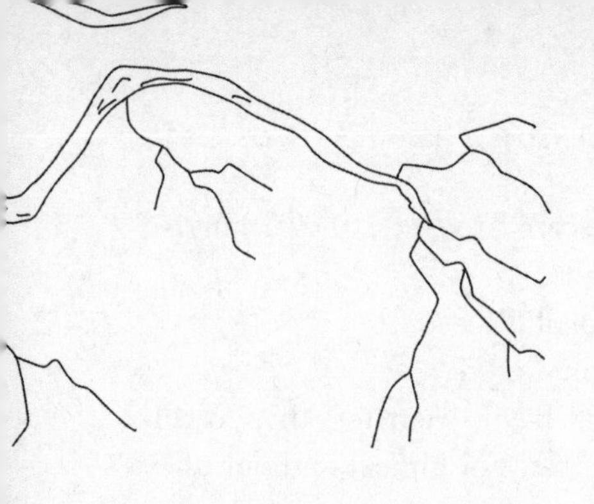

7

ADAIR

2010

I dreamed in stories.

When I was in the hospital fighting summer pneumonia, the fever pulled me into the one about our family.

Culleton had known for a century that my family was cursed. Boys die. Girls live. At least this was how they put it before the disease was called by its proper name: hemophilia. From the Greek: *haima* = blood + *philia* = to love. Though "to love," in this context, is interpreted as "tendency to." The blood doesn't clot properly. Tendency to bleed. Women are carriers. Their sons get the disease but their daughters don't.

Helen Dunleavy brought the broken gene over from Ireland.

Of Helen's daughters, Clara was either not a carrier or very lucky, because the disease did not appear in her family, but Lucy was, and it devastated her family with the loss of her two sons.

The diagnosis had been missed then, and whether it should not have been is an open question. One boy died in a fall that had not seemed serious. The child might have looked fine while hemorrhaging internally. Even if the symptoms had somehow come together for the local doctor, nothing could have been done to save him. The other boy died as an infant, hardly unusual for the time. Yet infants with hemophilia can die of birth trauma that is not typically fatal.

Lucy's daughter also lost a son, leaving her with one daughter, Bevin, who would have one girl herself, and then no more children. And so a generation passed without the disease appearing. Lucy–Anna–Bevin–Cecilia, carriers all.

When my grandparents Darragh and Cecilia married, they were aware of the old superstition but did not comprehend its danger, until their two-year-old son was diagnosed with hemophilia. Five years later, they decided to have another child. They needed a girl. A daughter's blood would clot.

Both their sons, Cathal and Michan, grew up learning how to manage their illness. Their parents' devastation was tempered by the knowledge that their sons would not face the dire prognoses of earlier eras. Factor VIII was a blood product manufactured as a powdered concentrate that caused blood to clot. Instead of whole-blood transfusions to treat bad bleeds and lives tied to the emergency room, hemophiliacs could self-treat at home.

Cecilia had prayed and prayed and donated what money she could to Saint Thomas Garnet, patron saint of blood disorders, and he had answered her. Hemophilia was not cured, but it was far less likely to be fatal. Hepatitis C, which both boys had contracted from their treatments, as had most hemophiliacs, she and Darragh chose not to think about. The threat was not immediate, and without blood transfusions, surely one of her sons' bleeds would have killed them. Future liver damage was the tradeoff, the thing to worry about if and when the time came.

The summer after Cathal graduated from college, Jorie Pearse asked him if he would teach a drawing class at Moye House. It could be held outside on the grounds in good weather, and on rainy days in the old carriage house, which she'd been meaning to clean out anyway.

When Cathal told her he'd never taught before, Jorie told him that making a living as an artist was going to be difficult unless he found a rich old woman to support him, and she was not available, considering that she had her hands full with Moye House. He would probably have to turn to teaching at some point. Might as well start with students who would not be demanding, as they'd be mostly widows, looking for an afternoon of company.

The class, advertised in Culleton, sold out so quickly that Cathal agreed to teach another. Several students in both classes were his own age, or close. When Cathal teased Jorie about getting it wrong, she told him crisply that it would have been a different story—the one she told of a post-fifty student body—if she hadn't published his picture with the course description.

One of the women in the class was nineteen. Her name was Lissa—just Lissa, not short for anything—and she was a photographer. She wanted to learn to draw, she told him, to sharpen her eye.

They married in 1982, when he was twenty-three and she was twenty-one. Far too young, both sets of parents said, but neither of them cared. Their daughter was born the following year.

If "gay cancer," or GRID (gay-related immune deficiency), registered at all for Cathal, the newlywed, or Michan, the college student, it was no more than a puzzling story on the news. Soon it had a new acronym. Soon it was a disease that not only gay men got, but also drug users who shared needles. The human immunodeficiency virus destroyed the immune system.

Picture a castle where the moat has evaporated, the knights have all gone and there is no one left to slay the dragon.

The nation's blood supply was full of HIV. Of course it was.

I've tried to imagine not knowing this. I have, but it's like the surprise ending of a movie that was in front of your eyes the whole time. If you watch the movie again, every clue is a shout. Of course hemophiliacs were going to get AIDS, exposed as they were to the blood of thousands through their medication.

Three doctors told my mother, Lissa, that she was getting sick because of stress. She was run-down. She needed to relax. Being a mother and attending graduate school were too much for her. No one thought of AIDS because women didn't get AIDS. Then a fourth doctor asked if she'd ever had a blood transfusion. No, she said; blood transfusions were her husband's thing. She understood from the expression on the doctor's face that the rumors they'd begun to hear from the hemophiliac community were not panic over *isolated cases.*

I picture Darragh and Cecilia, my grandparents, lying beside each other in the dark at night, trying to both be alive and be alive knowing that their entire family was going to die.

Not long after my father died, my mother retreated to her childhood home on Long Island with me. Cecilia had died in her sleep by then. Possibly broken-heart syndrome, my grandfather had said; it was a real phenomenon, thought to be caused by stress and grief. I've wondered if he believed it, or if he was trying to make one death make sense.

The night of my father's funeral, Michan got in his car and drove to the town of Culleton. On their childhood visits to Moye House, he and Cathal loved that Jorie Pearse let them have the run of the place, never treating them as invalids, never even flinching when they slid down the banister of the front staircase or played tag in the garden. She was not happy to catch them climbing over the railing of the loft that overlooked the library and making their tremulous way along its outside. If they fell—never mind a bad bleed, internal or external—death would come from a broken neck or cracked skull.

Michan arrived out of the rain after midnight in a drenched black suit.

One of the residents let him in and then called Jorie on the phone to come down. Even in this situation, I guessed, the thought of running up the stairs, it was unthinkable to breach the third floor where Jorie lived.

Jorie asked the confused writers to please leave the parlor, where they'd been gathered around the fireplace. One of them had gotten a fire going. The glasses they'd been drinking from sat abandoned on the side table, and the firelight lit the bourbon, turning them into amber candles.

When they'd gone, Jorie led Michan into the room, where he sank to his knees.

"I'm immortal," he said.

Jorie touched his red hair, so like his father's.

"You can't possibly be," she said.

"I've been tested and tested. I don't have it. I can't die," he said. "My whole life I've been told I could bleed to death from a fall, but it's never been true."

"Michan." Though he was over six feet tall, Jorie pulled him up and guided him to a chair.

She put her face near his so he could not look away.

"You will die of AIDS. You will."

"Listen to me. Please." Michan shook his head. "I am immortal."

Jorie lay her hand against her cheek.

"Stay here forever, then."

He did. Jorie gave him a room on the third floor, down the hall from her own, and she gave him a job. He drove the shuttle van. He repaired sinks and splintered steps. He did grounds work, mostly raking leaves and performing other easy tasks that the landscapers gave him.

Michan also began writing poems again, a pursuit begun in college, one he was too embarrassed to tell his family about. He had abandoned writing, though, lost it in the terror of his brother's last months and then his death. Renewed at Moye House, Michan left his poems on Jorie's desk, the sheets of paper folded and unsigned. Jorie made comments and edits and suggested books for him to read. She left the pages right where he had, for him to collect.

If Michan could have kept my HIV status a secret, he might have considered it, though he was not entirely sure of the ethics. But the question was moot, because Culleton knew what had happened to the McCrohan family. Each loss had been thoroughly and sympathetically reported in the *Culleton Beacon.*

When Michan tried to enroll me in the public school, the principal told him that they had to consult with doctors and the parents of the children who would be my classmates. Homeschooling was suggested. Michan turned to the Catholic school.

Sister Regina, the principal of St. Maren's, declared that Adair McCrohan would be admitted. All necessary precautions would be taken, but she would be allowed in. Monsignor Fitzgerald let it be known that he would not overrule Sister Regina, less on moral grounds and more because he did not have the energy for a fight with the nun. He did, however, make it clear that only she would be accountable, should anything happen.

Yet as fierce as Sister Regina was, she could not make my classmates step aside and open the circle when I came near. Rowan was the only one who patted the bench beside her at the lunch tables. She didn't avert her eyes when we passed each other in the hallways.

For so long, I had expected to join the dead. I dreamed of my uncle and myself, two relatives who would have seen each other only on holidays, together surviving the plagues of history. The black death of the Middle Ages, smallpox and diphtheria. Influenza and polio and tuberculosis.

There we are, me sitting up in a feather bed one morning, healed of noxious blisters, a swelling throat, limb paralysis and sticky, bloody lungs. Michan, in a chair beside me, unscathed. We stare at each other as he wishes I were his brother, and I want only my parents.

I dream of the two of us in a burning forest from a fairy tale full of eyes and back-throated growls. The wind is a hiss. Sometimes I'm grown but Michan is still a young man, and other times I'm small but his red hair is tinged with white. We can see the smoke and hear the flames and we are always running. When I'm a child, I reach for his hand, and when he is older he is reaching for mine. Neither will leave the other alone. The smoke thins. The roar of the flames ceases and we stop, and when we stop, I have his hand or he has mine and the forest is ash and we are alive but everyone we love is dead.

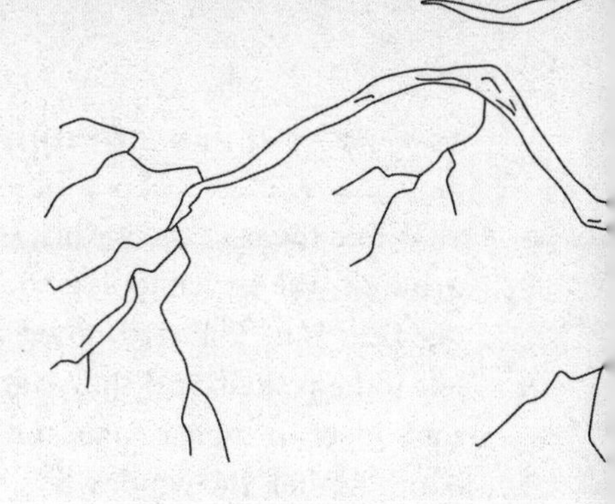

8
JORIE PEARSE

Quicken Day might have remained an antique holiday, a footnote in Culleton's history, if not for the fact that Moye House was sold in the spring of 1946. For a decade it had been vacant, the façade aging, the garden growing toward the woods. The empty house became an illicit drinking spot for the more daring high schoolers.

The daughter of the poet and the writer had abandoned the property because she could no longer afford the upkeep. As a child, she'd seen her parents forgo their own work in service to the estate and those who came to stay, trapped by their good deed in publishing *The Lost Girl and Other Stories.* They could not have known that they'd lose their own names to it. In October, when Cassius's grave was heaped with marigolds, she would steal a few bouquets and arrange them on her parents' graves, which lay in sight of the Moye family plot.

When the news broke that the house had finally been sold, the assumption was that the buyer intended to turn it into a hotel. Culleton had its own stop on the railroad, making it ideal for those who wanted neither city life nor suburbia. A train ride into Manhattan took about two hours. The town's literary history and its proximity to Degare Mountain State Park were additional draws.

While the necessary work was being done on the house and grounds, the buyer took a room on the top floor of the Falling Leaf Inn. The staff noted the addresses on the letters she left to be posted, and they watched her when she sat down to eat supper in their restaurant. They began saving the corner booth for her, the windowless one, best for privacy. She always brought along something to read while she ate. No company ever joined her.

Jorie Pearse made for an unlikely hotelier. She spent her first weeks in Culleton riding around town on the red bicycle she bought from the shop on Vine Street. She answered questions about her life without elaborating. Thank you for the information about Mass on Sundays, but she was not Catholic. She didn't need directions to the Episcopal church either, or any religious establishment.

She was thirty years old, though from a distance she was often mistaken for a girl, partly because she favored loose clothes and partly because she wore her hair short, over her ears but well above her shoulders.

When she went to the barber in Culleton to get her hair trimmed, he asked if she was sure, as though he thought her hair a mistake she was beginning to correct.

She told him she was quite sure. "There are two reasons. The first is that I should have been a flapper, but I was a baby then. Some of us are born in the wrong era. Second, if I wear it long, I'm distractingly beautiful."

The barber laughed then, and every time he told the story.

The rumor that Jorie had been widowed by the war persisted until it became a fact. Eventually she volunteered to the bartender at the Falling Leaf, where she had one cocktail every night after dinner, that there was no late husband, early husband or right-on-time husband. She was a rich daughter, not a rich widow.

Not until she paid a visit to the library one Saturday afternoon late in November did Jorie reveal that she was putting together an anthology of stories that had been written at Moye House. She had seven already, she told the librarian, and was hoping for at least three more. The librarian said they did not keep any records of writers who had stayed "up the hill" over the years. Then she went back to steadily stamping newly arrived books. Jorie thanked her (or, rather, the part in her steely hair) and set off to see what she could find on her own.

After scanning the sole Local History shelf, she brought her selection to the front desk, only to be told that in order to get a library card, she needed a piece of mail with her address on it, and, no, a hotel address wouldn't suffice. Jorie put the book back on the shelf and left. A man was shoveling the sidewalk in front of the store next to the library. Several inches of snow had fallen the night before, an unusually early storm, she was assured by a waitress in the Falling Leaf's restaurant. "Excuse me," she said, "do you live in town?"

When he turned, she saw that he was younger than she'd thought.

Darragh McCrohan, who was eighteen, looked over his shoulder, but the sidewalk was empty. He'd watched her go into the library and slowed his pace, normally rapid, since the quicker he finished one spot, the sooner he could move on to the next. He had fierce competition from boys still in high school who went out in pairs. They had to split the money but could get to twice as many houses. Before the war, Darragh and his brother had been such a team. Now that he was solo, Darragh stuck to downtown, hitting the stores whose owners were old men and those who had already cleared their driveways at home and were glad of the break.

The chance to get a close look at the woman who bought Moye House was worth losing a few bucks. But he had never expected to talk to her. His face was frozen, making it hard to form the words.

"Yeah," he said. "My whole life."

"Do you have a library card?" Jorie asked. "I want to take out a book, but I'm not a resident yet."

He shook his head. "I have overdue books. Once the fine is over two dollars, you're not allowed to take out new stuff."

He had a strange laziness when it came to returning the books he borrowed. Even the ones he didn't much like he had trouble surrendering.

Jorie stepped closer, tilting her head to look up at him, and Darragh lost track of his sentences. He had heard the barber repeat her remark about long hair making her beautiful, and he'd taken it as a plain woman's joke. But now he saw that she had not been kidding.

"I'll have to find another solution, then," she said. "It's called *A History of Culleton, New York*. It won't be found in a bookstore. Maybe I should borrow it without asking."

"Long as you get it back in fifty years, nobody'll notice."

Jorie laughed. "Maybe I will, then. If you hear it turns up missing, well, we never spoke."

She turned to go, walking carefully in her regular shoes with a little heel. Maybe she lived somewhere warm most of the year and didn't own a pair of snow boots.

Later, after he'd shoveled in front of every store that was open, Darragh returned to the library. The librarian glared at him as he went in.

"Ten minutes until closing," she announced.

Darragh found his way to Local History. There he found *A History of Culleton, New York*. That the woman had not, in fact, made off with it disappointed him, which in turn surprised him. Why should he care what some rich woman was up to?

The book's binding was black with gold stamping, and the author's name wasn't familiar. Darragh wondered why anyone, if they were going to write a book, would pick Culleton for a topic. Wondering if the author had explained his reason in the introduction, Darragh took the book down from the shelf. He plucked what he'd thought was an abandoned bookmark from a spot halfway through and found himself holding a pale yellow card with a name and address on it in cursive script. The address was in New York City, but Darragh barely noted it.

Marjorie Moye Pearse.

"Attention, patrons, the library is closing!" the librarian called. "You can't check anything out, Darragh McCrohan! You're on the list."

He put the card in his pocket and stuck the book back on the shelf.

Darragh memorized every word on the card. He dreamed of approaching Jorie Pearse in town, crossing the street to speak to her, handing her the pair of snow boots he'd bought for her. That he had no money to buy her boots didn't stop him from trying to guess her size.

About two weeks after he found the card, Darragh was riding his bike home from Magee's, where he played the button accordion in the Saturday-evening *seisiún*, and though it was a deeply cold night, just a week out from Christmas, he turned his bike off the straight route home, an unplanned detour. The clear night had turned cloudy, hiding the moon.

Darragh stopped his bike outside the front gate of Moye House.

He and his older brother were eleven and twelve when they began coming here at night, leaving the house before their father came home from the bar. If he wasn't drunk enough to pass out, he might drag them from their beds to shout at them for leaving dishes in the sink or their schoolbooks on the kitchen table. Sometimes he called out for his wife, their mother, though she'd been dead three years by then.

Later, in high school, they'd buy beer and drink it in the old chapel. It was always the same crew, him and his brother and four or five of their friends. Sometimes a couple of girls tagged along.

The chapel doors were never locked. When they went in, they caught the stale scent of beer from either their own spills or others'. Except for one lone church pew, the space was empty. Darragh always thought his friends found the place as creepy as he did. His mother used to tell him about the woman who'd lived here, the Irish widow. Some believed the lost dead were still drawn to this place, looking to pass a message through Helen, even though those who'd grieved for them were no longer among the living.

Now Darragh's brother was gone, and their friends went out to the bars.

At the start of Chapel Road, which was little more than a barely-there path, he lay his bike down and walked on without it. As he was beginning to worry that the beer he'd drunk at Magee's had made him veer off course, the spire of the chapel rose up out of the dark.

He was half expecting to find the door chained shut now that the big house was occupied, but when Darragh hesitantly turned the doorknob, it opened with a sound like the cry of a bird.

Leaves littered the floor. The blankets he and his brother had kept were still in a heap in one corner. Darragh set his button accordion down on the floor. He unfolded one blanket and shook the dirt out and probably a few bugs. It was dry at least. Uncomfortable as the floor was, it would have been worse if he were sober.

Shapes formed from the dark and moved toward him, but when he looked away and then back, they were gone. Darragh knew he should get up and go home; when the beer wore off, he'd be freezing. Instead, he shut his eyes to better picture his brother after his dark red hair had been cropped close, turning him into a stranger. He had not believed he'd come back from the war.

"Don't stay here, Dar," he'd said on the night before he left to fight. "Fuck Pop. Get out."

Darragh sat up from a dream, shaking, to see Jorie Pearse—Marjorie Moye Pearse, according to the card she'd left in the book—standing in the doorway. Darragh realized the shot of fresh cold from the open door had awakened him. His muscles ached. He must have shivered through the night.

"That's your bike out by the road?" she asked.

Darragh nodded. He stood up, gathering the blankets. "I didn't break in. The door was open."

Jorie rubbed her arms. She wore a coat, but no hat or gloves. "Come into the house. I don't have a housekeeper yet, but I can manage coffee."

She asked him to take off his boots in the small room off the kitchen. In a regular house, it'd be a mudroom, but here he imagined there would be some fancy name for it. He pulled his boots off and tugged on his sock until the hole was hidden between his toes.

Jorie Pearse asked Darragh if he would build a fire in the first-floor parlor. She'd had the wood chopped but she was nervous about the chimney, though she'd been told it was in working order. He wondered what she thought might happen and why she wasn't worried about it happening to him. But he went ahead and did as she asked.

Mismatched armchairs faced the fireplace. She gestured to the better one of the two and he sat, uneasily. She sat across from him.

"What's your name? I guess we start there."

"Darragh," he said. Then, resigned, he spelled it so she would stop picturing D-a-r-a.

"It's Irish."

"Irish," she repeated. "Your grandfather was in the old works?"

Startled, he nodded. "We're further back, even. Before the Civil War. We're called foundry families. Like a play on 'founding.' But nobody new knows what it means. The foundry's closed a long time now. I guess you'd know that."

She nodded absently.

Darragh sipped the coffee to keep himself from asking what she wanted with him. If she was going to have him thrown in jail, she would have called for the sheriff already. Houses like this had to have a phone.

"This isn't bad," he said.

She smiled. "Surprised?"

"Yeah," he said, and she laughed.

"What's that called?" Jorie asked, pointing.

He turned and looked.

Unable to abandon it as easily as his boots, he'd carried the instrument with him, and now it sat against the wall.

"It's a button accordion," he said.

"May I see it?"

But she was already on her feet.

He watched as she inspected it. Even when quiet, the fiddle and the penny whistle were pretty to look at, but the button accordion was a big block of an instrument with round white keys, awkward to hold at first. Only those who learned the exact spot on the lap to rest it, the precise angle to hold it at their side, could ever play it well.

Darragh waited for her to try to play it, or to ask him to, but she did neither. She gently set it down.

"Why were you asleep in the chapel?" Jorie asked.

He'd begun to relax, but now she seemed suddenly like a teacher.

"Me and my brother used to go there sometimes. Before the war."

"The war," she repeated, and then said, "He was killed?"

"Far as I know, he's alive," Darragh said. "He came home for a while, then he took off. I don't know where he is."

Jorie sat back down. "It's hard getting back a different person. Not as hard as losing them completely, but still—not easy," she said.

Darragh stared down at the china cup he was holding. He bet he could break it with one hand. If he shattered it, he might be able to admit that he had indeed wondered if a brother who was a dead hero might be better than one who had let the war do to him what their mother's death had done to their father.

"You—you had someone in the war?" Darragh asked without looking at her.

"My brother didn't go," she said.

"But—"

"He has poor eyesight. But he sees things very clearly. He says I'm impulsive, but since I act like I'm sure about things, it makes people assume I'm right."

"Okay," Darragh said.

"I've caught you trespassing and I've invited you into my house. Now I'm thinking about offering you a job."

"You can check my pockets. I didn't steal anything."

"I don't need to check," Jorie said. "You found my card in the book?"

Darragh nodded.

"I've been to town a few times since then. Not one person has hinted that they know my second name. You didn't tell anyone. Don't tell me you have no one to tell. If you'd wanted to, you'd have picked somebody."

"I never thought of it." Darragh shrugged.

"Would you accept a job?"

"Yeah," Darragh said.

"Without knowing what it is?"

"Shoveling your driveway? Chopping firewood?" he asked.

"Yes, and also yard work. I plan to restore the gardens," she said. "Now, you'll never ask outright, but you'd like to know exactly who I am."

Darragh nearly said it was up to her what she wanted him to know, but instead he nodded.

"Cassius Moye was my grandfather's first cousin," she began.

She first saw the house when she was eleven years old, when she and her family were on their way home from a weekend trip to Degare Mountain, where they'd stayed in one of the resort cottages nearby. On an impulse, her mother asked the driver to take them by Moye House.

From the car, they stared at the estate that should have gone to Jorie's grandfather Augustus, but instead Cassius left it to the friends who'd published his book.

In the library, Jorie found a copy of *The Lost Girl and Other Stories.* Within a week, she'd read it twice. She studied Cassius's picture. Villains were supposed to be ugly, but she was fascinated to see that Cassius was quite handsome and that there were traces of her own features in the shape of his dark eyes and his chin. Later, Jorie read his letters and his journal.

Cassius wrote of how he'd wanted nothing but to get away from home when he was a child but now couldn't fathom living in any city. He was glad to offer other writers the chance to experience the kind of peace he'd been born into.

When Jorie bought Moye House with her inheritance from her father, her mother was pleased. But then she found out that Jorie intended to establish Moye House as a writers' retreat, to revitalize and formalize what Cassius had begun. To create it, she'd have to pull in sizable donations, and she had to do it while her looks still held. Because once she'd drifted into middle age, every action would be seen as a grab for a husband.

She could wait until she was elderly. Spinsterhood, a tragedy for a woman past thirty, became a choice again after sixty. An old, rich woman would be considered eccentric, and indulged accordingly. She had seen it again and again in her parents' circle.

But Jorie did not want to wait. If the man existed who was selfless enough to follow her to Culleton, then it was her bad luck and his that they had never met. She would settle there alone.

Darragh listened to her story without comment, and his silence continued after she'd finished. Jorie sat, her hands folded lightly. He didn't understand why she'd want to lock herself into Culleton when surely she had her pick of a hundred cities to live in, and it made him wonder if there was something about his hometown that he was blind to. He'd always planned to leave. The Marines would have been his way out, but seeing what war had done to his brother, he'd let that idea go and nothing else had risen to take its place. Except Jorie. Maybe she, and Moye House, were it. Maybe he was meant to help her build something right in Culleton.

In September of 1953, Jorie welcomed the first group of residents to the Moye House Writers' Colony. The program was administered by a board of directors, who read the required applications and then invited the writers who were selected to come for a six-week stay. Each got his or her own room. Quiet hours were from 9 a.m. to 6 p.m. Only the evening meal was communal.

She returned to *A History of Culleton, New York*, checking the book out with her new library card. Whereas before, she had only skimmed it, now she read the whole thing. The story of a ghost-sighting in the woods intrigued her.

One morning in early October, Darragh found her waiting to talk to him about it.

He had entered Moye House through the kitchen door, the old servants' entrance, shortly after nine o'clock. Darragh had learned to arrive when the residents were most likely to be at their desks. Later in the morning, he had a good chance of running into two or three seeking out more coffee, or taking a head-clearing walk on the grounds. The writers did a lot of head-clearing. Jorie said they were supposed to. For many, it was the reason they'd come here.

He found Jorie in her study, seated at her desk.

"We're going to have a reading and talk about 'The Lost Girl' on the twenty-seventh," she said before he could even greet her. "Like in the old days. I didn't realize there used to be a town holiday built around it." Her tone was slightly accusatory.

"A town holiday?" He sat down on the couch.

"Quicken Day. I think it should be brought back again."

"Oh, that. What for?" he asked, amused by her interest.

"Tradition!"

Darragh thought she might be happy if they got rid of electric lights and cars and could all live the way long-dead Moyes had.

"I read about the girls and the ghost in the woods. Can you tell me what really went on? Or what people say at least? What did they see?"

"They didn't see anything," Darragh said. "They heard footsteps, I think."

Jorie pursed her lips. "Who told you about it?"

"My grandmother. My mother," Darragh said. "It's just a story that gets told around here, like Santa Claus."

"The two girls were never named, even in the old newspaper articles—"

Darragh laughed. "They're no girls now. I was in school with one of their daughters. Kids gave her a hard time. Called her mother crazy. Called her crazy. They say—" He stopped.

"What do they say, Darragh?"

Darragh frowned. "That the family's cursed. Girls live but the sons die. As kids, I mean. Not off fighting wars."

"Children did die a lot more frequently, once upon a time," Jorie said.

"But it was never girls." Darragh rubbed the back of his neck, trying to remember. "They say that's why Bevin only had one, Cecilia. To stop the curse. Cecilia's dad moved out when she was something like ten or eleven."

"Can you talk to this Cecilia? Ask her if she thinks her family is cursed."

"What does Cecilia Burke have to do with Quicken Day?" he asked.

Jorie tapped her fingers. "I want to write about it, for the paper. People have to be reminded of what Quicken Day was. A little town pride, some mystery. You'll go and see Miss Burke? She might close the door in my face, but my guess is she won't do that to you."

The success of the first celebration ensured there would be a second, and the second established Quicken Day firmly on the town's calendar.

Jorie's article did indeed revive interest. Her mention of the ghost-sighting in the woods included a quote from the daughter of Bevin Burke. Her mother, Cecilia stated, still did not waver in her account of that night. It was neither prank nor hysteria. She'd told the truth in 1911.

There was a parade in Culleton, though instead of teenage girls it was the younger children who wore homemade costumes and marched through town. Afterward, families drove out to Moye House for a party in the garden, with pumpkin carving and bobbing for apples and a ribbon for best costume. In bad weather, the party moved to the basement of St. Maren's Church. The bars in town were filled by afternoon and remained so late into the night.

On the morning after the second Quicken Day, Darragh went to see Jorie, though he was not scheduled to work that day. He paused in the parlor where they'd first spoken, and where writers now gathered for drinks after supper. Jorie joined them, not every night but often enough to elicit suspense.

The room's wooden floors had been sanded and were now polished regularly. The mismatched chairs were gone. The mantel held two small vases of flowers cut from the garden. Because it was October, there were marigolds and chrysanthemums.

Darragh left the parlor and, after hesitating slightly, went up the main stairs. On the second floor, typewriters clacked behind closed doors.

He assumed Jorie was in her study, which he privately called the bluebell room, for the bluebells painted on the wall between the windows. Jorie's door was open, but he knocked anyway. She was at her desk, reading a book, which she closed without marking her place when she saw him.

"You're leaving Culleton?" she asked.

"Yes," he said, surprised. "How did you know?"

"You buttoned your shirt cuffs. You've also ironed your shirt, or someone did it for you. I suppose this was bound to happen."

"I am twenty-five." Darragh sat by the window, on the small couch Jorie had bought on one of their Sunday outings to antique shops and estate sales up and down the river. A fainting couch, it was called. Jorie had said she doubted women were actually passing out from tight corsets. They were pretending, if only for a few minutes of peace.

"Twenty-five," Jorie answered. "I always thought aging wouldn't bother me, but now I see that I didn't think it would happen. You're leaving with Cecilia?"

Darragh had always been shy about Cecilia around Jorie, as if he were betraying her somehow. They'd met only a few times. Jorie made Cecilia as nervous as a school principal.

He nodded.

"I suppose you're getting married? I'm not an expert on marriage, but, I don't know, wait a little longer. Sow some wild oats, Darragh."

"We want to get out of here. Start over. Ceel won't leave without us being married. Said she won't do that to her parents."

"And how do they feel about this?"

"Her father'd feel better if I had a job lined up, but I'm not too worried," Darragh said. "Cecilia's mother's the one. She doesn't want Ceel to marry anyone. Thinks she shouldn't have children. The family line ends with her."

"Oh, the supposed *curse*." Jorie sighed. "Cecilia doesn't believe it?"

"Hell, no. She wants ten kids. She hated being an only child." Darragh grinned. "I'm not so sure about that."

"Ten children is about eight too many, but that's just my opinion."

"Maybe six too many. I like kids," Darragh said. Then he hesitated.

Jorie could usually guess when he had something to say and simply waited for him to get it out. If he didn't open his mouth for half an hour, they'd still be sitting in the same places at the end of it.

"Her mother, though," he finally said. "It makes me wonder. If Bevin did really hear something in those woods, maybe she does know things we don't. "Also—" He put his head in his hands for a second. "Maybe I'm the one who's crazy."

"Why?" Jorie didn't sound worried, only curious.

"I dreamed I was with my grandmother and we were walking down the road to the house where I grew up. Back then, there was space between the neighbors. There wasn't even a sidewalk. My grandmother wasn't just telling me not to get married. She was telling me not to marry Cecilia. Because of her family. I can't remember the exact words she said, but you know how, in a dream, you know things?"

Jorie crossed the room. She squeezed his shoulder. When he reached for her hand, she neatly stepped away.

"Darragh McCrohan, you're too smart to believe in curses," Jorie said.

"I guess it's normal to have doubts—"

"You're not having doubts," Jorie said. "Your instincts are telling you it's a mistake. Don't do it. Go, if you have to, but go by yourself. See some of the world."

Darragh looked up. He had trouble holding Cecilia's face in his mind when he was with Jorie. Ceel faded, the way the picture did at the end of a movie. He suspected she knew it, and this was one of the reasons she wanted to leave Culleton.

"I can't do that to her," he finally said.

Jorie returned to her desk. "Well. You know you can come back anytime you like. As long as the residency is up and running, you'll have a job here."

"We'll visit," Darragh said.

"Come on Quicken Days," Jorie said.

Darragh promised he would, and then he left, this time by the back staircase.

By the late 1950s, the holiday had become a blend of St. Patrick's Day and Halloween, drawing crowds from neighboring towns. Vendors who sold Irish products, like clothes, jewelry and books, set up tables in the yard of St. Maren's Elementary School, or in the gym, depending on the weather. A postparade gathering was still held on the grounds of Moye House.

The date for Quicken Day was moved to the Saturday before Halloween. Purists had long argued that this defeated the purpose of celebrating the story, with its specific opening date of October 27, but the practical argument won. A weekend would draw far more people from outside Culleton.

For decades, Quicken Day remained a point of town pride, a draw for foliage tourists and families from nearby towns looking for a weekend activity. It became the official start of the holiday season, which then began in earnest the Friday after Thanksgiving, when the town Christmas tree was lit. The ghost story was told and retold, and it lent a sense of mystery to the occasion—and also the notion that something eerie might yet happen.

9

ADAIR

2010

Several days after I told Emily my status, I went to the ER at Methodist Hospital in Park Slope. They admitted me, and I was in the hospital for three days with pneumonia (regular pneumonia, not pneumocystis), which Michan spent by my bedside.

At one point, I woke up to see him reading. He looked up from his book.

"You don't have to manufacture a crisis to come home," he said.

"I didn't manufacture anything," I said, pushing a hand through my unwashed hair, which felt like it was full of sand. "I just took a treatment holiday."

Treatment holiday: a break from the medication regimen. A benign term for something proven unsafe, like "cigarette break" (lung cancer) or "sunbathing" (melanoma).

I should not have used that term. It betrayed my comfort at being in the hospital, where I could freely speak medical jargon, my first language. The doctors and nurses were not afraid of me. I was their business.

Michan slammed his book shut. "You can't. You *cannot.* You know that. Enough with the bullshit."

All told, I'd been a bad long-term survivor for almost a year, since I moved into Sarah's, first adhering poorly to the drug protocol and then stopping altogether. This wasn't like drinking Coke instead of orange juice with breakfast. It's hard to explain how you can simply avoid doing the thing that will keep you healthy. My hand reaching for the drawer where I kept the meds, and then drifting away like a meandering bird.

The day before I checked out, the doctor gave me the long version of Michan's admonishment: "HIV is highly mutable. You have to take your meds every day, within a two-hour window, or you could find yourself with drug-resistant HIV. And that could be a huge problem. I know I'm not telling you anything you haven't already heard. You are old enough to remember the way it was."

Before 1996, she meant. HAART—highly active antiretroviral therapy, the cocktail of drugs that kept the virus from replicating. When I adhered, HIV was nearly undetectable in my blood. This meant I was barely contagious, or possibly not at all. My next few counts would be critical.

Michan drove me to Moye House on Saturday afternoon, and I slept most of the way, waking only when the car slowed to turn into the parking lot. I got out of the car and the scent of damp grass hit me, a verdancy I was no longer used to, since I only ever came back at Christmas, when Culleton was either gray with cold or dressed in snow.

I leaned against the car for a moment as Michan slammed his door.

"Can you make the walk?" he asked.

"If I can't, what will you do, carry me?"

"I would run up to the house for a pillow and blanket and make sure you're comfortable sleeping in the car."

I laughed.

"Or I would drive you to the front door, which I should have thought to do." Michan held up the car keys, but I shook my head. I'd walk.

That night, I went to bed at 9 p.m. and didn't wake up until Sunday morning. My alarm woke me at 8 a.m. to take my pill, which I did, chastened, hoping shame as a motivator would last until something else emerged. Then I went back to sleep for another two hours. When I woke, the room was so bright that the light hurt my eyes because I had not drawn the curtains.

Moye House was quiet. There were no residents from mid-August to the last week in September. The fall residency was now timed to avoid the first two weeks of school. For parents, taking four or six weeks to focus on their writing was difficult enough. A late-September start date helped ease the guilt.

My room looked like a resident's room, cleared out after a stay. I had not left much behind when I went off to college. But even when I was a kid, it had the look of a guest room, with its heavy mahogany furniture and queen-size bed that was so high, Michan had to buy a portable step so I could climb into it. Neither Jorie nor Michan ever mentioned redecorating it for a child, and I never thought to ask.

I got out of bed and went to sit at the vanity. Jorie had kept it in her bedroom, and when she died, it came to me. It was a beautiful piece made of cherrywood that was likely worth a good bit of money. The oval mirror rested on hinged supports carved to look like vines. The mirror was tipped toward the ceiling. I'd never liked to catch accidental glances of myself, so there was that, but a writer, a resident from long ago, once told me quite seriously that mirrors were magnets for ghosts. Even as a grown-up in daylight, I was uneasy.

But when I lowered the mirror slowly, I saw only myself and the unmade bed behind me. I ran a finger down my cheek.

It looked like a whittler had been at work on my face. Sharply. I turned away and headed downstairs in the plaid pants and T-shirt I had slept in.

Michan was in the kitchen, pouring himself a cup of coffee. I sat down at the island as he wordlessly took another mug from the cabinet.

My dog came over, wagging his tail, and I leaned over to pet him. When I was home, Poe usually slept in my room, but I'd tricked him by going to bed so early. I hoped he hadn't been scratching at the door and I hadn't heard.

Michan placed a mug in front of me and sat down.

"Feeling better?"

I nodded, though my chest still ached and the walk downstairs had left me slightly short of breath. In the crook of my elbow, there was a green and yellow bruise from the IV.

"You look like shit." Michan raised his coffee cup to me.

I raised my cup back.

"I'm going to be working most of the day, but if you need me, knock," he said.

I knew he was deep into the edits for his latest book. I looked away guiltily. By giving me permission to interrupt him, he was telling me how much I'd scared him.

"Are you teaching this semester?" I asked, mainly to fill the silence.

He was a professor at Gilbride College and well known enough for his classes to be a draw. It was said of him that he began to write after his brother's death, and though he tried to explain that this wasn't so, that he'd wanted to write long before HIV, he could never correct the impression. Either way, he was still never quite comfortable with the way he was known not only for his work but for his grief and his good fortune.

Once the doctors confirmed, to their astonishment and Michan's weary I-told-you-so, that he was, indeed, immune to HIV, or at least resistant (theories varied), he offered himself to science. Take whatever you need, he'd said. He meant blood, but if they'd asked for an arm or even his heart, I think he would have gladly given either.

Used to be, at his readings, Michan would get at least one question about it during the Q&A, specifically asking him to explain, but that was rare now. He avoided terminology and simply said that his cells were essentially in HIV lockdown. The virus could not get in.

"I'm teaching four classes," he said. "Gin says it's too much."

Gin, his longtime girlfriend, dark-haired and nearly his height, was protective of Michan's health in a way nobody else thought to be.

I smiled. "How is she?"

"She's fine. Busy. She doesn't need anyone in the bookstore now, but said possibly around the holidays," Michan said. "You could work food prep."

"Food prep?" I repeated, certain I'd missed something he'd said.

"You can't possibly think I'm going to let you live here without putting you to work," Michan said, smiling.

Moye House did not deliver lunches to the writers' doors like some other writers' colonies. But the refrigerator was kept fully stocked, and residents were free to make their own food or help themselves to leftovers. There were also dorm-size refrigerators in each room. The truly focused and organized could bring lunch upstairs with them after breakfast so they didn't have to leave their rooms at all. Many did do this at first, but after two weeks there was a fall-off. That was because they'd gotten to know one another by then, Michan said. They sought each other's company around lunchtime. He didn't quite approve.

Moye House had a cook with a staff who made the dinner every evening. Michan never joined the residents. As a child, I believed it was so he could eat with me in the corner nook of the kitchen, in a real-family sort of way, but I'd been gone for a long time now and he still didn't eat with the others.

Most of the house's rooms and furnishings remained as they were in Cassius Moye's time, but the kitchen had been remodeled and modernized so that it was possible to cook for a large group.

Food prep, I knew, meant slicing vegetables and shredding lettuce.

"Hey, does the job come with health insurance?" I asked.

Michan didn't laugh. "If this is your way of asking if I will pay for your meds, the answer is yes, for now of course, but not forever. You need to be self-reliant. I don't know how else to say it."

I won't be around forever, he meant. No HIV, but still hemophilia, hep C. He didn't like to talk about either, which made it easy for me to pretend that he was perfectly fine, always.

"You're okay, right? I mean—"

"I'm okay," Michan said more gently. "Don't worry about me. I was saving this talk for when you'd been home for a few days, but since you brought it up, yes, you need to stay insured. You just do."

"And if someone objects to me touching their food?" I said.

My status was not a secret here. It was the rare resident who was unfamiliar with Michan's biography. If anyone did come here not knowing, then they soon found out.

Michan tugged on a lock of my hair, which meant he was in big brother mode.

"Our writers are *generally* an enlightened group. Which you know. Besides, if you do food prep without wearing gloves, Mrs. Penrose will throw you out of the house. She won't care that you live here. Try another tactic."

"The gloves won't be made of steel. They're not going to help if I cut my finger open with a knife."

"Then the best practice is not to cut your finger open with a knife," he said. "But Shannon can always use help in the office. We've talked about hiring a part-time assistant, but we've never gotten around to it. She's too busy to write up the job description."

"Why don't you do it?" I said.

"She does more work in a day than I do in a week. I wouldn't know where to start." He smiled, but it was probably only a slight exaggeration. "I'm going to leave it to you to figure out." Michan stood up.

"Because I'm so good at figuring things out," I called after him.

"Try harder."

After tugging once again on my hair, he left the kitchen.

Alone at the counter, I looked up at the servants' bells, which hung near the ceiling. The wires no longer connected them to the upper floors, to stations where the Moye family would have reached out to ring them, summoning the girls and women at work here in the kitchen. They must have grown to hate the sound.

I went to stand beneath them for a moment before opening the narrow door that hid the servants' staircase, which went all the way up to the attic, where the maids had slept.

I climbed the stairs and paused by the window on the landing. Ivy grew up the wall on this side of the house, and it covered the window except for a spot almost directly in the center, where there were no leaves. The story went that long ago, the servant girls had cut away enough of the ivy to create a peephole for themselves. Eventually the plant began to grow that way. It was said that the girls peeked at the men who worked in the stables, but I didn't believe that. They would only have had glimpses of the men coming and going. I always thought they gazed out at the gardens.

Care of the gardens was paid for by the town, an arrangement that worked because then Culleton could advertise Moye House as a tourist attraction. The grounds were open to the public on weekends year-round, and in the spring, summer and fall, couples could book weddings of up to fifty people for a fee, and only in the morning before the grounds opened. Rowan and I used to sit on the steps and watch weddings in the rose garden through the ivy window.

Remember the bride who wore the ring of flowers on her head instead of a veil? And all the way up the aisle, the petals blew away?

Rowan's voice, very near.

Like it was raining roses.

You've been gone so long.

I didn't turn around, but instead pressed my forehead against the glass.

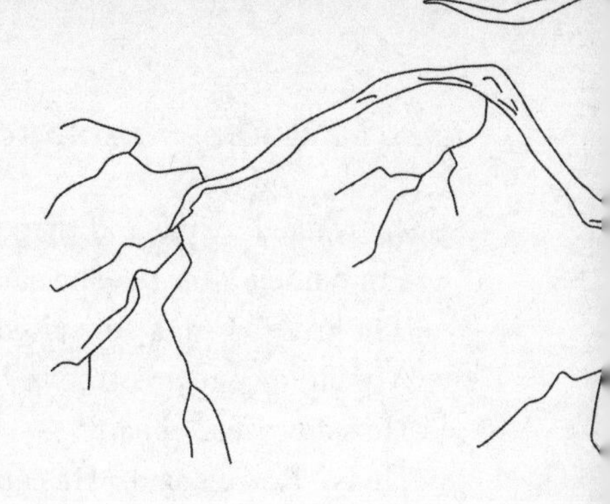

10
ADAIR
November 1994

I walked past the chapel, not far, until I came to the quicken tree, where I lay a hand against its trunk. The bark felt good against my palm, solid and rough. I sat down on the ground about a foot away and opened my sketchpad. Never sure how to begin, I circled the pencil above the page, trying to decide where to set the first line. Michan had told me he would show me the chapel, but I'd been at Moye House for almost a month and he hadn't mentioned it again. I didn't want to ask, afraid of bothering him, so one Friday after school I decided to go on my own. We had no homework on Fridays. I had nothing else to do.

I had erased three false starts when I heard a noise, nothing nearly as definitive as a footstep. Turning, I saw Rowan Kinnane wearing jeans and a black hooded sweatshirt.

I had not seen her since the day I'd arrived at Moye House. Her mother apparently didn't like to bring her by. Rowan had a habit of taking off to explore the house, and Evelyn could hardly abandon her work to search for her daughter.

"It's about to rain."

She said it as though plans we'd made together would now be ruined, and I wondered for a moment if I had invited her to meet me here and had somehow forgotten.

She walked by me and then, as I had done, touched the tree.

"I'm named after it," she said.

"The tree?" I said, surprised.

"My father put this tree in his story—"

"He's a writer?" I said.

"He is," Rowan said. "He came to stay at Moye House a long time ago. That's where he met my mother. And he wrote about this tree and named me after it."

"Quicken?" I said, wondering if it was her middle name.

"Rowan tree. Quicken tree. It's the same thing. My sister's name is Elizabeth, but we call her Libby. It's David who started calling her that. I said, Why give her a pretty name like Elizabeth and call her Libby? Why not Beth, if there has to be a nickname?"

"David's your—"

"Stepfather," she said grimly. "I have a half brother too, by my father. There is a saying that the middle child of three has second sight. But I'm between two halves, so it may not apply to me."

"Two halves—"

"Two half siblings," she said impatiently. "I'm not sure if that really makes me a middle, since they're both related to me and not to each other."

I tapped my pencil against the sketchpad, interested in the problem in spite of myself. "Because you're in two families of two kids, and not one family of three?"

Rowan smiled, pleased that I understood. "Yes! That's exactly what I mean."

"Well, have you ever seen the future?" I asked.

But Rowan looked away and shrugged, as though she'd lost interest. She did that, I'd learn, when she didn't want to answer a question.

She pointed at my sketchpad. "Were you drawing the tree?"

"Trying to," I said, covering the page with my arm.

"I can't draw," Rowan said. "I can't sing either. But I have a good memory. That's what I'll get voted in high school. Best Memory."

Then the rain began. The drops hit the leaves with small smacks that sounded like faint applause. Rowan pulled her hood up over her dark hair. "Time to go," she said.

"The chapel," I said, pointing to it.

Rowan glanced over her shoulder. "It's locked."

I reached into my pocket and withdrew two silver keys.

"You stole them!" she said, delighted.

"I'm putting them back. That's borrowing."

"Without asking."

I shrugged and Rowan laughed.

I unlocked the chapel and pushed the door tentatively, but Rowan, shifting from one foot to the other behind me, reached over my shoulder and shoved the door open.

Laughing, she pushed her hood back and shook out her hair.

I unzipped my jacket. The wooden floor was bare. Even the center aisle was uncarpeted.

There were eight pews, four on each side, put in when Jorie had the chapel renovated so it could be rented out for weddings and baptisms.

Above the altar, there was a round window of green glass. There were two plain glass windows on either side of the chapel, the kind that came to a point at the top, like the flame of a candle or a teardrop.

Between them was a square stained-glass window, its image the view beyond the wall. The woods in autumn colors, the trees shedding leaves. In the corner, the quicken tree with its dark red berries. Even if it weren't the reason I'd swiped the keys, I would have gone to take a closer look, so striking it was to see a stained-glass window that was not of a saint or a familiar religious scene. The wedding at Cana. Veronica and her veil. The Good Samaritan.

As Rowan wandered the space, I went to the window to read the plaque beneath it:

IN DEAR MEMORY OF NICHOLAS AND GABRIEL,
THE SONS OF EDWARD AND LUCY ADAIR

Rowan swirled her finger in the holy water font and made a face as she wiped her hand on her sweatshirt.

"Nasty. I bet nobody ever changes that water."

I sat in the last pew on the left side of the chapel. In the corner were the votive candles. She picked one up and rolled it in both hands.

"You don't have any matches, do you?"

"Matches? No," I said. "Why would I?"

"I don't know you," Rowan said, "so I thought I'd check."

Did she think I was a smoker or an arsonist? I was rehearsing the comeback when she dropped the candle in its holder and turned to me, folding her arms over her chest.

"We should come here at night," Rowan said. "It's haunted."

I thought, We? But I only said, "Haunted?"

Rowan nodded. "Helen, the maid who worked at Moye House a long time ago? Helen, our ancestor, spoke to the dead, and, they say, sometimes the dead still come here looking for her."

Rowan spoke in her husky voice and kept her eyes averted, as though listening to someone I couldn't see or hear. I kept glancing around. We hadn't turned the lights on—I didn't see a light switch—and besides the rain-darkness, the afternoon was nearly over.

I pulled my hands inside my sleeves and held on to my cuffs. The rain suddenly fell in a torrent, pounding the roof so hard that Rowan and I both looked up, alarmed.

"Bells," Rowan said absently, still staring at the ceiling. "People have sworn they heard the sound of a bell ringing in the woods." Her great-grandmother Elspeth had told her that.

"We'd better go back," I said. "It's getting dark."

She was about to say something, I think, when the door opened.

I gasped, but Rowan, much closer, leapt back with a scream.

A man stood there, looking at us both. He was young, not a teenager, but not long past.

He wore jeans and a green jacket. On the jacket, in white, there was a round logo that I could not make out, though I could see the words beneath it clearly: *Degare Mountain State Park.*

"Jesus, Rowan," he said. "What the hell is wrong with you?"

"What are you doing here?"

"Evelyn asked me to come find you."

"I know, I know. She's waiting for me."

"She already went home."

"She left me here?" Rowan said.

"The babysitter had to leave. She had to get home. Come on." He started walking.

Rowan scowled at him, struggling to regain her dignity. "I thought you lost your driver's license."

"Got it back. Now let's go."

He went outside and we followed him. We went down the three steps, Rowan ahead.

He turned around. "I can give you a ride too," he said to me. "Where do you live?"

"She lives here," Rowan said.

"Oh yeah? She lives in the woods?"

"She lives at Moye House," Rowan said.

The blank look of disinterest disappeared. He looked at me again, this time with his eyebrows raised.

"You're Michan's niece?"

I nodded shyly.

"I'm Leo."

Gently test people, Janus advised the men in his HIV support group. And my mother, and me by extension, because I overheard, and I understood even then that I was one of them. When you meet someone new and they know (because you've told them or because it's obvious), it's fair to find out where you stand. Put out a hand. Reach over as if to touch their wrist. If they recoil, well, then, what's next is up to you. Begin the work or walk away.

Many grown-ups hid their hands in their pockets when they met me, or they crossed them behind their backs as if about to be handcuffed. Receptionists at the dentist's office and at my school did this, and friends of my mother's had when they still visited, before she began to look like a person with AIDS.

I'd never tested anyone before, not my teachers and not my classmates. But I extended my hand to Leo. He was the first.

"Adair McCrohan."

Leo accepted my hand. His fingers rested against my pulse. He squeezed, just slightly.

When we let go at the same time, he did not wipe his hand on his jeans. He cleared his throat self-consciously, which told me that he knew, he understood.

Then he turned to Rowan and scowled. "Okay, I've got shit to do, so let's go."

"Oh, right, I'm sure," she said. "You're that busy."

"I can't wait for the day you graduate charm school," he said and started walking.

At that, she laughed, surprising me.

We walked in silence until I moved closer to whisper, "Will your brother tell that we were in the chapel?"

"My what?" Rowan didn't whisper, and then she laughed. "Leo's not my brother. He's our landlady's son."

She explained that she and her mother rented the house where Leo's grandmother had lived. Leo and his mother and sister had lived there for a while, after the divorce. Now the grandmother was in a nursing home, and they couldn't sell the house until she died, though she'd never live there again. She, Rowan, slept in Leo's old room.

My real father, Rowan said, went home to Ireland a long time ago, and that was where her actual brother lived.

"Ireland?" I said faintly.

"Ireland," she said firmly. "I'm going to live there someday too."

Later, after dinner, I was in the upstairs living room, where all the lights were on, and the television too. Michan sat in his chair, reading a thick book. Jorie was in her rooms at the end of the hall, probably reading as well. She may have been north of seventy-five, but she was still a night owl. We were, the three of us, sequestered from the life downstairs, the writers drinking and talking in the front parlor.

"Michan?"

He looked up, the flash of irritation quickly replaced by a friendlier look. Raised eyebrows. Yes?

"Do you believe in ghosts?"

He closed the book, saving his place with his finger. "Been talking to Rowan?"

"Well, yes," I said, annoyed that he'd guessed. "But do you?"

He wasn't laughing at me, I saw, but appeared to be thinking about it.

Finally he said, "I would like to believe that something comes after this. I don't mean heaven, like the Church says. Some change of energy. We're one thing now, and when our bodies die, shazam, we're something else."

"Shazam?" I repeated, rolling my eyes.

He grinned. "That's the best I can do. What about you? Do you believe in ghosts?"

I thought about it, staring at the commercial on the television. Michan left his book closed in his lap.

"No," I said, and he laughed, but what I meant and could not explain was that, like him, I wanted to believe. But to see a ghost seemed too much to ask for, like the ability to fly.

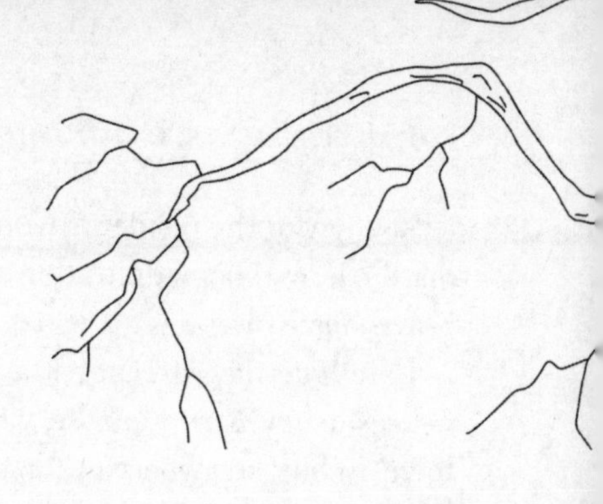

11

ADAIR

2010

To earn my keep, I would serve as a kind of Girl Friday for anyone who needed me, be it the office or kitchen staff. The on-site administrative office was a fifteen-minute walk across the grounds, in what had once been the gardener's house.

The gardener's house handled residents' issues as they arose. It booked Moye House weddings and other special events. I asked Shannon to please not put me on the phones, a job I'd had one summer in high school. Shannon had advised me then to keep in mind that the callers didn't know the answers to their questions. I'd laughed, but soon found that she was right. It did start to feel personal, like a stalker was calling to torment me by asking the same ten questions over and over, using an array of different voices.

I didn't give the answers I wanted to, of course.

How do I apply? *Go online and read the instructions.*

Can my husband/wife/kids come? *Why would you want them to?*

Can I bring my dog? *Can the dog write?*

Can I bring my cat? *The cat can probably write, but no.*

How good a writer do I have to be? *Better than the cat.*

Nor did I want to work directly with the food. I was sure at least a few of the residents would be uncomfortable with it, no matter how much admiration they might express for me, the brave survivor.

Late Tuesday afternoon, a few days after the start of the fall residency, Mrs. Penrose, who ran the kitchen, sent me into town to buy strawberries for the next day's breakfast. It was usually a mistake to buy fruit from the supermarket, but she'd been running late, she told me. Now the ones she'd chosen were already going bad.

I walked through town slowly, my hands in the pockets of a denim jacket I'd found in the back of my closet. This morning, the brisk weather had caused a buzz in the house. There had been some worried talk about the summer extending all the way into October, but overnight, the weather arrived that the residents had come here for.

I left the fruit store and stood on the sidewalk for a moment, looking at the bookstore across the street. It still surprised me sometimes to see Wild Books, neat and inviting, instead of the old Byrd's New & Used Books, with its peeling paint and cracked windows.

Gin had the quote from which she took the store's name stenciled on the front window.

> Second-hand books are wild books, homeless books.
> —Virginia Woolf

Wild Books and Doyle's Pub, beside it, were once a single private home that had been divided when the street turned from residential to the town's business district. The two were connected by a sliding door that had once been the divide between the parlor and the dining room. The bar and bookstore were written up on the Moye House website under Local Attractions, and when the resident writers entered the bookstore for the first time, they always sought out the door. The black handle was recessed and barely a shade darker than the wooden wall, easy to miss, and because of the way the door slipped behind the magazine rack, it had the look of a secret passageway.

At four o'clock on a weekday, the bookstore wasn't too busy, and I was glad I didn't see anybody I knew.

"Hey, Adair," Gin said as I approached the register. "Good to have you home."

Almost as soon as Gin began working at Byrd's New & Used Books, she'd resolved to buy the store someday, and once it was truly hers, Gin gutted the place as if it had been an entirely different kind of business, like a butcher's or a haberdashery. She'd made Wild Books practically an annex of Moye House, always making sure to stock the books of past and present writers who had come to stay and scheduling open mics and readings.

"I'm taking a break," I told her, though I knew Michan would have told her everything. "Recharging."

As if Culleton were a tropical island. I vowed not to say that again.

"How's the new crew?"

I shrugged. "It's early days. I haven't met too many of them yet."

"I saw one in town this afternoon."

"This afternoon?" I said, surprised. "Too soon to be panicking."

For many of our residents, Moye House was their first experience at a writers' colony. Some, as much as they'd dreamed of being alone with their thoughts, couldn't make themselves sit still at their desks. Usually it took a full week before they began wandering around the gardens or stealing into town to go to the bookstore or the movies. Still, it didn't happen very often. The personal statement and writing samples required with the application mostly separated the dreamers from the focused.

"He could be settling in," Gin said.

Both of us always ignored the fact that Gin might have been my sort-of stepmother. Step-aunt, as it were. But even the well-meaning town busybodies had stopped asking when she and Michan were going to make it official. Gin, who'd been married and divorced young, liked to say if she'd gone skydiving once, and her parachute failed, she sure as hell wouldn't go skydiving again. She lived on the edge of town in an enclave called Cottages. It was a neighborhood of small houses that had once been summer rentals for the rich.

"Okay, I'm just going to—" I gestured to the store in general.

"Surely," Gin said. "Let me know if you need help."

After browsing for a bit, with a wave to Gin, who was with a customer, I left. On the sidewalk in front of the store, I hesitated and then turned down the alley. I could cut through the parking lot and walk one more block to the elementary school and my car.

As I headed down the cobblestone street, I checked my phone for the time. It was only four thirty, though it would hardly have mattered if it were midnight, since I had no place to be. I dropped the phone in my purse and looked up to see a tall man holding a lantern coming toward me. I looked away and back, and saw that it was not a lantern, but a black shopping bag he held loosely by the handles.

As I passed him, he put out a hand as if to lay it on my arm, but stopped.

"Adair?" he said.

"Yes?" I answered automatically and stepped back. This is how it happens, I thought. He calls your name, and even though he's a stranger, you answer.

"I'm sorry," he said. "God, I'm an idiot, coming at you out of nowhere." He moved his hand in a gesture that I guessed meant the alley but might have included all of Culleton.

He had an Irish accent.

"My name is Ciaran Riordan. I'm at Moye House for the fall, ah, term? Residency, I guess we're supposed to say, since it's not school. I emailed you over the summer," he said. "Of course you don't know me, but I saw you at the house—" Ciaran stopped, as if he'd run out of words.

I'll be there in fall, I remembered. The email I never answered.

Michan greeted the new arrivals. As a child, I had too, but once I became a teenager, I'd always preferred to meet them when we ran into one another in the hallways of the house or out on the grounds. I didn't like being the center of their collective attention, even briefly.

"Adair!" the residents would say with surprise when we were introduced. Though they knew I couldn't still be a child, I was still like a character in a book. I was Beth from *Little Women*, if she had grabbed hold of the pen and crossed out the paragraphs that ended her life.

"I'm sorry I didn't answer your email this summer," I said. "There was a lot going on—"

"I'm the one who's sorry," Ciaran said, fixing his gaze on the ground. "I'm not in the habit of emailing women I don't know."

"It's fine, really," I said.

Ciaran relaxed, which was my intention.

"How did you get into town?" I asked. "Did you take the shuttle van from the house, or did you bring your car to the residency?"

"I don't have a car. I live in Brooklyn too. Don't need one. I walked into town. Walking helps me think," he said.

"About your novel?" I asked.

"I'm writing nonfiction, actually," he said.

"Oh, well, if you're done—"

He laughed. "Done thinking? I am, yes."

"I can take you back home," I said, and then added, "To the house, I mean."

Moye House was not his home, of course.

I drove back to the house and parked the car in the lot. As we walked to the house, Ciaran asked how far we were from Rosary Chapel.

"It's not far at all," I said. "You can go and take a look and be back in time for dinner."

"I'm not much for that sort of thing. We were told it wasn't required."

"Required, no, but it's sort of expected, this early on at least," I said.

"It's a hard sell for me," Ciaran said, "sitting at a table for an hour, made to chat with whoever I happen to be beside. Drinks together after, I can get behind that because I can move about. I can leave if I want."

I started to give him directions to the chapel, and when I paused, he spoke.

"Will you come with me?" he asked.

Friendships formed quickly at Moye House, because the

residents were together so much when they weren't working. I used to try to guess on arrival day who would pair off, who were bound to hate each other. Ciaran was the youngest of this group by several years, and I wondered whom he was spending his off-time with. Maybe no one. Maybe that was why he was talking to me as if I were one of them.

"I haven't been back there in a long time," I said, and then, "Yes."

He put his shopping bag inside his backpack, which I saw held a laptop, and we headed off.

I led him off the grounds, to the edge of the woods. The trail was unmarked, but visible if you knew where to look. Ciaran walked beside me with a silence I recognized from my uncle Michan and so many of the writers who'd come to stay. I'd seen them wandering the gardens with the very expression Ciaran was wearing: his head tilted slightly, listening to his own thoughts to the exclusion of everything else.

Because I knew, of course, how long it took to get to the chapel, I glanced at Ciaran to see his expression at the moment the tree line broke and the chapel appeared. He stared. Even when you were expecting to see the small church surrounded by woods, as if it had grown there like one of the trees, it was still startling.

Rather than trailing behind him, I sat on the chapel steps as Ciaran walked around the building, studying it.

"Where's the quicken tree?"

I stood and led him to it, the mountain ash, the quicken tree, a few feet away. In the spring, the tree was covered with white flowers, but now, in autumn, the berries were in bloom.

"Are you using Culleton's history in your book?" I asked.

Ciaran rubbed his arms as though he were cold. "Yes. It's

—I'm sorry. This isn't an easy thing to explain, since I'm hoping you can help me. That's why I emailed you this summer. Then when I got here and saw you'd moved back in . . . I've been trying all week to think of a way to approach you."

"I don't know what I could possibly help you with," I said, baffled.

Ciaran gestured in the direction of the chapel. "Can we sit for a minute?"

We settled on the chapel steps. The key, I thought, and curled my fist as though it were in my hand.

"I told you I was writing nonfiction," he said.

I nodded.

"My book is about missing children," Ciaran said.

"Rowan." I did not intend to whisper, but it came out that way.

"Yes. Rowan Kinnane."

If I turned around, I'd see her, grinning at me.

"You must know the case has never come close to being solved," I said coolly. "I don't know what you're going to write about."

"The angle of the book is to spotlight cold cases," Ciaran said. "I know there was speculation in the press about Rowan's mother and the landlady's son. One or both of them were guilty."

"The police never arrested anybody," I said. "It's Evelyn you should be talking to. She's Rowan's mother."

"I hope to," Ciaran said. "Research is part of the reason for coming here. Getting a feel for the town, talking to people who remember. I know the boy across the street said she didn't leave for the parade with her mother. And I know you told the police you saw her in town that afternoon. In the bookstore."

He's right, you did. I could hear her voice, raspy, like a child smoker.

"The police figured out I was wrong almost right away," I said. "My name was never in the papers. How do you know something that wasn't even worth reporting?"

Ciaran sat very still, as though afraid he might startle me into bolting.

"The lead detective who worked the case is retired now. I've interviewed him. Some of the police argued that with all the people out that day for the parade, it was possible that Rowan simply went unnoticed, but this detective thought the opposite. He said that the more people, the better the chances that somebody else would've seen her too. He thought she never made it into town."

Detective Huyser. He'd kept running a hand over his head, as if he'd forgotten he was balding. His belly jutted out over his belt, and his brown eyes were moist and sad, like a beagle's.

We need you to tell us the truth, honey. Think hard. What was Rowan wearing? Are you sure it was Saturday that you saw her? If you're mixing up your days, that's a mistake and that's okay. Nobody else seems to have seen her. We need to find out what's going on here.

"Did he tell you I was lying or that I was crazy?"

"Mistaken," Ciaran said crisply.

I liked that Ciaran didn't reflexively protest that I was neither a liar nor crazy. He didn't know me.

"He said Adair McCrohan was confused and nobody could blame her, with all she'd been through already," Ciaran said. "He said you were sick that week."

I sidestepped my health. "He gave you my name? Is he allowed to do that?"

"He had a heart attack last year. I'm not sure if he cares much what he's allowed to do. He was glad to talk to me. Said that nobody'd asked him about Rowan in years. He told me you were the poet's niece, who lost her parents."

The girl with AIDS was what he'd said, I had no doubt. I let it go.

"Eyewitnesses are unreliable. It's been proven. You invent details without meaning to and you're convinced they're real," I said. "I don't have anything to say. I'm sorry."

"You were cousins," Ciaran said. "You share a four-times great-grandmother who once worked at Moye House as a maid."

"It makes us very *distant* cousins. Fifth, I think."

I started jiggling my foot, and I saw Ciaran glance at it.

"Fifth, that's right," he said.

Boo, I heard her say in my ear.

Go away, I thought, afraid to turn my head and feel her cold breath on my cheek.

"You found Rowan's case online?" I moved my head slightly to the left as I said her name, though I sensed she'd retreated. Indeed, I saw only the trees, unbroken by the figure of a girl.

Rowan had an entry on *Missing in New York* and another on *The Perdita Blog,* an online encyclopedia of the missing. I pictured Ciaran browsing a list of missing children and clicking on Rowan's name, if only to see if she was a boy or a girl.

Ciaran unzipped his backpack and took out a gray folder. He held it, closed, in his hands.

"There's not too many who'll tell you off the top of their head that two people who share a four-times great-grandmother are fifth cousins," he said.

"Rowan told me," I said, confused.

"She told me too," Ciaran said.

He opened the folder and drew out a white envelope. I reached for it and then pulled back, as if the paper might burn, but Ciaran held it out further and I accepted it.

Ciaran Riordan
Ballyineen, Galway, Ireland

The postmark: January 4, 1995.

There was an air mail stamp but no return address on the front. I turned the envelope over. It had been torn open from the top. On the intact flap I saw the familiar signature, with its oversize R and K, the two letters exaggerated, almost interchangeable.

ROWAN KINNANE

Under that was her address, and beside the zip code was a smear of blue, a blurred fingerprint. I touched it carefully, as if I might erase it, though the ink had set long ago.

"Who *are* you?" I asked.

Ciaran looked, for a moment, like he wasn't sure. "I'm her brother."

My blood jumped. But instead of pressing two fingers to my hammering pulse, I smoothed the envelope over my lap and studied Ciaran's face anew.

The chin, its cleft slightly off-center, the thick, dark brows that Rowan hated, though I believe she might have grown to like them as a teenager for the dramatic way they framed her eyes. Those eyes, the tell. Ciaran's were the same light blue that I guessed also turned silvery in certain light.

"Half brother," I said.

"Half, yes," Ciaran said. "We have the same father. He and Evelyn never married. Kinnane is Evelyn's maiden name."

"I know that," I said.

"My father was a resident here a long time ago."

"I know," I said, raising my voice slightly. "It's where he met Evelyn. She worked in the office then."

"I'm almost three years older," Ciaran said. "I don't want to make excuses for my father, but there are reasons—" He shook his head. "Ballyineen and Culleton, you know the connection?"

Ballyineen, where so many of the foundrymen had emigrated from. The relationship between Culleton and Ballyineen had been formalized decades ago by pronouncing the two sister towns.

"My parents were separated. That was the reason he'd come to the States. He wanted to get away."

"They were getting divorced?" I asked, glad for Rowan. Neither parent was quite an adulterer.

Ciaran shook his head. "There was no divorce in Ireland back then. You could live apart for the rest of your lives, but there was no legal way to end a marriage."

I was silent for a moment, absorbing that. In 1982? No divorce?

"When did you find out about Rowan?" I asked.

"When she was born," Ciaran said defensively. "My father never lied about Evelyn, or her. He wasn't coming back. He'd made that plain."

"But he did," I said. "He did go back."

"Yes, when he and Evelyn broke up." Ciaran smiled bitterly. "Rowan was about two. It fell apart quick, after she was born."

"You met her," I said, as if to prove that we had been close, even though, moments earlier, I'd been pretending we'd only been fellow citizens of Culleton.

To twelve-year-old girls, something that was simply not discussed had the gravity of an actual secret. Because my friendship with Rowan had not aged, I remained in the place where the whisper in which a thing was told had more weight than the words themselves. I met my brother, she'd said.

"Once," Ciaran said quietly, "Evelyn brought her to Ireland, the week after Christmas. She'd just turned four."

And I saw them, the dark-haired boy and the smaller girl, sitting side by side on a blue couch. They were neither looking at each other nor touching.

"That visit was the last time my father saw her and the only time I ever did." Ciaran looked down at his hands. "Then one day I get a letter from America, from Rowan. I wrote her back, but all I could think was, What do I have to say to an eleven-year-old girl? I was fourteen."

I stared at the envelope in my lap and turned it over again.

"Adair? There's this, too." Ciaran reached into the folder and withdrew a greeting card.

I looked at it without touching it. It was a pumpkin patch beneath a full moon. *Halloween Greetings*, it said.

"It came the first week of November."

I looked up. "If there's proof Rowan mailed a letter the day she disappeared—"

"I didn't save the envelope. I don't have the postmark. I tossed that one in a drawer to save for the address. There's no way of knowing when she mailed the card."

"The police should still know."

"They do," Ciaran said. "The police have had my letters from the beginning."

"You don't remember if the envelope the card came in—" I stopped.

"If it was red?" he asked. "She was holding a red envelope. That's what you'd told them."

"Red, yes," I said. "Red."

Me in an aisle of Byrd's New & Used Books. Those disorganized shelves. The piles of books on the floor that Charley Byrd never bothered shelving. Rowan, appearing at the end of the aisle, then vanishing. In her hand, a flash of red.

"I don't remember. I tossed the card on my bed with my schoolbooks and then ran back down the stairs."

The envelope for a Halloween card might be orange or black or even white, but certainly not red.

I tried to remember, to focus on Rowan's hand, but the image in my mind flickered like a reflection in water. I breathed through my nose. With a panic attack, there was time to stave it off, but usually only seconds, to retreat from the cliff's edge.

"Are the other cases you're looking at like Rowan's?" I asked.

"They are." Ciaran gave a trace of a smile. "Narrow windows of time. A lot of theories but no solid evidence pointing at a suspect. 'Vanished into Thin Air.' Nearly every article about a missing person's got that headline."

I knew what he meant. The sentence was constructed as though thin air itself were responsible, like quicksand.

"But in Rowan's case, and the others I'm writing about, it's nearly true," Ciaran said. "Their shoes being left behind like they walked out of them would be less mysterious. We'd know exactly where it happened at least."

"I don't know how I can help you," I said.

"You knew her," Ciaran said. "And I didn't."

Together we went back to the house, slowly retracing our path in the dark. Ciaran didn't speak, and I was grateful. We walked beside each other, and I turned to look over my shoulder so often that he began to do it too. But there was nothing behind us but the woods, beginning to fill with darkness. His words played over and over in my mind. *You knew her, you knew her.* But if it had not been her mother, and I never believed it was Evelyn, then it was a lightning strike under circumstances I couldn't put together. I didn't even have the pieces. Nobody did. But if the crime had been random, then it had not been about Rowan, only where she was standing, when. It would have been some other girl. Knowing her, having known her, was useless.

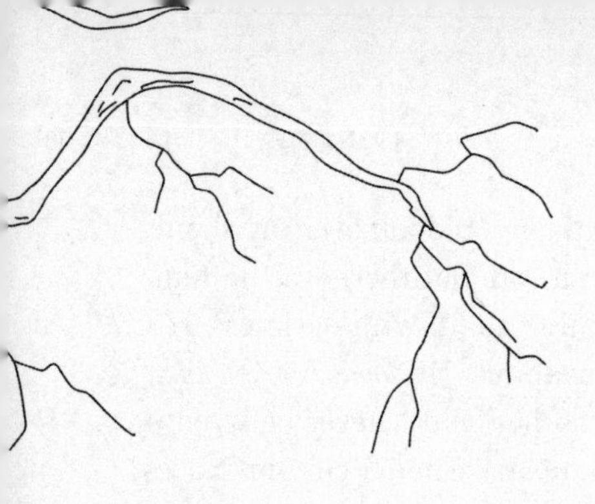

12
ADAIR
2010

Quiet hours were due to start in five minutes, but mostly everyone had already finished breakfast and retreated to their rooms to begin the workday.

Mornings, after I helped load the dishwasher, I took the dog for a walk off the grounds, across the road. Poe kept glancing behind him to make sure I was there. I was glad to see him too, though I knew that Michan took good care of him and he had company from the staff and the residents who were dog people. Poe's existence was addressed upon acceptance, and notations were made as to residents' allergies and fears. If certain residents couldn't abide him in any common areas, we accommodated them.

Still, Poe was a Moye House fixture. Poe at the feet of a writer sitting on the back terrace. Poe waiting at the foot of the stairs for the residents to come down for dinner. Poe at evening drinks, nudging hands to pet him.

After touring his usual spots, we went back home. I settled down on the steps to the side door, the old servants' entrance, and produced a tennis ball from my jacket pocket. Poe chased it and brought it happily back. We wrestled for the ball for a minute, until he released it and waited for the next throw. He was far slower than he used to be, I noticed with dismay, but that was only to be expected.

The dog and I had been playing for ten minutes, no more, when Ciaran came around the side of the house, holding a mug of coffee. He might have been out for a walk on the grounds, but from how slowly he approached, I assumed he'd come looking for me.

Two days had passed since he told me of his connection to Rowan, and we had not run into each other since, for which I was grateful. I needed time to process who he was and what he'd come here for.

Talking to him had been like watching lights going on in dark rooms, one by one. Part of it might have been that I was still recovering. I had been sick often enough in childhood to recall the strangeness of being well. It's how keenly you feel the absence of labored breathing, or the confusion of a fever when you are burning up but cannot stop shivering. It's having a night's sleep work and not wear off in hours, like aspirin.

The day before, I'd learned that my viral load had risen but was not dangerously high. My doctor didn't believe I had developed a resistance to the medication. She also lectured me:

- 2010 is not 1985
- We will never go back to 1985
- But you are not cured
- There is no cure
- There will someday be a cure
- Probably in your lifetime
- This is not someday

But my clear-sightedness was more than a return to health. It wasn't until this morning, after I took my meds and began brushing my teeth, that I was able to place it. I felt the way I had when I went into Byrd's Books for the first time after Rowan disappeared. I walked down every cluttered aisle and saw that she was not there. I realized then that no answer was imminent. Rowan had not been the victim of some inexpert magician who would soon figure out how to reverse his trick. She was gone.

Now, I didn't want a return to hope, and I didn't want to talk about Rowan using the comfortable crutch of grief. I didn't want to assume she was dead. I wanted a return to urgency.

I pictured Rowan: the sly grin and the silver-eyed glance over her thin shoulder to make sure no grown-ups were watching. Anger replaced acceptance. What happened? Who took her? Where was she?

Ciaran sat on the step beside me. He'd cut himself shaving. There was a small spot of dried blood near his ear. Poe bounded over, dropped the ball at Ciaran's feet and ran a few steps before he turned around, tensed, waiting.

"Traitor," I said mildly. "He makes me fight for it."

Ciaran threw the ball much farther than I had managed to, and we watched Poe scramble after it.

"Who do you need to talk to?" I asked.

"Rowan's mother, of course. Her stepfather."

"They've been divorced a long time."

"I know," Ciaran said. "Evelyn and my father talk sometimes on Rowan's birthday. The anniversary. If something comes up with the investigation."

"Do things come up?" I asked, surprised.

"Sometimes the police show Evelyn a picture of some man

who's been arrested for some kind of sex crime. They'll say take a look, have you ever seen him before? Nothing's happened for a long time, though," Ciaran said. "I already talked to the boy who said he didn't see Rowan get in the car with her mother that day."

"Brian Kelly," I said.

"Brian, yes. I spoke to him. He didn't have anything new to say. He was playing basketball in front of his house. Evelyn came outside and put the baby in the car seat. She went straight to the driver's side, got in the front and drove off."

"And there you go. Rowan was never in town that day."

"You saw her," he said.

"I was wrong."

"What if you weren't?" Ciaran asked. "What if the police decided to believe the wrong kid?"

Ciaran was frowning, his slightly furrowed brow unnervingly like Rowan's. It felt as if she were speaking through him. That the detectives had made choices was not something I had ever considered. Instead of the traumatized orphan, they'd picked the one with the stable home life, calm and confident. Instead of the girl, they chose the boy.

As if to escape the thought, I stood up. "Have you seen the rec room yet?"

"In the carriage house? No."

After I put Poe in the house, we walked over. Like the tour guide I supposed I was, I explained that the carriage house was not where the horses had once been kept, only the buggy. The truly wealthy might have had carriage houses big enough for two or three carriages, but this one was single. The structure was two stories tall and made of brick. The large double doors were painted red with black trim. I went to the small black door beside them and unlocked it with my key.

In the main room there were several colorful throw rugs on the wooden floor and a sectional sofa facing a flat-screen television. A small bar stood in one corner with four stools in front of it. In another room there was a combination pool table–air hockey table.

"Some writers never set foot in here. They're afraid that if they do it once, they won't stop," I said. "This used to be used for storage."

"Let's put the TV outside of the house, make the writers hike to it," Ciaran said.

"That was the idea."

Ciaran stepped further into the room. He looked up at the beamed ceiling. "Procrastination Station. I heard that's what it's called."

"Gabby Lundy is the one who first called it that. Her books are over there." I pointed to the wall of built-in bookshelves. "This is known as the residents' library."

Ciaran moved to look at the bookshelf. He crouched down to search, but after a moment stood.

"What are you looking for?" I asked.

"My father published a short story in an anthology of stories that were written here," he said. "His story was called 'The Quicken Tree.'"

"Rowan looked for it too. Michan said we must have had it at some point. Somebody probably took off with it."

"She looked for it?" he said, stricken. "I promised to send her a copy. I never did it, though. I brought one with me, for all the good it'll do now."

I sat down on the edge of the couch. Saying her name out loud, and casually, felt strange.

"Did you tell them on your application who you were?" I asked.

"I didn't," Ciaran said. "You're supposed to come here to write. To say that I came here to do research, I wasn't sure how that would have been looked at."

"Research is part of writing," I said, though I wasn't sure either.

"But going out in the day, interviewing people." He shrugged uncomfortably.

Why are you here, I wanted to ask, but I decided to put it differently.

"Did you consider renting a place in Culleton?" I asked.

"If I hadn't been accepted, I would have," he said. "But six weeks where it happened, without having to pay rent or buy meals? I had to try."

"But nothing happened here," I said.

"This is where Evelyn was that afternoon."

The last happy hours of her life. Or hours of suspense, waiting for the proper time to begin her lie. Depending on what you believed.

"Can I ask you a personal question?" Ciaran asked.

I tensed, but nodded.

"Was there ever any thought of you and your uncle taking this place for yourselves? You'd have had your own house but still on the grounds."

I wanted to laugh at his idea of a personal question when I'd been asked so much worse: HIV? How did you get it? Is HIV in your tears? Is it in, you know, all your blood?

"Jorie wanted him to do exactly that," I said. "She told me once."

"He didn't want to?" Ciaran asked. "It had to be hard, being a child here."

"It's not a hotel," I said.

"It is a public place, though. This would have been private."

"Up on the third floor, you can't hear a thing going on even one floor below. He can lock himself in his office for hours. Sometimes I'd think he was in there working, and he'd walk in the back door. Just went down another set of stairs, out another door. If we'd lived here, we'd never have been able to get away from each other," I said.

No one could fault Michan for needing some distance from the child he'd been left.

I didn't know how to explain that Michan had, at least in part, given me over to the house to raise. On my way to bed, I would pause to rest my cheek against the banister. I'd open the back door slowly to draw out the syllables of the creak, my home-from-school greeting.

"I think Jorie hoped that he'd eventually get married and we'd move to our own place."

"No, though. Committed bachelor?" Ciaran asked.

I hesitated. Michan considered himself a private person. He sometimes seemed not to remember that he'd put his life into writing. When residents mentioned some personal episode, he often seemed surprised. Your brother, your poor parents.

"He's never wanted kids," I said.

"Because of hemophilia?" Ciaran asked. "He'd pass it on?"

"His sons would be fine. His daughters would be carriers. Because they would get his X with the hemophilia gene on it," I said. I waited for him to realize the significance of that, what it meant for me, the daughter of a hemophiliac.

But he said, "You can choose the gender of a baby nowadays."

"I'll be sure and tell him," I said, and Ciaran laughed.

I wasn't going to explain. Though a fluke of genetics had spared Michan from HIV, I believed he was afraid of what else might lurk in his cells, that he might pass on something that was no saving grace.

Late the next afternoon, near the end of quiet hours, Ciaran found me again outside the servants' door with the dog. He tossed Poe the ball a few times and then asked if I wanted to come with him to Deering Road, where Rowan had lived. I said that I would. I opened the door and brought Poe up to the third floor by way of the servants' stairs. I kissed the top of his head and promised to be back later.

When I returned, Ciaran and I walked to my car. I saw several gardeners turn their heads to watch us as we passed by. I looked away. The house itself seemed to be watching us, resident and resident. There was no rule against the staff and the writers socializing, but it rarely happened on more than a casual level. The writers cocooned themselves in their time here, bonded by their purpose. The last two people to bend this unwritten rule in the way Ciaran and I were may well have been Evelyn and his own father.

I pointed out St. Maren's Catholic Church. Michan and I only went to Mass on Christmas Eve, and Rowan and Evelyn had not even bothered with that until David. I slowed down at the corner of Winter Hill Road.

"The house that Rowan's stepfather bought is right up there. See the red roof?" I said.

Ciaran wanted to get a closer look, so I obliged.

Twenty-two Winter Hill Road was at the crest of the hill. The house had four bedrooms, a wraparound porch and property of nearly a half acre.

Ciaran made no move to get out of the car. "Did Rowan want to move?" he asked.

"She did," I said. "She said it was the one good thing about

David. Her room was going to be much bigger. She was excited about having a big backyard."

"David and Evelyn never lived here either, am I right?"

I shook my head. "Once the work was finished, David wanted to move in, but Evelyn wouldn't leave where she'd lived with Rowan. He finally gave up and put it on the market. He left her not long after that."

"When I read about the new house being under construction, I was convinced I'd solved the case."

"Solved it?"

"I thought Rowan came here that day. It was a Saturday, and the workmen wouldn't have been here. She went in a window or an unlocked door and had some kind of accident. One of the workers covered it up because he knew they'd get in trouble."

"It's plausible," I said, "as a theory, but—"

Ciaran looked at me. "Wrong. I know. I had some fantasy of confronting the detective and then he calls in the FBI to shut me up. They find her somewhere in the house or yard."

"They searched it back then," I said, gazing at the house that was to be Rowan's compensation for putting up with David. The shutters were painted dark green and the curtains behind the windows were white.

"I know that now," Ciaran said. "Detective Huyser told me that all the men who were working here were looked at. He was nice about it. Didn't ask if I thought the investigators were so stupid they'd not thought of it."

I wasn't sure how to answer, but then Ciaran asked abruptly, "How did Rowan talk about David Brayton? Did she not like him only because he was her stepfather and he made her eat her vegetables and go to bed at nine thirty?"

David. Rowan's lip practically curled each time she said his name.

"And me—he wouldn't let me in their house. Rowan was mad about that."

"You're not serious," Ciaran said. "Because of—"

"Everyone thinks the worst was over by the nineties. It just stopped making the news," I said. "He didn't want me around Libby. Babies' immune systems aren't fully developed. That's what he told Evelyn."

Ciaran frowned. "That shouldn't matter, right?"

"It isn't the flu," I said wearily.

I remembered my humiliation when Rowan explained to me why I couldn't come over to her house. Furious as she was, she had not considered my feelings in quoting her stepfather.

Ciaran was watching me closely. "But you were still friends?"

"Rowan liked the idea of defying him. If we went to the movies, we'd buy tickets separately and meet in the balcony. I went along, but I don't think he'd have much cared. He just didn't want me in their house."

Ciaran looked down at his hands. "That's an awful thing to do to a child."

"I was twelve," I said.

"Do you mean you weren't a child, or you were?"

"I mean I'd had twelve years of it already," I said. "And that's a lot of practice."

He said no more, and I was pleased to have made it sound like a thing you could get used to.

On Deering Road, Ciaran had his door open before I'd pulled the key out of the ignition. I dropped my keys in my purse and followed him. He was surveying the neighborhood as though it were a mysterious landscape and not an ordinary block of houses with sagging eaves and shingles missing from their roofs.

He stopped before a house of red brick with navy-blue trim, like a house in a uniform. Number 4.

"Has it changed much?" he asked.

I rubbed my arms as I sorted the house into shapes as if preparing to draw it. The sharp triangle of the roof and the circular attic window. The twin rectangles of the second-story windows, Rowan's bedroom.

"No, not really," I said. "The front window is different. The porch railing was white back then, not blue. But otherwise, it looks the same."

I glanced behind me, at the mailbox beside the curb, also the same. One newspaper article had called the path from Rowan's front porch to the mailbox her "final walk," as though she'd opened her front door and stepped off the planet.

Ciaran went down the driveway and paused by the side door.

I glanced up at the house. "I'm not sure who lives here now—"

"No cars in the driveway. I don't think anybody's home," Ciaran said, unconcerned. "Would Rowan have come out this way?"

"She might have," I said. "But it doesn't matter if she came out the side door or the back door. Evelyn never pulled up this far."

Before Ciaran could answer, we both turned to watch a tan car pull into the Kellys' driveway, across the street. When the driver's door opened and a dark-haired woman got out, I believed for a moment that Brian's mother had arrived, even younger than she'd been in 1995. But Mrs. Kelly must have been at least forty then, and this woman was near my own age.

"That's Molly," I said.

Ciaran glanced at me and then back at the woman as she closed her car door and paused, keys in hand, watching us. I hadn't seen Brian's sister in years. She was wearing a dress and low heels and her hair was pulled back with a headband. Ciaran and I met her at the edge of the driveway.

"Adair," she said before turning to Ciaran expectantly.

I introduced them. "This is Ciaran Riordan. He's a writer staying at Moye House."

Molly's expression didn't change. "You're Rowan's brother. My brother told me you called him. You're writing a book. Well. We thought Rowan was making you up."

After hesitating a moment, Ciaran said, "We?" As though he had many questions and chose that one.

"The girls at school," she said and then looked at me. "Not Adair. Adair always believed her."

Her tone was casual, even friendly, but it rankled.

"She wasn't a liar," I said.

Molly raised her eyebrows and hoisted her purse higher on her shoulder.

"How well did you know Rowan?" Ciaran asked.

"We were summertime friends," Molly said. "We roller-skated and rode bikes. The usual."

As far as I could recall, Rowan had only ever mentioned Molly in passing, as a girl who lived on her block.

"But once Adair moved to town, forget it," Molly said. "I couldn't compete."

"Compete with *me?*" I said, my eyebrows raised.

"You were way more exciting than I was," Molly said.

"Lucky me," I said.

Molly shrugged. "That's the way her mind worked."

I thought, uncomfortably, that there was something to that.

"What do you know about the day Rowan disappeared?" Ciaran asked, deciding to bypass the twists of childhood friendships.

"Absolutely nothing," Molly said archly. "I didn't see Rowan at all."

"When did you last see her?" Ciaran asked.

Now Molly hesitated, with a look at her house as if afraid of being overheard.

"Two, three days before she disappeared," Molly said. "I looked out my bedroom window and she was sitting on her roof."

"The roof?" Ciaran repeated. "Of her house?"

Molly pointed. "Yes. Between the windows."

Molly explained that it had not been late, but she couldn't remember if she'd looked at the clock. That night, something had woken her up. A car door slamming. A barking dog. A dream. She only knew she had not been asleep very long and that she had keenly felt the need to go to her window, as though to check the sky on Christmas Eve. And there was Rowan, her legs stretched out in front of her. The roof was flat there, a cover for the porch below. Rowan had been wearing pajamas and no sweater or jacket, though it was a chilly night. She might not have been wearing socks, but given the distance, that was hard to say definitively. Next to her was a lit candle.

"What was she doing?" Ciaran said.

"I didn't know. She couldn't sleep? She'd gone out there to read instead of the typical flashlight under the covers? But I didn't see a book either. She wasn't doing anything," Molly said. "After she disappeared, I told my mother about it, because the thought was in the back of my head, even if I couldn't put it into words then, that she was hiding."

"From her stepfather?" Ciaran asked intently.

"No," she said. "He wasn't home that night."

"He was away on business most of that week," I said. "Then went to his mother's that weekend."

"You never told the police?" Ciaran asked, his eyes on her.

Molly shook her head. "My mother said it couldn't have meant anything and we didn't need to be more involved than we were. That used to be Leo's room. My mom said he always did the same thing. He probably told Rowan and she was copying him. I always thought she had a crush on him."

After we left Molly, Ciaran headed back up Rowan's driveway, then walked without pausing to the end of the street and climbed over the short brick wall that marked the block as a dead end. I followed him down a steep embankment to where a stream ran, shallow and cold. He squatted and put his hand in the water.

"Even with a lot of rain, it wouldn't get much deeper than this, am I right? One newspaper mentioned a search of the river behind her house. But this is no river."

"In the summer, we put our feet in," I said. "No, it's not enough to drown in."

"Sure it is, if someone held you and you couldn't get free," Ciaran said.

"They'd have to move the body, after."

He nodded. "There's this case, an old case from the fifties or sixties, here in the States. A two-year-old boy was playing with his dog in his backyard and the mother went inside to answer the phone. She came back and the boy was gone. There was a river behind the house, and I mean a real river with a strong current. The police were sure he drowned and was swept away."

"Because they never found him?"

"Because of the dog. The mother found the dog, barking like mad on the riverbank," Ciaran said. "The family never believed it, because the body never surfaced. They were sure he was abducted."

"What do you think?" I asked.

Ciaran stood up. "Occam's razor—do you know what that is?"

I shook my head.

"It's a rule of philosophy that says the simpler solution, the one that takes the fewest assumptions, is more likely to be true. Did a two-year-old wander out of his own backyard, or did a kidnapper wander *in* without being seen and without the dog barking? Then not a single neighbor hears or sees anything as the boy is taken, and all of it done in about ten minutes? Maybe, but it's far more likely that he fell in the river. His body sank and then snagged on something underwater, so it never rose up."

Occam's razor. Did Evelyn kill her daughter and then have her lover dispose of the body?

Or did Rowan cross paths with a kidnapper that afternoon?

But before I could frame the question, and ask which answer was the simpler one in Rowan's case, because I honestly didn't know, Ciaran turned and climbed back up the embankment. I followed. He stopped in front of Rowan's house and started to speak, but then stopped, staring at the window. A young woman with long hair was watching us, one hand holding back the curtain.

Not Rowan, I thought wildly. Never Rowan. The lost don't simply reappear in their homes.

The front door opened and a girl in a Gilbride sweatshirt came out on the porch in her stocking feet.

"You're here about the missing girl, aren't you," she said, as if Rowan were indeed in the house, waiting for us to collect her.

"I'm writing about the case," Ciaran said, and the ease with which he said it surprised me. Though he wasn't lying, this woman surely had no sense of what he was leaving out.

"Do a lot of curiosity seekers show up here?" he asked.

"Not a lot. We've been renting this place since sophomore year, and it's happened a few other times. We can tell because the people, like, stand out front and stare. Then there's a guy who gives ghost tours of the Hudson Valley in October. This is a stop." She leaned on the doorjamb. "Last time, he gave us forty dollars to bring the tour inside the house."

"And you let him?" I asked.

She laughed. "We're college students. He could've given us a six-pack and we would've said sure."

"I've no cash on me," Ciaran said. "I'd be happy to send a pizza over later if we can come in and look around."

She laughed again but shifted from foot to foot, surely weighing her mother's warnings about not trusting strangers. Then she studied me and, a moment later, opened the door wider.

She had decided my presence meant Ciaran was safe. Obviously, she hadn't spent enough time in the murky trenches of the internet. She had not read about girls who went to their fate together, assuming two could not be harmed at once, or girls who thought the woman in the passenger seat of a car meant the man driving was as harmless as he appeared to be.

"Come in."

I started to grab Ciaran's sleeve but he was already up the steps of the porch. Given his need to reconstruct what he could of Rowan's life, he would not turn down the chance to see where she had lived. I'd intended to tell him that I would sit on the step and wait for him, but he was already inside and it now seemed worse to be alone, so I followed, at first slowly and then fighting the urge to run inside shouting for Rowan. She would not answer her brother, because she barely knew him. She wouldn't come if her mother called, because in life she never had. But me, she would answer.

The kitchen's color scheme was different, yellow and beige instead of blue and green, but the cabinets and the placement of the table were the same. The stove and refrigerator were new. Evelyn's furniture was gone, of course. The living room held only a couch, facing a big-screen television, and a coffee table.

"What did the tour guide say?" Ciaran asked. "I'm sorry. I'm being rude. What's your name?"

"Sophie," she said. "The tour guide? He said the girl disappeared and was never found. Most people think she died here."

"Where?" I asked, and as I thought she would, she pointed to the stairs that led from the front hallway to the second floor. They were narrow and uncarpeted.

"An old tenant used to hear footsteps running down the hall and a banging on the stairs. Like someone falling? That's why they moved out, and that's why the house is only rented and never sold." Sophie paused. "But that's not true, because my dad asked about buying it, figuring he could fix it up and sell it once I'm done with school. But the lady who owns it said no."

"Have *you* ever heard anything?" Ciaran asked.

He sounded almost stern, as though it were not the tour guide he disapproved of, but Rowan, as if she were indeed performing her death nightly, and he, her brother, had finally arrived to make her stop.

"Me? No. But I don't believe in that stuff. One of my roommates said lights have turned off and on, but she's kind of a liar."

Silently, I agreed. Rowan was not here. But then why would she be? Her mother and sister were gone. Strangers moved in and left again. More strangers came.

"Can we take a look upstairs?" Ciaran asked.

Sophie shrugged. "Sure. Nobody else is home."

She started up, with Ciaran behind her and me last. She paused on the landing and pointed.

"See how steep these are?" she said. "It'd be easy to fall, especially if you were a kid and you were running."

I'd forgotten how short the hallway was. Both bedroom doors were open. She gestured to the room at the front. Rowan's room.

"It's kind of a mess," she said unapologetically.

It *was* a mess, I thought. Clothes and books were scattered over the floor and the bed was unmade. Rowan had kept the room very neat.

Ciaran went to the window, to look out at the roof. He parted the curtain, as if hoping to see whatever Rowan had been looking at that night.

I stayed where I was, on the threshold. Ciaran didn't speak or move. Minutes passed.

Finally, Sophie coughed. "Hey, sorry, but I have to get going soon," she said, as though she'd just realized it was a bad idea to let a strange man stroll right into your bedroom.

Ciaran snapped the curtain closed and started back across the room. Then he stopped at the open closet door. The inside light was on, revealing hangers jammed with clothes and a jumble of shoes.

"Adair?" Ciaran said and beckoned me to look.

I went over. On the inside of the door were crooked marks, some in black pen, some in blue. There were no dates beside them, only numbers. Eight, nine, ten, eleven.

"Her height," Ciaran whispered.

My fingertips climbed the marks like a ladder until I reached the highest one, twelve, which was level with my shoulder.

"No," I said. "Rowan was never this tall. This is Leo."

"Leo?" Ciaran said, raising his voice.

"That's our landlady's son." For the first time, Sophie actually looked at me. "Do you *know* him?" she breathed.

"I grew up in town," I said, turning away from her.

"Do *you* know him?" Ciaran asked. "Does he live around here?"

"We mail our rent checks to his mother—it's a PO box," she added, as though afraid he might ask for the address. "I have no idea where they live. He was, like, a drug dealer. We didn't know that before we rented this place. My dad said to tell him immediately if the guy ever comes around. I never told him that Leo what's-his-name was a suspect in this case. You know that, right?"

"I know they think he knew more than he was telling," Ciaran said. "I know the whole story, except what really happened and the ending."

It sounded as if he were expressing only a writer's frustration, not a brother's. But it made me wonder if Ciaran had come here not to write about Rowan but to find her, in spite of his insistence otherwise. Maybe he believed the case was his to break.

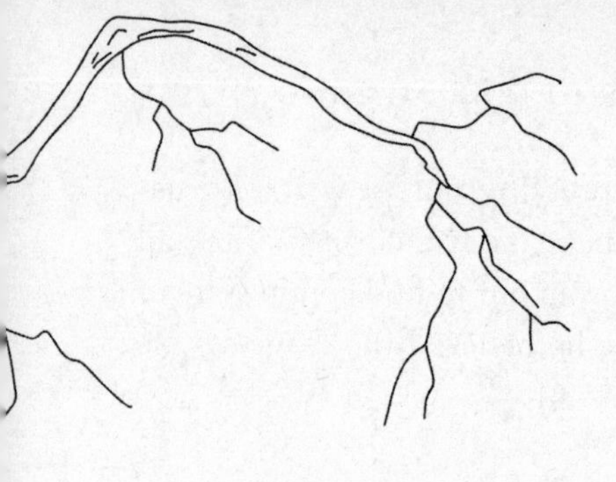

13

The oaks that lined the streets of the neighborhood were so dense with leaves that the sidewalks below were dark, the glow of the streetlamps caught in the branches.

The neighborhood was on the far edge of town, so residents could go grocery shopping either in Culleton or in the more anonymous Onohedo.

I drove slowly. All the lights in the houses were lit, it seemed. It was only seven o'clock. In the summer, children would still be out playing, but this deep in autumn, everyone was indoors.

I pulled into the driveway of a corner house. Smoke drifted from the chimney. A pickup truck was in the driveway, the kind with an open bed, the better to carry rakes and shears and all the other gardening tools I could not name.

I climbed the steps and stood on the narrow porch. In the dark, I shivered, as though I were at a stranger's door to ask directions. There was a hole where the doorbell should have been. I knocked, and when there was no answer, I knocked again, a second set of three.

When there was still no answer, I pulled my keys out of my purse. There were only three: my car key, the key to the servants' door at Moye House and this one, which I had not used in five years, since I was twenty-one.

The short hallway was uncarpeted, and though my soft-soled shoes made little noise on the wood floor, the sound was amplified by the quiet in the rest of the house. There was a small eat-in kitchen and then a living room with a bedroom off it that had a bathroom attached. The firelight was visible before the fire. I reached the end of the hallway and paused on the top step of the three that led into the sunken living room.

He was feeding the fire. Even kneeling, it was clear he was tall, as those marks on his closet door had predicted. The kindling caught with a soft roar and the fire surged.

"Leo," I said.

"*Adair*," he said, still kneeling, watching the flames.

I was cold where I stood, but I didn't move until he got slowly to his feet and sat in the chair beside the fireplace.

"How have you been? I think that's what old friends are supposed to say."

I went down the stairs, and after dropping my purse by the couch, I sat down on the floor, not quite at his feet but close. I stretched my legs out in front of me. Leo would be thirty-five soon, but I thought those who didn't know him would probably guess older.

Though still slim, he had thickened since I'd last seen him. We'd been right here, lying together on a blanket I'd fetched from his bed. A fire was going then too. It was a freezing January night, and I'd been home from college on winter break but due back at school the next day.

"What did you say to Molly when you saw her on Deering Road today?" he asked.

"She called you? I should have known."

"She called my mother," Leo said. "Who then called me, crying that it's going to start all over again. Is this guy really Rowan's brother? He's really writing a book about her?"

"He is," I said. "But it's about other missing kids too. He's not making the case for anyone's guilt," I said. "I think you should talk to him."

"Jesus, did he send you here?" Leo asked.

"No!" I said, angry that Leo would think that. "I just think he'll listen."

"Even if he believes every word I say, he still has to write that I was a suspect. *Am* a suspect," Leo said.

"And he still has to write that I told the police I saw her that morning when nobody else did."

"Your name never got out," Leo said. "Don't fucking try that."

"It will this time," I said. "Ciaran is going to write everything, I think."

Leo shook his head and stared at the fire. I waited patiently for him to answer, just as I'd been waiting these past weeks for him to break away from the grounds crew at Moye House as I crossed the lawn, or to come find me at the end of his workday. But maybe that was asking too much. Leo was too grateful to Michan for reaching out to him in the first year of his parole, when he was living with his mother, searching for the kind of work a man with a prison record could get. In 1995, he'd begun to consider formally studying horticulture, creating a real career for himself. Postprison, however, he was sure that was all over. He didn't know, still, that it was me who got Michan to pull strings with the head gardener, who then offered Leo a job, with the caveat that at any time in the first three months Leo could be let go if he wasn't working out.

I was seventeen then. Michan thought I was acting out of pity, and there is truth to that. I never tried to explain to my uncle that, even more than pity, it was a gift of gratitude for a handshake.

"Does this Ciaran think I did it?"

"He doesn't know," I said.

"He knows what he thinks. He's just not telling *you.*"

I shook my head. "He doesn't think the police should've based their whole theory on Brian Kelly. He's said that. If you think Brian's wrong, then maybe I'm right."

Leo tilted his head, in acknowledgment, I thought.

"And—I don't know. He seems to want me to be right."

"Why?" Leo asked. "Are you sleeping with him?"

I half smiled. "No. Even if he wanted to, I think he wouldn't risk compromising his book. Otherwise, he might ask. He's noble enough."

"Noble enough?" Leo said. "Give me a break, Adair. You aren't that special."

"You always get nasty when you're mad. I mean, he knows about me and would pretend not to care."

"Or, try this, he *really* wouldn't care," Leo said.

"No guy wouldn't care."

"I didn't."

"You knew me a long time, before."

I wanted to say that he had been in a dark place, and though free, when he closed his eyes he was still there in his cell. The stares on the street, the whispers. He'd been approached in the supermarket by old ladies, who put a hand on his arm. *Tell where she is. She deserves a Christian burial.*

"Did you really come back home because you're getting sick? I heard you were in the hospital."

I pulled my knees up to my chest. "Don't listen to the village gossips."

"If all I had to do to fix my life was take some pills every day, I'd stop feeling sorry for myself and do it," Leo said.

"Maybe you're the one who should stop feeling sorry for yourself."

"I spent two years in prison, Adair."

"Well, Leo, you were guilty."

He looked up and laughed. We sat quietly in the heat from the fire until I said it was getting late and I had to go. He barely nodded and didn't try to stop me.

At Moye House the next day, when it was four thirty and still light out, though early-winter darkness was beginning to encroach, I went up the front staircase to the second floor.

With an hour and a half before the end of quiet hours, the residents were still at work. Jorie used to talk fondly about visiting the second floor just to hear the clack of typewriters behind closed doors. The doors were still closed, but keyboards had put an end to the sound of writing. Most of the hallways in the house were bare, but on the residents' floor thick carpeting was meant to muffle the comings and goings during quiet hours.

The hallway ended in a full-length mirror that was set in a cherrywood frame. The keyhole was obscured by the design of the woodwork, an intricate swirl of leaves. I took the key out of my pocket, quickly unlocked the door and shut it behind me.

This room, my studio, was above the library, though half its size. It had once belonged to Maddy Moye, Cassius's mother, who had used it for reading and sewing and writing letters to her son, away at war.

The library's recessed windows kept the room dim, so leaving the library and coming up here was like trading the underworld for heaven.

I was eleven when I first learned about the quality of light and how important it was to an artist. How in a room where the light shifted as the day aged, colors might take on different hues. A shadow might fall over a canvas.

North light was best because it was consistent. North light: light from the sky, not the sun. It was my grandfather Darragh who told me this.

On the last day of the December residency, Darragh had turned up at the servants' door of Moye House with his square suitcase. He had come to stay with Michan before, often during the break between one set of residents leaving and the new ones arriving. Sober, but promising nothing.

Previous visits, he'd slept in the small sitting room off the kitchen. The couch there was a sofa bed. It was fine, he said. But this time he moved into Jorie's old suite. "Suite" was her word, he'd told me with a sad smile.

If Michan resented his father, and I thought he must, he set those feelings aside in exchange for a break from being my sole guardian. Perhaps he hoped that this time Darragh would not leave, which would give *him* the chance to be the runaway, at least for a little while.

On Christmas Day, Michan came out and asked his father how long he would be staying, which Michan had never done before. Darragh only said he'd see. I understood why Michan asked, though. There was a difference in Darragh, and it was not that he had aged. There were no changes that a year might not have brought. Rather, it was his willingness to talk about my father and his ability to look directly at me while doing so. Then, I believed it was a trick he had taught himself, as if since I'd last seen him, he'd done nothing but practice saying his son's name without looking at the floor or closing his eyes.

Darragh came upon me drawing at the dining room table, and he told me that my father had liked to draw in the rooms at the front of the house because he'd read about north light. The residents' reading room was his favorite spot. When he was recovering from a bleed, Cathal would spend hours drawing to distract himself from the pain.

The writers loved that room. They'd sink into the couch or one of the two green chairs. In good weather, they'd step out onto the balcony that was directly over the front door. That room was like being cocooned from the rest of the house.

Then Darragh said we should turn it into a studio for me. There were dozens of other places for residents to park themselves. The new ones wouldn't miss it, and returning ones, well, too bad. When Michan said he'd have to get a change like that approved by the board, Darragh told him he could explain what he'd done after the fact. If they objected, let them undo it. Let them be the ones to take the room away from me. Michan let it go, and in fact the project brought on a togetherness like a fever shared between them.

Darragh hired a pair of local brothers to move the furniture out and empty the bookshelves. They removed the old wallpaper and painted the walls. Darragh chose a shade called Shadow White, which had overtones of gray. The name thrilled me. The throw rugs were rolled up and taken away to be set down on other floors, leaving the wood floor bare so I could paint. The balcony doors were replaced. The new ones had glass that was smooth, not divided into panes, so the light arrived unbroken.

When finished, the room held a drafting table and an easel. The easel Michan bought new, but the drafting table he found after calling antique stores up and down the Hudson Valley, going to check out three at least before settling on one that was also a desk. In that same store he found the mirror that became the door, a secret entrance to a secret room.

The room was well used now. The bookshelves were cluttered with supplies that I should have thrown away years ago. Clotted paintbrushes that I'd failed to clean properly after use, the way you were supposed to. Pencils worn down to a size too small for my hand. But I had a way of crediting the instruments for work that went well. Tossing them seemed a poor reward. They deserved retirement.

Michan first called the room North Light when it was only half finished, and by the time it was done, that was its name. When Darragh left, he told me, "Keep North Light, Adair."

It was the middle of January, and he'd been with us more than a month, his longest visit ever, and his last. He never mentioned heart trouble, the opposite of the kind that had left him a widower. Cecilia had died without a chance of rescue, but Darragh was told his options (stents, surgery) and refused them. Michan learned this from his neighbor, the only friend Darragh had, as far as we knew. When he died, she was the one who called to tell us.

After I moved away, North Light was the place in Moye House that I'd missed the most. Since coming back, I'd only briefly visited the room, afraid to see the work I'd left behind, the good as well as the bad. Afraid to remember what I'd been thinking back then.

My sense of time felt off-kilter, as though my years away

had been an interlude that had come to its natural end. If I belonged anywhere in the world, it was here.

I went to a pile of my old sketchbooks, which were stacked in the nonworking fireplace. I found a couple from when I was twelve or thirteen and began leafing through them. It wasn't until then that I admitted to myself that these sketchbooks were the reason I was here.

I had not started putting dates on my sketchbooks until I was fifteen, and none of them were organized, which I cursed myself for now. In Brooklyn, I'd tried to keep a corner of my living room as a bit of studio space, but it never worked. Clutter crept over the invisible boundaries.

I took out my phone, and after only a moment's hesitation, I texted Ciaran: *Go to the mirror at the end of the residents' hallway.*

If he was working and had his phone put away, he might not see it for some time. But quiet hours were almost over. I was not surprised to hear the tap on the door not more than ten minutes after I asked him to come.

I opened the door and stepped aside to let Ciaran in, resisting the urge to ask if anyone had seen him. The hallway was empty; I didn't think so. As he passed by me, I caught the faintest tang of cigarettes.

"I've been thinking there had to be a room at the end of this hallway. Otherwise, there's no way to get to the balcony above the door," Ciaran said, gesturing to it.

A few residents over the years had noticed this, but most hardly paid attention to the length of the house. I shut the door and turned around to see Ciaran studying the sketches of mine that I'd hung on the wall. He pointed at one, a girl staring up at a grinning cat in a tree.

"That's the Cheshire Cat. But that's not Alice. Is she anybody, or did you make her up?"

"She's not Alice from the illustrations, with the blond hair and the headband," I said. "That's Alice Liddell, who Lewis Carroll wrote the story for."

Blunt black hair. Hard stare. The sort of girl who was described as handsome rather than pretty and didn't care. In nearly every photo I'd seen of her, I could imagine Alice Liddell giving the finger.

Ciaran studied the other sketches of mine, which were mostly of Moye House from different angles or close-ups of things like the curio in the parlor. My grandfather's button accordion, which had come to me though I couldn't play it. The servants' staircase. Other ordinary things. Ciaran moved next to my drafting table. He touched the edges with his fingertips.

"This is North Light, isn't it?" he said quietly.

Neither my grandfather nor I had known that the construction of this room would be turned into poetry. "North Light" was probably Michan's most well-known poem. His party piece, he called it, the one he was always expected to recite at readings. An elegy for me.

"Did you mind him writing it?"

I sat down at my drafting table, remembering. The slender book with its blue cover and the title in a black font: *North Light and Other Poems.*

"Why would I mind?"

"If someone had imagined my death, I might mind."

"You must understand why he was thinking about it."

"Yes. But that wasn't the question," Ciaran said.

"Yes," I said, almost inaudibly. "But not for the reason you're thinking. In the poem, I'm full of all the promise in the world, the way only the dead can be."

"You're very talented," he said.

"I'm also alive," I said, and then went out onto the balcony to stand at the rail, feeling as though I'd taken off my clothes. Ciaran followed, leaving the door open behind us.

"Do you believe Molly Kelly about Rowan being on the roof?" Ciaran asked.

I nearly smiled. We were done, then, talking about me. I was alive, yes, and so able to answer his questions.

"You think she's making it up so you'll put her in your book?" I asked.

"Maybe to get one up on her brother, the star witness? Possible star witness, I mean," Ciaran said. "What do you think?"

I considered Molly's puzzlement, and I wondered how many nights she'd lain awake wondering what Rowan had been doing.

"I think Rowan was on the roof," I said.

Ciaran was silent for a moment. "Waiting for someone? Hiding?"

"I've been thinking about it," I said, but I meant remembering. "Looking at the moon is my best guess."

Whatever Ciaran had been expecting to hear, it was not that. "Looking at the *moon?* Why wouldn't she just look through her window?"

"She'd found a book, about spells and curses." I frowned. "Well, I don't know if there were any curses. Spells definitely. Irish spells."

"What are you talking about? Witchcraft?" Ciaran asked. "'On the night of a full moon, say this three times—'"

"That kind of thing, yes."

Ciaran took out his phone and typed quickly. "The full moon had already passed, but on October 24, 1995, there was a new moon. Does a new moon have some kind of meaning?"

"I have no idea," I said.

Ciaran started to type again and then stopped. "What was the name of the book?"

"It had 'Irish' or 'Ireland' in the title, and the word 'charm.' The cover was sort of *Book of Kells*–ish."

Ciaran sighed and put his phone in his pocket. "At least it wasn't a leprechaun."

"Maybe it doesn't mean anything. It was almost Halloween."

Ciaran nodded, an acknowledgment.

After a brief silence, I said, only because I'd been wondering, "Have you told the other writers here what you're working on?"

"Not specifically. A couple of them keep asking me, and I give out my answer that gives away nothing, and we don't get much further."

"You're talking to me," I said.

"You know who I am."

I didn't care for how he made it sound, like I'd found him out. As though I'd gone through his things when he wasn't in his room.

"Because you told me," I said.

"Because I didn't want to lie to you," Ciaran said.

Because you think I might know something, I thought.

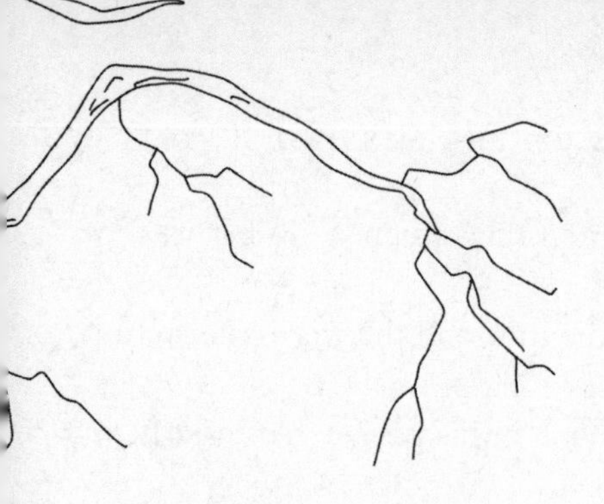

14
ADAIR
December 1994

Rowan and I sat on our sleeping bags, which were spread out beneath the Christmas tree in the front parlor. The tree, a concolor fir, was so tall that the wings of its angel brushed the ceiling. The room's only illumination were the tree's clear, unblinking lights. The ornaments—red, silver, green bells and stars, spheres and spirals—swung gently in the draft seeping in around the windowpane. The curtain was left open to display the tree, a tradition meant to welcome lost travelers, though certainly there would be no one on the road by Moye House at close to midnight.

In the near-dark I could almost see a hand from another era rising to wind the ancient clock on the mantel, as ever two hours behind. No one living could fix it, not even my grandfather Darragh, who had often tried.

The sleepover was to mark my twelfth birthday. Michan had bought the sleeping bags especially (one of my gifts, I thought) because he had somehow realized it would be more fun for us to sleep beneath the Christmas tree. But then Rowan told me that it was the only way her stepfather would agree to let her stay over. My double bed was more than big enough for the both of us, and this was the problem. Twin beds or bunk beds might have been deemed fine. "I keep telling him there's nothing wrong with you," Rowan had said, disgusted. "There is," I'd argued, but she shook her head.

I held the cards, a deck abandoned by a writer from years ago, who had sat at the dining room table long after breakfast was over, dealing himself hand after hand of solitaire. When he took off only halfway through his residency, he left the cards behind.

"Hit me," Rowan said.

"King plus nine equals nineteen," I said, exasperated. "You'll go over."

She grinned. "Hit me!"

I tossed down the jack of hearts. "See?"

Rowan laughed and sat back on her hands. "My mom once won money at blackjack in Las Vegas."

"When did she go to Las Vegas?" I asked. Rowan, and sometimes Evelyn herself, revealed interesting fragments of Evelyn's life, the years between high school and Rowan's own birth. I pictured Evelyn as she must have been then, her smile not the polite work-smile but an expression she never used anymore.

Rowan shrugged. "Twenty? I forget. This woman told her she should stay and work in the casinos because she could make a fortune, even as a cocktail waitress. Mom said she thought about it for half a second, but it was so hot out there that raindrops would evaporate before they hit the ground."

I nodded, a yawn pressing at the back of my throat. It was too early for bed, though. Sleepovers, I'd heard, went on until dawn. They were wild. I didn't want to disappoint Rowan.

One day, home from school with a fever, I was sitting in Evelyn's office as she worked, something Michan allowed because Evelyn said she didn't mind. I sat on the loveseat by the window with a book. After a morning of listening to her field phone calls and watching her type letters, her fingers flying over the keyboard as if she were playing a piece of music, Michan came to see if I was hungry, and Evelyn asked what the plan was for my birthday, which was in a week.

"Plan?" Michan said with that touch of panic he always tried to pass off as a joke.

Evelyn suggested the sleepover. She probably hoped that if she arranged this for Rowan, Rowan would leave her be about letting me stay over at their house.

Now Rowan stood, apparently not at all tired, and pointed at two open boxes in a corner of the parlor. "Are those more Christmas decorations?"

"Those are books," I told Rowan, "for the residents' library."

"The what?" she asked.

I explained that it was going to be built in the old carriage house, and it would be far less formal than the one in the house. At least one section would be books that had been written in Moye House, and another would be other books by authors who had been residents.

Rowan looked at me quickly. "The book my father's in could be there," she said, and I realized this was probably why her mother had not mentioned it to her. Evelyn didn't want to talk about Jamie Riordan.

Rowan went over to the boxes and dropped to her knees.

For all the stories I'd heard about sleepovers, none of them included sorting through old books.

"So?" I said.

"So I've never even seen it," Rowan said. "My mom doesn't have a copy. I always look in bookstores but it's never there." She leaned over so that her hair hid her face.

Rowan began taking books out, glancing at the titles and then setting them aside.

"You have to put those back," I said.

"I will," she said. "Help me. I'll get done faster."

I stepped off my sleeping bag and went to kneel beside her.

"Will he ever come back to America?" I asked.

"He can't," Rowan said. She sat back on her heels and, with a book in her lap, explained that her father was locked out. When he first came over, it was supposed to be for only a few months. But he'd met her mother and overstayed his visa, Rowan said, repeating the words as though translating them from a foreign language. He could not work legally in the United States. If he'd been pulled over for a speeding ticket, he might have been taken straight to jail. Then, when Rowan was two, he'd gone back to Ireland, and this made returning to New York almost impossible. Whatever list they kept of those who overstayed their visas, Jamie Riordan was on it. And once you'd been in America illegally and were caught, you were banned for ten years. He could hardly go to the airport and buy a ticket to come back.

In that case, I asked, why had he taken such a risk? Rowan turned away and explained that by then, Jamie and her mother had broken up, and he hadn't seen his son, her brother Ciaran, in almost four years. She said no more, but I understood. With children in two different countries, her father had to choose between them. "But if you were two," I said, "that means it's been ten years. He can come back."

Rowan set aside the book she was holding and took another one from the box. "Well, sure. But he has a job and everything now. He can't leave."

I started to ask why not, just for a visit, but Rowan spoke first.

"Somebody stole a library book." Rowan put the book close to her face to read the title: *A History of Culleton, New York.*

I leaned over.

The plastic cover crinkled as Rowan opened the book to flip through it. She stopped abruptly and tapped the page.

Rowan tossed the book aside and continued searching. I went back to my own hunt. After several minutes of silence, she held up another, slimmer book with a green cover edged with Celtic knotwork: *A Charm for Lasting Love: Spells and Cures from Ireland.*

I shifted close to Rowan as she opened the book to the middle. She read, "'This beauty spell will make you think you're more beautiful than you are.'"

"That's a dumb idea," I said.

"Really. Walking around ugly and thinking you're not? At least I know."

"You're not ugly, Rowan," I said.

She shrugged. "I'm not you."

It was too close to a thought I'd had, staring in the mirror —that I did indeed resemble my grandmother Cecelia, who had been so pretty.

I pretended not to understand. "With this spell, a girl wouldn't know, though," I said. "Even if everybody told her, she'd think they were wrong."

"I guess," Rowan said, already moving on. She turned the pages, skimming them. "Too bad we don't have a rooster," she said, and, "Is it a full moon?"

When I had gone to the window and reported that the moon was only half lit, she flipped a page, annoyed.

"You can make a bracelet out of your hair and give it to a man, and if he takes it, he's your true love," she said and grinned. "You should give one to Leo. See what happens."

"That's a stupid thing to say. I don't like Leo." I was grateful for the darkness, because she couldn't see me blushing.

"I don't care if you do. It's better than liking any of the idiots in our class."

I didn't like any of the boys in our class either, but Leo was unthinkable. He was in high school, as out of reach as a movie star.

"I don't like anybody," I said.

She laughed as she bent her head back over the book. "Whatever."

Rowan read quietly for a moment and then stood, stomping her foot to wake it.

"We need matches."

"We can't use the fireplace. Jorie would kill us."

"We don't need a whole fire," Rowan said impatiently. "We need a candle."

I followed her into the hallway and through the dark to the dining room, where she plucked a red Christmas candle from the holder on the table. Those candles were never lit. When it was time to set the table, they were carefully moved to the sideboard.

Rowan rolled the candle between her palms. "Matches."

That was easy. The top drawer of her mother's desk. I eased it open, as though afraid of tripping an alarm. I slid my hand inside, and there among the rubber bands and paper clips, I found a matchbook.

Rowan laughed when I held it up. "She smokes?"

"Sometimes," I admitted.

She snorted. "So much for 'I quit for you and Libby.'"

I started to defend Evelyn. I was going to say it was only occasionally, sometimes after lunch, but Rowan was already heading back to the hallway and I quickly followed.

Back beneath the Christmas tree, we sat cross-legged on our sleeping bags, which had grown cold in our absence.

Rowan held the candle and I struck the match. The flame arrived with a hiss. She tilted the candle and the wick caught. I blew out the match as she recited the spell.

We sat in the small light, listening for the sound of the stairs creaking or a door opening, some sign of the house accommodating the dead. I turned and looked at the round Christmas ornaments to see if the same room was reflected back. Red wax dripped over Rowan's fingers.

I jumped when she abruptly blew the candle out. The smoke drifted between us.

"Oh," she said acidly. "I should have told you to make a wish for your birthday."

Rowan set the candle on the mantel. She climbed inside her sleeping bag and I did the same, relieved to tuck myself away, to be cocooned.

"What now?" I asked.

"We wait," she said.

But it wasn't long before her breathing slowed and deepened, and I closed my own eyes.

"Do you hear that?"

I turned my head away from whomever I was with in my dream, and the dream retreated as if I were walking backward, toward the whisper above me, which turned from the question to my name.

"Adair? Adair?"

I opened my eyes to see Rowan hovering above me, propped up on one elbow.

"What?" I asked, instinctively whispering as well.

"Listen," Rowan said.

I heard the bell then. One bell, ringing faintly, as though it were not the ring itself but an echo.

She said, "It's the servants' bell."

"The servants' bells are disconnected," I whispered.

With one hand, she groped behind her and came up with her glasses. She slipped them on and said, "It's saying our names."

Fear pushed against my rib cage like two hands. I did hear it.

RowanAdair.

Four quick syllables in a voice like light, calling us both.

Rowan rolled away and I grabbed for her, but she was already on her feet. She reached down and I gripped her hand and she pulled me up. I was holding her so tightly that when she released me I nearly fell, but she was already walking to the door.

"Rowan!" I called, but she didn't look back, and I followed her into the hallway. The temperature dropped, and it seemed like we'd stepped outside. Her red pajamas nearly glowed. They were new, bought for this occasion. I'd heard Evelyn tell Michan this, and I'd felt a kind of pity for Rowan to think she put this much importance on me, only me. All the way down the hallway, I stayed behind her as the bell continued to ring our names.

Rowan opened the kitchen door slowly, as if afraid of striking someone hiding behind it. The room was dark and felt the way a kitchen did outside of mealtimes, like a museum. The stove an artifact, the kettle quaint, the toaster a strange, useless thing. Only the refrigerator lived, as told by its steady hum.

Though the ringing was clearly coming from the kitchen, a detail we'd always agreed on, the sound got no louder when we were in the room. As one, we looked up at the bell line near the ceiling, something the girls who had made their living in Moye House a century ago must have done a hundred times a day. The old bells were still. The ringing continued.

"It's not outside?" Rowan asked.

"No," I said. "It's too loud."

The windows were shut tight.

She opened the door to the servants' staircase, and with that, the ringing ceased.

Rowan extended a hand into the dark of the stairwell, palm up, pressing against the dark.

The grief of the house pressed back like a sigh. She stepped back and closed the door. I tugged her sleeve.

We didn't speak the name out loud. Helen. Helen, grandmother, skipping over the four "greats" that lay between her and us and then passing by our mothers, the one who was living and the one who was dead, and then moving further back until she was only a girl herself, not much older than we were when she first came to live here. We had, all three of us, perhaps traversed all the eras between us, landing in one that none of us had ever seen.

Rowan and I did not have a holding-hands kind of friendship, but we hitched closer to each other inside our sleeping bags until our foreheads touched. Like that, we slept.

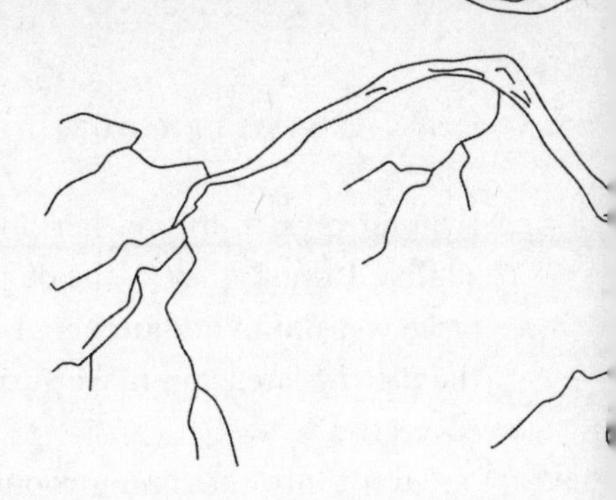

15

ADAIR

2010

The residents' dining room was furnished with one long table, not original to the house but bought at an estate sale years ago. Above the three tall windows there was a stained-glass window, but not the kind found in a church. The panes formed no picture; they were only colored glass. On bright mornings, the sun cast fractured blue and green light on the dining room table, but this day was cloudy.

I was working in the kitchen, unloading the dishwasher and returning the dishes to their places in the pantry, half listening to the banter of the two women who worked with Mrs. Penrose. Most of their work was done for the moment. Soon they'd go out and clear the table.

Usually the residents left the dining room by nine o'clock, when quiet hours started. But Michan, who rarely had anything but coffee, had gone out to say good morning. They would linger as long as he did, to remain in his company.

In the kitchen, we could not hear the conversation, only the hum of voices, broken by laughter.

Mrs. Penrose handed me a fresh pot of coffee. "Bring this out there before someone comes in here asking, will you?"

I had no desire to interact with the crowd, but she was already impatient with me, as though I were a cat who kept twining myself around her ankles. There was some old sensibility, I think, that as the de facto daughter of the house, my place was not in her kitchen. I had no doubt she would go into the pantry later and make sure the dishes had been put away correctly.

I went into the dining room and the conversation stopped, as if I'd pressed a mute button. Ciaran was there with a man and two women.

"You *are* real, then," the older of the women said. "I was starting to wonder if you were made up."

I sensed the others collectively wince.

Michan winked at me.

I was sure he was thinking, as I was, about how Jorie used to say that in each group there will be one person everybody likes and one person everybody dislikes.

"I've been real for some time," I said, picking up the empty coffeepot and replacing it with the full one.

"Who became real, in literature?" Hal asked, and I glanced at him gratefully. "Pinocchio? The Velveteen Rabbit."

"Any grown-up books?" Michan asked. "And I mean where the transformation is literal."

After a short silence, Ciaran said, "We're a sad lot. Can't think of one."

"It's early." Hal picked up his mug and stood, but I brought the coffeepot to him. He thanked me. I raised the pot, and Ciaran picked up his mug.

"Thanks. Maybe this'll help."

"Since we need to clear out for the cleaning crew this afternoon, some of us are going hiking," Hal said. "Unless it pours, which it looks like it might. What is there to do around here in the rain?"

"Not much," I said, and they laughed.

"You can work in the library. Go out to the rec room. Come in here," Michan said.

"I need a break," Hal said. "None of that 'write every day' bullshit for me. Is there a bowling alley around here?"

"Not in Culleton. There's one in Onohedo, though," Michan said.

"Well, I'm going hiking, even if it's pouring," the younger woman, Brooke, said. "I need to move my legs. Exercise increases circulation to the brain."

"So does red wine," Michan said.

"Since it's nine o'clock in the morning, I'll go for a walk," Brooke said. "I read about Degare Mountain Park's wildflower tour where they take you on a hike and the guide identifies all sorts of species of flowers."

"Adair, didn't you do that for a birthday party once?" Michan asked.

"That was a class trip," I said.

"Same thing," Michan said.

It wasn't, since you had to be invited to a birthday party, but I only pressed my left hand against the warm coffeepot.

"Ciaran, are you coming hiking?" Brooke asked.

"Afraid not," he said. "I've got some research to do."

"Research, for your mysterious book that you won't tell us about," the older woman said. Her tone annoyed me, but Ciaran seemed unfazed.

"That's the one." His tone was detached.

"Too much research and not enough writing can be dangerous," Hal said.

"So can not doing enough research when you're putting real people in a book," Michan said, looking directly at Ciaran as if expecting him to agree. When Ciaran didn't answer, Michan wished them all a productive and/or a relaxing day and reminded them to stick to the trail if they were going hiking. Years ago, a resident had gone off by himself to Degare Mountain, eager to write in complete solitude.

"He went into the woods deliberately?" Brooke said.

But Michan was serious. Luckily, the writer had told him of this plan. Michan, aware that the man had been raised in a city and had no hiking or camping experience, suggested that he not go far. Settle for the illusion of solitude. The woods could easily disorient. The man had replied that he had an excellent sense of direction.

When he hadn't returned by dinnertime, Michan contacted Degare Mountain State Park. There was still enough light to begin a search, and he was found within a couple of hours, a few miles west of a popular trail—but heading in the opposite direction.

Michan had told me privately that if dark had fallen and the city boy had still been out there, he probably would have been too grateful to be embarrassed, but the relatively quick resolution made him feel foolish. He'd guessed that he would become a Moye House cautionary tale.

Michan came with me into the kitchen. He told Mrs. Penrose that some of the residents were heading up the mountain. They'd probably be coming in to gather food for a picnic. She sighed and said she'd move the sandwich things to the front of the refrigerator, so they wouldn't be calling her every five minutes to ask where the cheese was, or the mustard.

I went outside and sat on the step, Poe by my feet. He was peeved because I'd forgotten to bring the ball. When he was younger, he'd have fetched a stick, but I supposed now he was content to sulk. Michan joined me and closed the door behind him. He was holding a newspaper, and I hoped for a minute that he'd want to read and not talk. But he sat down next to me, and though I considered dashing into the house on the pretense of getting a ball for Poe (and not coming back), I decided not to be a coward.

"Ciaran told you about his book, I guess," I said.

"No, *Ciaran* didn't tell me."

Michan unfolded the newspaper and handed it to me. It was the *Culleton Beacon.*

"Page five," Michan said.

I opened it and considered reading out loud, "PTA Meeting Gets Heated," but it would only annoy him further.

Brother of Missing Culleton Girl Writing Book

In the article's four brief paragraphs, Molly Kelly was quoted confirming that "Rowan's brother" had spoken to both her and her own brother. Ciaran was also quoted, but all he said was that he preferred to finish the book before commenting on it. The case was still open. Anyone who had any information should take it to the police.

I folded the paper and handed it back to Michan, who set it down.

"Gin called me this morning to ask if I'd seen it. She told me that you both talked to Molly."

"We did, yes," I said defensively.

"Why?" Michan asked. "Ciaran and Molly speak the same language. They hardly needed you to translate."

"I knew Rowan," I said. "Ciaran only met her once, when she was little."

"Writers write about victims they never knew all the time. That's how it usually goes, and I know you know that."

"Ciaran's not some journalist looking for a story. She was his sister. He wants to know who she was."

"Is that the only way he wants you to help him?"

"What is that supposed to mean?"

"Rowan's been gone a long time now."

I recalled the first weeks, crying into my pillow, Michan sitting helplessly beside me, at first saying she would be okay, and then that they'd find out soon what happened because something had to break, and then finally nothing at all.

It's my fault, I had told him at one point.

How is it your fault? he'd asked.

I'm cursed.

The ones left behind always think that, he'd said. You're not.

That was the last time I cried in front of him.

"Why does it matter how long she's been gone? What does that have to do with anything?" I asked.

"Because the odds of finding out what happened, or even uncovering new information, aren't good," Michan said. "Ciaran's going to need more than what people can find online. What's his book really about?"

"He's not only writing about Rowan's case," I said. "He has several. A lot of it is going to be about what it's like to live with no answers."

"Okay, that could be a whole book, in the right hands," Michan said. "Has he contacted Evelyn?"

"Yes. She emailed him back saying she would think about talking to him. He's hoping she'll decide she wants to have her say. He thinks she will, since she would have said a flat-out no."

"And if she does say no?"

"I guess he writes around her," I said uncertainly.

Michan was silent for a moment. "Has it occurred to you that he needs you? I don't know how he's structuring this book, but he'll need an axis to spin each section on. The mom. The dad. The sibling." He paused. "The friend."

"He could be the center of Rowan's chapter. Again—he was her brother."

"Who wasn't here. Who barely knew her."

I shrugged to hide my uneasiness. "If new information comes out, it'll be worth it."

"Let me ask you this. Do you even know for sure there is a book? Has he shown you any of it?"

"Why would he lie?" I asked, baffled.

"Does he think Leo was involved?" Michan asked. "Is that why he's here?"

I turned my head to watch a crew of gardeners at work, raking. Each wore green cargo pants and a darker green T-shirt, the standard uniform. They moved in tandem too as they drew the rakes over the grass, back and forth. There was one woman and three men, too far away for me to see their faces.

"You think he's here to get to Leo so he can beat him up? Kill him?" I asked.

"We don't know him," Michan said.

"We don't know any of the people we live with."

Michan laughed. "True enough. Any writer who comes here could be a maniac."

I hugged my knees.

"But maybe he's planning to write from the angle that Leo did it," Michan said

Leo, the lovesick accomplice. Leo, the child rapist and murderer. Leo, his proximity to a crime inadvertently revealing a crime he did commit.

"Maybe he's going to dig into Leo's life these past fifteen years."

We sat in silence for a while and then I asked, "What do you want me to do?"

"Leave," Michan said. "Go back to Brooklyn. Go someplace else."

"I'm broke, remember?"

"Your inheritance."

My parents' estate became mine on my twenty-first birthday. The government had eventually reached a settlement with the hemophiliacs infected by factor VIII.

For years, Michan had been cautioning me not to spend all the money on rent. Save it for drugs, he'd say. What if something happens and you can't afford your meds anymore and I can't help? What if the cure is found and you can't afford it? Insurance may not cover the shot or the pill. It may cost a fortune with insurance. It may be approved in Switzerland years before the United States. You may have to travel to get it. I'd roll my eyes and repeat: chronic but manageable. Yet his words had done their work, and I was afraid to touch a penny. I shook my head.

"Then I'll give you the money," Michan said. "Free ride. Until you find a job."

I shook my head again. "I can't go."

"I wish you would." Michan shuffled his feet, a sign that he was reaching the limits of his patience.

"Would you have tried to block Ciaran's admission if you'd known who he was?" I asked.

After a long pause, Michan said, "Admissions are not up to me."

"Come on, if you said, 'Don't let this guy in,' the admissions committee or the board or whoever would listen."

"They shouldn't," Michan said. "And I'd never ask."

That night, near ten o'clock, I stole up to the second floor, where the residents worked and slept, Michan's warning playing in my head like a song.

I knocked softly, hoping nobody else on the floor would hear. When there was no answer, I put my hand on the doorknob but then withdrew it. I rested my forehead against the closed door and knocked more boldly.

Ciaran opened the door and peered out, maybe reluctant to engage with the other residents. Perhaps someone had been trying to befriend him. But then I realized that I'd woken him up.

"Adair?" he said, his voice thick with sleep, though he was wearing jeans and a T-shirt.

"Are you really writing a book?" I asked.

Perhaps he was still too foggy to ask why I would even think that. He pressed his palms to his eyes, then opened the door wider and stepped aside. I went in. All three windows were open and the curtains rose and fell.

A painting called *Writer at Work* would have had the desk buried under a blizzard of papers and splayed books. But on Ciaran's desk, the books were stacked neatly beside his keyboard, and there was a single open notebook, the page half filled with a gallop of words.

I saw *Lost Girls.* The subtitle, in smaller print, said, *An Anthology of Stories Written at Moye House Writers' Colony.* I picked it up. On the book jacket was a photograph of Moye House.

"I've never read it."

"You can take it. I'll need it back, though," he said.

"Of course." I set the book down and looked at the cork bulletin board on the wall beside the desk, as in every writer's room. Before the start of each residency, Shannon pinned up fliers for nearby businesses, a calendar and a list of Things to Do—a printout of the Local Attractions tab on the Moye House website. This time, it had been my job.

Ciaran had removed all of it, and he'd used the pushpins to put up pictures. First I saw only Rowan's Missing poster, but then my eyes jumped to the others.

A boy, about twelve, in a collared shirt and longish hair that spoke of the seventies. A teenage girl wearing a wide headband, the ends of her hair flipped up, the late fifties or early sixties. A boy of about six whose photo might have been taken last week. His was the only one with a solitary picture. Each of the others had an age progression beside their original photo, a computer-generated leap into a future that likely did not exist.

When Rowan's first age progression was released, I'd studied her features closely. One minute I was certain I'd know this eighteen-year-old if I saw her, and the next I believed I'd pass her by without a glance. Ciaran had the most recent one: Rowan at twenty-three. Eighteen and twenty-three were not very different, except the artist had darkened her hair and made it shorter, to her shoulders.

There were clippings, printouts of newspapers. My scanning eyes found all the trite phrases from the missing-person thesaurus. Gone in Minutes, Search Continues, No Leads, Baffling, Without a Trace.

"They're all missing, and I'm putting their stories in a book. I don't know what made you think I wasn't."

Ciaran didn't sound angry, only curious.

I looked back at the board, specifically at a newspaper clipping. "Culleton Man Sentenced." The picture was of Leo leaving the courthouse. He was wearing a suit that was slightly too big for him. His eyes were wide and frightened, his jaw clenched tight. Leo told me that he'd been trying not to cry, but at the same time he'd wondered, if he did cry, would they be sorry and let him go?

"Did you come to Culleton to find Leo?" I asked.

Ciaran sat down on the bed, which was still made, though the red comforter was creased and the pillow dented.

"Yes," he said, but before I could speak, he added, "And Evelyn. And you."

In one drawing class I took in college, the students had taken turns being the model, and I felt the way I had when it was my turn, as if it were not only eyes on me, but hands, too.

I pulled out his desk chair and sat down. "Do you think Leo was involved?"

"My father does. He thinks Evelyn married David for his money, and he blames himself for that. She never had much help with Rowan. But he says she wouldn't be sleeping with a goddamn kid."

"But if your father thinks it was Leo—"

"He thinks it was Leo alone," Ciaran said. "One thing that was said, you must know, was why didn't Leo point the finger at Evelyn after he was arrested? If he only helped cover up whatever the hell Evelyn did, she's the one on the hook for murder, not him. My father thinks Evelyn is telling the truth and Rowan did go into town that afternoon. She ran off, went home. Leo turned up at the house and he found Rowan there alone."

Ciaran was watching me carefully.

I shook my head. "Leo wouldn't. He didn't. He never showed

any special interest in her. She was a kid who was sometimes funny, sometimes annoying."

"Like a little sister?"

I hadn't thought of it that way, but it fit. I nodded. "More or less."

I waited for him to say, Where is Leo? But instead he said, "Zachary Zengerle. The boy in the top row."

I turned and looked. Zachary Zengerle. Missing from Haynestown, Connecticut, August 30, 1981.

"He took off on his bike about six o'clock on a summer evening to meet up with friends at the local park. Somewhere along the way, he and his bike vanished," Ciaran said. "Right before I left to come here, I had to drop him from my book. I should take his picture down, but I've been looking at it for two years now. I'm not ready yet."

"They found him?" I asked, and I didn't mean alive.

"They found his bike," Ciaran said. "Red bike with a bell that had the initials ZZ scratched in the paint. It was in the basement of a house around the corner, which the police searched a few months ago, after the man who lived there was arrested for trying to sexually assault a boy. The boy got away. This man was a lifelong bachelor. Took care of his mother until she died, then stayed on in the house. Churchgoer. The usual pillar-of-the-community bullshit."

"He was never a suspect?"

Ciaran shook his head. "Questioned and cleared. From what I understand, it was a routine did-you-see-anything-unusual questioning. He had no record. He was only in his twenties then. He helped with the search. You never know."

I thought of the men of Culleton, popping fresh batteries into their flashlights and heading out in their hiking boots and raincoats.

Rowan, they'd shouted.

Rowan! Can you hear me! Over and over, as though they were some strange, verbose flock of birds, calling only to one another.

"A psychic told Zachary's mother that the boy had been taken by a couple to raise as their own, to replace the son they lost. He was afraid to come home because they'd threatened the family."

"She believed that?"

"Mrs. Zengerle told me she would know if Zachary were dead. She could feel that he was alive. He'd make it back someday."

"Psychics came to Culleton," I said. "Evelyn talked to them."

"Yes, I know. My father told me they came out of the woodwork."

I realized he was echoing me when he said something that I certainly knew. We both kept forgetting that our missing girl was the same girl.

"She's near water. She's with a man with an accent," Ciaran said. "A man whose name begins with S. A man with facial hair. Two women. Evelyn kept letting them in the house, and they'd go up to Rowan's room and hold her hairbrush and sniff her sweaters. She'd call my dad and tell him. It was David who finally put a stop to it."

It was hard for me to believe he let even one in the house. Desperation, I supposed. Perhaps he'd been unable to say no to Evelyn.

"There was one who came to see my father in Ireland," Ciaran said softly. "She showed up at the house."

"Did your father talk to her?"

Ciaran shook his head. "I did."

One day, in the hours between after school and his mother's

arriving home from work, the bell rang and he answered it. The woman was young, in her early twenties, her black hair in a loose bun. He'd never seen her before and thought that she had to be selling something, sweets or makeup.

She asked if this was indeed the house with the girl gone missing in America. The first anniversary had just passed.

Ciaran said it was, in a way. He lived here with his own mother. His father was nearby, but he was at work and would be for another two hours.

She introduced herself as Una. She told him that she'd had dreams about the girl. Because she hadn't the time to wait for his father, since she had to get the bus back home, could she tell him?

Ciaran invited her in, curious, even as he recalled his father's bitter complaints about this lot. Ghouls with their hands out, Jamie Riordan called them.

Una settled herself at their kitchen table and he made tea, his eye on the clock. She had to be done in an hour and a half, before his mother got home.

"I don't have any money," Ciaran told her as he set the mug down in front of her.

She'd never take money, she told him. Neither had her grandmother.

Three nights in a row, a week earlier, Una had dreamed about a rowan tree. Three times—that was how she knew she wouldn't be free of the dream until she passed on the message.

Ciaran tried to keep his face impassive, as he thought his father would.

The numbers five and two, which might mean May and February, or someone fifty-two years old.

Ciaran thought: If we're adding, it might mean seven. If we're subtracting, it could be three.

Una was speaking so softly that he had to lean in to hear her. He sensed she'd rather be anywhere else, as if she'd choose the dentist, even, over his kitchen. Her hesitation was what made him listen.

The tree she saw was a flying rowan—that is, a rowan tree that's growing out of another tree. Rowan trees are powerful to begin with, but a flying rowan is more so, because its roots have never touched the ground.

There was a room with a slanted ceiling and two narrow beds. The windows were small and high up on the wall.

Ciaran had tensed at this. He had spent too much time trying not to think about hidden rooms in basements.

Una had told her mother about this dream, and it was she who connected it to Jamie Riordan from over in Ballyineen, that one who had a child in America with a woman not his wife. Nobody should talk about sins being punished. He was surely suffering enough without being told he'd brought it on himself. You wouldn't like to think of that sort of God. But in any case, the girl's name was Rowan and she'd gone missing.

"Is she dead?" Ciaran interrupted.

Una lifted her shoulders. If she knew, she would tell him.

It was easy to believe that ghosts can tell where their bones lie, and if it was murder, who did it. But they often can't. And the missing who are still alive can't say where they are.

"Ghosts are not alive," Ciaran said. "A missing person who isn't dead won't show up as a ghost, unless I'm not understanding what a ghost is."

Una sipped her tea, her blue eyes on his over the top of her mug.

Her grandmother had told stories about ships that foundered in storms, with all hands lost. The widows dreamed of their husbands and were comforted to know they were at peace. And then the men returned alive. It happened as well with parents who had lost touch with their emigrant children. Years passed without a word, and they believed there must have been an accident or an illness, because they saw the children appear like lightning in a dark room. A shadow behind the door takes form. A voice calling, clear as a bell. And then a letter arrives: *Forgive me. It's been so long.*

Ciaran asked Una, dryly, why she supposed that was.

Una chose to ignore his sarcasm. Instead, she answered: Ghosts of the dead are sometimes not aware they've died, but those they left behind remember. Ghosts of the missing, though, are lost in both worlds. It's a question, still, which one they belong to.

"A question, unless you're psychic," Ciaran said.

"I wish," Una answered sadly.

When she was done, Ciaran put out his hand for her to shake, and she smiled and accepted. He led her to the door. Having said what she'd come to say, Una walked more lightly. She pulled the elastic holding her bun. He wondered if she'd worn her hair that way to try to make herself look older and more serious. With her hair loose, he lowered his estimate of her age.

"I wrote down what she said, but none of it meant anything," Ciaran said to me. "She could have gotten Rowan's name from the newspaper. A girl is named for a kind of tree, of course you're going to say you saw a vision of that fucking tree."

Then, a couple of years ago, Ciaran continued, he'd come home from a night of drinking and instead of going to bed, he'd gone online. He'd begun gathering notes for the book, and had written most of a publishing proposal, but that was as far as he'd gotten. He searched for the names of a few missing children whose cases he'd thought he might like to include.

Then, on impulse, he Googled Moye House. On its website he clicked Gallery. Thumbnail photos, three rows of three. Without quite knowing why, since it wasn't any particular interest of his, he clicked on the one that was a black-and-white sketch of the house. Moye House: A History.

It brought up a slide show, and he moved through it quickly, until the photo captioned "Servants' Quarters" filled the screen.

Ciaran shut his eyes, and I realized what he'd seen: the servants' quarters where Helen Dunleavy had lived with three other Irish women.

It did indeed look much as Ciaran's psychic had described it, though surely skeptics could produce a list of reasons why it meant nothing.

The air in the room shifted as it went from two souls to three. Rowan, beside the desk and her own aged likeness.

I turned away from her. "Is that why you came to stay here?"

"The answers are here," he said.

"Rowan isn't hidden away in our attic," I said.

She tipped her head back. Her hair brushed the wall behind her. *I still can't make the bells ring*, she said. *I would like to.*

Ciaran opened his eyes, as though he heard her.

"You were her friend," he said.

I folded my arms. Behind me, Rowan did the same.

"You were her friend," Ciaran said again. "You'd have helped her."

"Helped her hide, you mean," I said. "If someone was hurting her."

"David," Ciaran said. "Leo."

Ah, Rowan said. *Imagine that.*

Yes, imagine Rowan living clandestinely in Moye House, moving from room to room ahead of any footfalls. Me, carrying food and clothes and books up the servants' stairs. Nobody would have asked where I was going or what I was doing. Nobody watched me closely when my health was stable. Imagine Rowan sleeping all day and emerging at night to play in the gardens.

Rowan smiled. *That would have been nice.*

"I want to go up and look," Ciaran said. "But if she isn't there, if she was never there, then she's probably dead."

I could have reminded him that had she lived past 1995, she'd be long gone from her hiding place.

Paris, Rowan said. *Italy. Ireland. Australia. New York. California.*

"She was never here," I said softly. "Not after that day."

Not alive. I didn't say it out loud, but I sensed he read the thought, because he leaned forward.

"I'm tired," Ciaran said.

"I'll go."

I was almost to the door when I remembered the anthology and went back for it. Book in hand, I left, closing the door behind me.

I knew about the ghosts of the dead versus the ghosts of the missing. The latter remain closer to the living, invested in the promise of discovery, the art of being found. Like us, the not-lost, the living, they want to know how it ends.

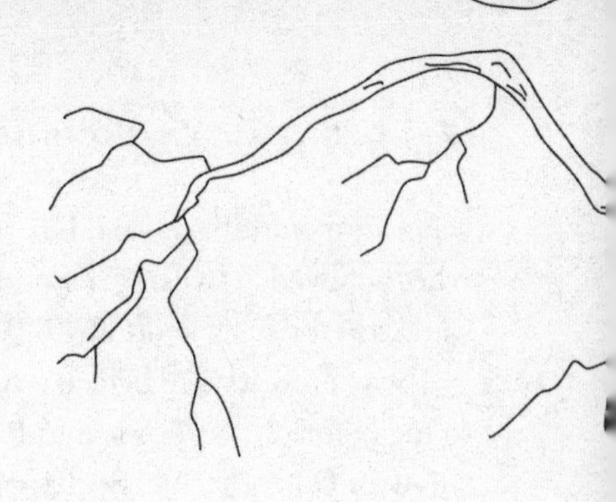

16
ADAIR
April 1995

When I'd first started school at St. Maren's Elementary, Michan would ask each day if there were any problems, and I'd shake my head, not speaking of the whispers that rose in my wake.

A different version of myself might have won them over. A funny or charming girl might have made them forget. But I didn't know how to be an inspiration, so I wished instead for invisibility.

I would have eaten lunch alone at the end of the table, using a book as a shield, if it were not for Rowan. We were not in the same class, but it was a small school and there was only one lunch period.

"I can't believe you're in here too," she said on my first day, like an inmate pleased to finally have company in prison.

The school uniform was a white blouse and navy-blue plaid jumper and blue knee socks. I didn't mind wearing it, but Rowan hated it.

Rowan transferred to St. Maren's in the third grade. Her mother had decided she needed more discipline. St. Maren's went straight through to eighth grade, and Rowan had been close to convincing her mother to let her return to the public school for middle school, but then Evelyn had married David, who believed it wasn't a good idea. Finish St. Maren's, he'd said, and for high school, we'll see.

I was an outsider because of something that had happened to me before I was born, and Rowan was alone because of who she was. Odd. Prickly. Stubborn.

Sometimes I imagined another life.

In this other version of the universe, Rowan and I were in the same school, and I could see my friends and me rolling our eyes when Rowan walked by, making fun of her clothes, her hair, her mismatched barrettes, her glasses, the core of loneliness evident to any child, though he or she might have been unable to name it.

Yet in the world as it was, I became Rowan's friend.

One Monday after lunch, Rowan and I noticed the girls laughing and looking over at us. Keeping as we did to the edge of the schoolyard, we heard only the inflection of syllables and the laughter that followed, but not words.

The chilly morning had become a warm afternoon, typical for early April. We'd taken off our jackets, and they lay on the ground like two puddles, one red, one blue. As Rowan and I talked about television shows, what mean thing the stepfather had done, Moye House gossip (two of the writers were having an affair and everybody knew), I kept up an uneasy surveillance, sensing that whatever was going on had to do with me. We knew the girls by name, and we knew who their moms and dads were and how many brothers and sisters each one had, in the casual intimacy of classmates. But when we saw them together, they were a single entity that moved in tandem the way a spider moved, all its legs at once.

As they began sidling toward us, I gauged the distance to the nearest exit as Rowan pushed herself away from the fence.

When they stopped, one of the girls, Gracelynn, stepped forward, slapped my shoulder and darted away, laughing. I put a reflexive hand to the place she'd hit, though it hadn't hurt. Rowan and I looked at each other and exchanged a silent question and answer.

What was that about?

I don't know.

We soon found out. The previous weekend, at a slumber party that neither Rowan nor I had been invited to, there was pizza and a chocolate cake, and after the parents went to sleep, three strawberry wine coolers, split among the six girls. And a game was invented, Truth or Adair. A question is asked. Choose: tell the truth or touch Adair McCrohan.

Over the course of the week, Truth proved the popular choice, though some followed Gracelynn's lead and picked Adair. Of them, a few merely jabbed me with a finger, others only pretended to do it.

Then the boys began to play.

They wouldn't have joined for ordinary risks, like climbing to the top of the jungle gym and leaping off or darting across the street as a car closed in. But I added a unique danger. Or at least the sense of it. Probably none of them believed they'd contract HIV from a touch, and not because of the letter that had gone home to parents that supplied the proper wording to explain HIV to children. And it wasn't because the posters in the nurse's office had done their job. *I have AIDS. Give me a hug!* said a stick figure with a red triangle for a dress, her mouth downturned. No, for them, contracting a disease was as unthinkable as their house burning down.

They say if a boy hits you, it means he likes you. But these boys didn't think of me as a girl, and they didn't consider it hitting. There were shoves, slaps on the shoulder, the daring pinch. Above the waist, from behind and through my shirt. Some days nothing happened, and others, three or four times, I heard the rush of approaching footsteps and crossed my arms over my chest.

I did not consider telling a teacher or my uncle, and Rowan never suggested it either. Rowan did not believe in tattling. She did believe in revenge.

On Holy Thursday, the day of the Last Supper, St. Maren's had a half day. The whole class was in a genial mood, looking forward to the long Easter weekend, and I had not been bothered once. Rowan and I had left the building and were crossing the schoolyard together.

It was Rowan's quick turn that made me look behind her, even as I kept walking. Because of this, I was off-balance when Brian Kelly, at a full run, slammed me right between the shoulder blades. My palms and bare knees hit the concrete. Rowan cursed.

On the ground, I was more disoriented than in pain, confused by the sight of the concrete with its mix of small pebbles, gray and white and pale blue.

"Shit, are you—" Brian started to say, but then Rowan wheeled around and he backed up with his hands in the air.

"Hey, it was an accident." He walked away. The boys who'd been watching were also backpedaling, fast.

Rowan put a hand under my elbow and pulled me up. Flecks of blood stood out on one knee.

"Do you want me to go get a Band-Aid?" I heard someone ask.

Molly Kelly, Brian's sister.

"Don't bother," Rowan said. "Just tell your brother he's going to be very sorry."

I nearly laughed at how serious she sounded. But Molly

only nodded, as though she relayed threats to Brian every day. She left, joining her friends, who began whispering when she reached them.

"Blood," I heard. Rowan started fishing through her book bag, saying, "I don't know why I'm looking. I know I don't have any tissues."

"It's fine," I said, dabbing at my knee with the hem of my skirt.

"Bet that doesn't come out," Rowan said.

"No one'll see it." I liked the idea of carrying around a few hidden drops of dried blood.

We started walking again.

Rowan said, "He's a jerk."

"It's not a big deal," I said, but the lump in my throat felt as big as a fist. Again and again, I swallowed.

"You're a bad liar," Rowan said, and she laughed.

We stood at Rowan's bedroom window as the May evening grew darker, peeking out of either side of the sheer green curtain. Rowan kept the light off, and she'd barricaded the door by jamming her desk chair beneath the doorknob.

We didn't want Brian and his friends to see us, Rowan had said. Ten minutes ago, the four boys had been playing basketball, two on two, but when Joe Reese arrived, they abandoned the game and retreated farther up the driveway. I supposed they felt invisible too, in the shadow of the Kelly house.

Two of the boys leaned against the wall and the other two against Brian's mother's minivan. His father's car was gone; he was working the night shift at the hospital and wouldn't be home until the next morning. Brian stood in the center of the boys. He took the two silver cans from Joe's book bag.

Joe, Rowan whispered, had an older brother with a fake ID. He'd probably stolen the beers from his brother's stash.

Brian didn't drink in the driveway when his dad was home, Rowan continued. If his mother caught them, she'd probably take the beers, but she wouldn't tell on them.

"I have to get home soon," I said.

We'd gone to a movie together, and afterward Rowan insisted that I go to her house. She ducked inside (reconnaissance) and came back to report that her mother and David were in the living room with the baby. I tried to protest. Sneaking into Rowan's house was far riskier than meeting up at the movies. But I didn't want to be called a coward, so we slipped into the kitchen, through the dining room and up the stairs to Rowan's room.

When Rowan didn't answer, I spoke up. "It's almost seven thirty."

"It's dark enough. I'm ready," Rowan said. She pulled off her sweatshirt. Beneath it she wore a white T-shirt, tucked into her jeans. She pulled her hair out of its ponytail and combed it with her fingers.

Rowan dislodged the chair and we left the bedroom quietly, pausing to listen. The bathroom light was on. We heard the water running, filling the tub, and Evelyn's voice, low and soothing as she talked to the baby.

Halfway down the stairs, we paused again. The television was on in the living room, but David could be in the kitchen. I stayed behind Rowan as we passed through the dining room. The kitchen was silent. Rowan beckoned me forward. We crossed the expanse of linoleum and she eased open the screen door. Outside, I breathed again. I followed Rowan into the driveway and expected to stop there and say goodbye.

Alone, I'd trek back to the theater and call Michan from the pay phone on the corner to come pick me up.

Instead, Rowan said, "Follow me."

She crossed the street and I was right behind her. One of the boys saw us and stopped talking. The others turned to see what had caught his attention and they also fell silent.

Rowan stopped at the edge of the circle. I hovered behind her. She didn't look at Brian, her neighbor, but at the boy beside him with the can of Coors. Neil something.

Can I?

Neil looked from her to me.

He said, You. Not her.

Well, duh.

Rowan tipped the can to her lips. I waited for her to spit into it. But she finished and, without even a grimace, passed the can to Brian. She did the same thing when the second Coors came to her.

Rowan and Brian and the boys bantered. I listened with a feeling I did not, then, recognize as jealousy.

When the second can of beer was finished, Rowan announced that we had to go.

See you around.

Hang out, Brian said.

They could go to the playground. There were always guys there who'd get them more beer.

Rowan shook her head. Night!

She turned, tugging on my sleeve. In the safety of Rowan's driveway, we put our hands over our mouths and laughed.

I asked her what that was all about.

Just wait. Rowan said. Go down the driveway. Stand right behind the house.

I did, as Rowan darted to the curb.

Brian! she called.

He strolled down his own driveway to the curb, his friends frozen behind him.

She said she had to tell him something.

The boys snuffled. Brian crossed the street. The street was empty. There was not so much as a dog walker out.

Rowan and Brian talked briefly at the edge of the curb and then she led him partway down the driveway. She put a hand on his arm, guided him so he was leaning against the wall.

Close your eyes, she told him. He did.

Rowan came to me, peeking around the corner of the house.

She put her mouth close to my ear.

He's sorry for what he did. He wants to show you that he knows nothing bad can happen. Her words smelled of beer.

I stood in front of Brian, Rowan behind me.

Kiss, Rowan whispered.

Brian turned his head a fraction, as if he sensed her voice was not coming quite from the place it should have. Still, he leaned over and brushed his lips over mine. Barely a touch.

Boo, Rowan said.

Brian's eyes snapped open and he reared back, scrubbing his mouth with the back of his hand as he looked from me to Rowan, who was grinning, her eyes cold and luminous in the dark.

17
ADAIR
2010

Ciaran and I walked across the expanse of lawn. I studied him surreptitiously. There were shadows beneath his eyes, as though he hadn't managed to sleep after I left him the night before. When I asked a question about the psychic in Ireland, he shrugged and changed the subject.

We paused outside a small, gated garden. The entryway was an arch, and inside, wrought-iron letters spelled out *Kitchen Garden.*

I said, "It's also known as Helen's Garden."

"Did she plant it?" Ciaran asked.

I laughed. "No, no. The historical society proposed it in the early nineties—the 1990s, when they turned the foundry into a museum—and they worked with the head gardener to make it happen. It's an herb garden, because she was known as a healer. There's a story where one of the foundry wives was bleeding after childbirth, and Helen made a tea out of something and it worked. She found her plants on the mountain. If you haven't gone for a hike yet, that's not something you should miss, while you're here."

"I can't. No break for me," Ciaran said. "I realized this morning that this is the start of the third week, and that means I'm almost halfway to the end. It seemed like a lot more time in the abstract."

"Michan calls it the midresidency crisis. That's when writers realize they aren't going to finish the book here, or write five chapters, or whatever it was they hoped to do. Lots of them say it's only after they're back home that they realize how much they did get done."

"That's good to hear," Ciaran said ruefully.

"What's next?" I asked.

"Next," Ciaran said, "is Kit Sullivan."

"Who's that?" I asked. A relative of Rowan's stepfather, I thought. Some former teacher from before I moved to Culleton.

"A private detective."

I stopped walking. "You're hiring a private detective?"

"No. This one was hired when Rowan had been gone six months. Did you know there'd been one on the case?"

"Yes, I heard it at school," I said slowly. "I didn't know his name."

"Her. Kit's a woman."

"Is she coming here, or—?"

Ciaran said her office had been then, and was still, in Brooklyn.

I offered to drive Ciaran there, but he said it was much easier to take the Metro-North and then jump on the subway. He had notes to read over, more questions to add to his list. The monotony of train time was what he needed.

I felt like Poe when he saw me putting my shoes on and frantically fetched his leash.

"I would like you to come with me, though," Ciaran said. "If you want to. If you can. The detective doesn't know the town the way you do. There may be things you think to ask that I won't."

"I'll go," I said.

When Ciaran wrote this scene in his book, I thought he'd probably describe how we were standing beside the dormant garden. He would mention that my jeans had frayed cuffs and that my hair was in a ponytail and how I looked away as if unable to find the words to thank him. But I was mostly thinking about how this seemed like a quest, with challenges to overcome and a reward to win. As if at the end, if we did everything right, Rowan would be one of the lucky ghosts who returned alive.

Ciaran and I got off the F train at Bergen Street in Cobble Hill, a neighborhood not far from where I'd lived. We emerged to find that the overcast sky had given way to steady rain. Neither of us had thought to bring an umbrella, but we both were wearing jackets with hoods, and we pulled them up.

I made a nervous remark about being in disguise, and Ciaran hunched his shoulders and said we might look like private eyes ourselves, following a suspect. Because of the wet weather, the sidewalks were far less crowded than they would normally be on a Sunday afternoon in autumn.

I found myself searching for familiar faces the way I did in Culleton, where I was likely to find several. There were couples sharing umbrellas and parents pushing strollers shrouded in rain-guard plastic. But they were strangers, all. Since returning home, my time in Brooklyn had come to seem more like a long daydream, as if I'd never really belonged here.

"Will you move back here after you leave Culleton?" I asked.

"My place is sublet until December. I've got a student in there now who'll be leaving after this semester. It's worked out."

"But that leaves you with more than a month before you can move back in."

"I'll sublet something myself."

Ciaran was walking so fast that I had to hurry to keep up with him. We passed a Key Food supermarket, a pediatric dentist, a few bars and restaurants.

I remarked that a private investigator's office should be above a check-cashing joint or a fast-food place. Ciaran said it might very well have been, once. The agency had been in business for over twenty years.

He finally stopped in front of a two-story brick building. Between two storefronts were three doors. Two were recessed and made of glass, and the one in the middle was wood. Distinct as it was, because we were looking for a business, it took both Ciaran and me a moment of looking back and forth to sort this out.

"It has to be the middle one," Ciaran said, though there was no address on it.

He tapped a finger beside the first doorbell of three beside the wooden door. *S. I.* was printed in black ink on a narrow strip of white.

I grabbed his sleeve and then pushed my hood off.

"They didn't find out anything. We'd know, wouldn't we, if they had?" I asked. "If they'd uncovered any real clues, they'd have gone to the police and let them take over?"

"Yes, exactly," Ciaran said. "My father said they worked the case for months. Nothing came of it in the end."

His questions for the detective had more to do with theories developed and impressions of the key witnesses.

Ciaran pushed the bell and the door buzzed immediately. He opened it and glanced back at me. I raised my eyebrows back, echoing what I presumed to be his thought. We had not been asked to identify ourselves.

Ciaran didn't whisper but he kept his voice low. "Camera," he said.

I looked up and tried to find it.

"Adair," he said.

I stepped inside so he could close the door. The cessation of street noise and rain was so sudden, it almost made me dizzy. Ciaran pushed off his hood.

In front of us was a staircase and, in a repeat, three doors, all of which were white. There was a brass sign on the center door, bigger than the one outside.

Sullivan Investigations.

The door opened and a woman with long brown hair gestured us in. She was tall and wearing boots with a high, square heel.

"Ciaran?" she said, extending her hand. "Kit Sullivan."

She looked at me expectantly. Ciaran said, "This is Adair McCrohan, she's been—"

"Adair?" Kit's eyebrows went up. "The writer's niece. Well. Nice to meet you at long last."

Though I was used to being known by strangers, the intensity of her stare was unnerving. She put out her hand and I took it loosely, but she squeezed it and held on, so I thought for a moment she might turn my hand over to read my palm.

We followed her upstairs. Kit explained that the office was closed on Saturdays, which is why she thought it was the best day for us to meet.

The stairs led to a hallway. Through an open door at one end, I saw a table, its wood gleaming, and a gray row of file cabinets. We went the opposite way, into a high-ceilinged room that had one wall made of brick. Its two windows overlooked Atlantic Avenue.

"You're both good and soaked," Kit said. "Would you like some coffee?"

"When we left this morning, it was threatening to clear. I guess an Irishman should know better than to forget an umbrella," Ciaran said.

"I never carry one unless it's pouring. I make do with hats," Kit said. "And now that you're both picturing a female Sherlock Holmes, please take a seat."

She pointed to a dining room table between the galley kitchen and what looked like a regular living room, with a couch, an armchair and a coffee table. It did not, in other words, have the appearance of a waiting room.

Ciaran and I sat in chairs beside each other while Kit went to the kitchen.

In a corner of the room there was a spiral staircase that led to another floor. A cutaway in the wall above the kitchen revealed an office. The desk wasn't visible, only the glowing computer screen.

Ciaran and I accepted a sturdy white mug each from Kit, the kind used in diners. She sat down across from us. Ciaran reached into his backpack (which held his laptop), took out a tape recorder and set it down on the table. "Is it all right if I record this?"

"Sure," Kit said.

"To start," Ciaran said, "I understand your specialty is missing people."

"Specialty?" Kit said. "I don't know if I'd put it that way. Most of the time, with kids, we start out knowing who took them. It's one parent or the other after a bad custody fight.

When you do see stories on the news, it's because the kid was found after decades. But those are the exceptions. These folks cave and call their own mothers or a sibling because they're running out of money. They head straight for the town they used to vacation at," she said. "Then there are the cases that are impossible from the start. Without a lucky break, you're not getting anywhere."

I wondered if she was making excuses for her failure to find Rowan. "Some kids are just gone for good?"

Kit looked at me steadily. "Some are, yeah."

"That's pessimistic, isn't it?" Ciaran said.

"It's realistic," Kit said. "Most kids are killed by a parent or another person in their household. Most who are taken by a stranger are murdered within hours. Rowan had been gone for months when we were hired. That's a long time. It meant she was well hidden."

"Dead? Alive?" Ciaran asked.

I thought of Una the psychic's shipwrecked Irish sailors, making their way home after grass had grown over their graves.

"Either," Kit said.

The word lingered in the room, acrid as smoke.

"My grandfather," Kit said, with a glance at the ceiling, "used to have a saying. He was a cop. NYPD. When he couldn't crack a case, he'd say it's got bad facts."

I set my coffee cup down.

"No clear suspect or motive. No witnesses to the actual crime. No break in the first couple of days," Kit said.

"You thought Rowan's case had 'bad facts'?" Ciaran said.

"A mother who looked just good enough for it that the cops figured she probably did it. There's the gap in time from when the girl is last seen and the mother calling the police. They were never able to say with certainty when or where she disappeared from."

"They put together a timeline," Ciaran said.

"With the information they had. Speculation. Guesswork. Maybe good guesswork, but that's what it was," Kit said. "There's always the chance of finding something the cops missed, but early on I thought it wouldn't be solved unless Rowan's case was linked to a similar crime."

After a brief silence, I said, "But there haven't been any others?"

Kit shook her head. "I still take a look now and then, because the guy could've gone to jail for another crime. He gets out, goes back to his territory. But at this point, I have to tell you, it's not likely."

"Do you have a theory? Any suspects?" Ciaran asked.

"Let me start at the beginning," Kit said.

I tensed. Beginning signaled ending. Yet there was no ending.

"The beginning," Ciaran said. "Rowan disappears."

"For you," Kit said. "My beginning was a phone call from an Irishman who says a cop he used to know gave him my number. He says his daughter is gone."

Kit had gone to Culleton the day after receiving the phone call, but her first two full days of investigation had yielded little of interest.

On her second night, she went out onto the small terrace of her hotel to review what she'd learned so far. It was early April and chilly, but not cold. She had a view of the woods and, in the distance, Degare Mountain, fading into the dark.

Kit picked up her notebook and found the page she'd titled "Hard Sightings."

Hard sighting: a sighting that was credible, that fit in with the known timeline and was worth checking out. The mailman, who'd seen Rowan on Friday afternoon, October 27.

Kit had spoken to Brian Kelly. They'd talked in the family's living room, his parents perched at either end of the couch and Brian slouched in a La-Z-Boy. His answers didn't vary from the record. Kit thought uneasily that if an ambitious prosecutor decided to go for a murder conviction without a body, he might have a shot based mostly on this kid's testimony.

Kit flipped a page in her notebook. That left Adair McCrohan.

Walking into the bookstore on Vine Street was like walking into a book-filled cave.

Charley Byrd was behind the counter, reading. He closed his book when he saw her.

"Nothing I tell you is going to help find the girl," he said after Kit introduced herself. "But ask away," he said genially. "Practice on me."

Kit wanted to put her nose to his and calmly say that she didn't need practice, and do it in such a way that would make him think, if only briefly, that she was not a private eye but a paid assassin.

Instead, she smiled and said she had only a few questions for him.

The day of Rowan's disappearance, Charley had been alone behind the counter, which had a view of the front door. His sole employee, Gin, was helping to set up the reading in the yard. He'd told her if she wanted to host things like that, it was on her to organize it.

The store was busy. At almost all times, there were customers inside and also outside, browsing the discount racks in front of the store.

Michan McCrohan showed up with the other writers from Moye House. Charley had no idea who any of them were. Some people going to the reading walked through the store and out to the backyard, while others went in through the back gate.

To clarify, Kit asked if Charley meant the side door, which opened onto the alley between his store and the pharmacy. He said no—the back gate opened, the side door wasn't used. Sometimes he did open it, to let fresh air in, and then forgot to lock it, so though he couldn't say for sure the door was locked that day, he could tell you that it was closed. Anybody who tried to come in that way would've knocked over a pile of books.

Charley invited her to see for herself.

Kit walked over to the door, which was out of sight of the register. There was, indeed, a stack of books up against it. She turned the knob. The door opened out. If you didn't know the books were there, you'd trip over them as you came in. Yet for all that, the pile was only about as high as her ankle. If you knew to be careful, it would have been easy to step over them. And then you were inside.

Kit returned to the register and asked if this ever happened. Annoyed, Charley answered that his customers knew to leave that door alone. But Kit knew that twelve-year-old girls were not necessarily the best at following directions.

Charley picked up his book, but when Kit mentioned Adair McCrohan, he set it down again. Adair and Rowan came in together after school. Rowan had occasionally asked him if he had this book or that, but Adair barely said a word.

That fall, he'd heard that she was getting sick. For-real sick. Rowan had been in the store alone several times, and Charley had found out it was because Adair was home from school.

Rowan once asked Gin if they had any books on AIDS, and Gin suggested she go to the library. Later, Charley asked her why she didn't at least check—he wasn't mad about losing a sale, but only curious. Gin answered that even if she did find something on their shelves—and it wasn't likely—a library book would have more updated information. Also, it might be best if Rowan got a book that she had to return in two weeks. That way, it wouldn't be lying around her house when the worst happened.

"Was Adair here on the day of the parade, October 28?" Kit asked.

"With her uncle," Charley confirmed. "And like I told the police, Rowan didn't come in at all. The last time I saw her was a few days before. Tuesday, Wednesday. I don't know. But I know she was alone."

"The day of the disappearance—did Adair say anything to you about seeing Rowan?"

"About seeing her?" Charley repeated.

"You know, anything like, I saw Rowan. Did you see where she went?"

"She never said a word." Charley shook his head. "I didn't see any other kids besides Adair. They were all outside that day. You know what I mean? There was no kid in here Adair could have even thought was Rowan."

* * *

Kit added the notes of her conversation with Charley to the growing file. His employee, Gin, seconded him. Rowan had not come in the store that day. Adair wandered around alone while the reading was going on in the backyard, and she'd left with her uncle right after.

With Michan McCrohan not returning her messages, Kit resorted to a stakeout. She parked her car across the street from Byrd's Books and Doyle's Pub on Wednesday, Thursday and Friday afternoons from 3 to 7.

Charley had told her that Michan dropped into the bookstore most often on those days. Almost as often, he'd go to Doyle's Pub for their happy hour.

Kit had spoken to everyone else on her list except Adair McCrohan. She'd talked to Evelyn and David Brayton, both together and alone. Nothing either of them said varied from the stories they'd been telling since the beginning, and nothing they said triggered Kit's gut.

Friday, she was in place slightly before 3 p.m. While she waited, she used the time to read about Michan. She already knew enough about him to recite his life story to him, though it was probably not a story the guy wanted to hear more than he had to.

It was as if the entire family had been on the *Titanic* and only Michan and his niece made it to a lifeboat. She shook the thought away. Pitying Adair was not her responsibility. Her job was to uncover clues as to what had happened to Rowan.

Kit had perfected the art of dozing with her eyes open. When she saw Michan emerge from the alley between the bookstore and the pharmacy, she sat up and took a quick hit of her coffee, long grown cold.

"Yes," she said softly when he went in, not to the bookstore, but to Doyle's.

A full fifteen minutes later, she popped a peppermint Life Saver in her mouth and strolled over to the bar. When she first started out as a detective, she'd felt guilty about cornering subjects in bars. Taking advantage of a good buzz seemed like cheating. But she eventually accepted that more than half her good information was going to come on a cloud of whiskey. She made a practice of not talking to the very drunk, the ones where she could see her words entering in one ear and walking out the other. If she needed to ask follow-up questions, she didn't want to have to start from the beginning.

She saw Michan seated at the far end, talking to the bartender. She was confused for a moment, having so recently read about his life, to see him laughing over a beer.

Doyle's wasn't crowded. Kit could not have played coy if she wanted to. She went up to Michan and introduced herself.

"I'm looking into Rowan Kinnane's disappearance. Can we talk for a few minutes?"

Michan's eyebrows quirked as he shook her hand. Maybe she'd surprised him by not mentioning his niece.

He signaled the bartender for a refill.

"Can I get you something?" he asked.

"I'm good," she said.

She would get a beer if she thought the person she was talking to would be uncomfortable if she didn't. Michan, guardian of the child she needed to get to, would probably think better of her if she didn't drink.

Without glancing behind him to make sure she was following, he led her down a short, dark hallway to the empty back room. He sat in a booth, and Kit slid in across from him. She wanted to take out her notebook, but instinct made her fold her hands on the table instead.

The room was paneled in dark wood, and the booth was high-backed and rigid.

"Mr. McCrohan—"

"Michan, please," he said automatically.

She noted that he said his name carefully, and she figured he'd had a lifetime of correcting people who called him Michael.

"Okay, Michan. Can you tell me about October 28?"

Kit listened as he succinctly went through the day, tensing when he reached the afternoon.

The current residents of Moye House had done a reading at Byrd's, not amid the dust and clutter of the store, but out in the fresh air of the small yard. The reading had lasted an hour, an hour and a half. They'd gotten a good crowd. There was extra foot traffic in Culleton anyway in October, and this was increased by the fact that it was Quicken Day.

Adair wasn't interested in marching in the parade, so Michan had asked her if she wanted to accompany him and the others to Byrd's; he thought it would be good for her to get out of the house. She'd been home sick on Wednesday and Thursday. Her fever was gone by Friday, but she'd stayed home from school anyway.

Staring into his beer, he asked, "You do know about Adair?"

"I do, yes."

"I guess you'd be a bad detective if you didn't."

"I guess I would be," Kit said smoothly, tamping down her irritation.

Michan smiled and looked almost boyish. "I only meant Adair's status has never been a secret around here."

Anyway, he continued, Adair slipped into the bookstore at some point during the reading. When he turned around to look for her, one of the other writers pointed to the back door.

"So she wasn't sitting with you?" Kit asked.

Michan explained that he'd been introducing the readers, so he'd been sitting in the front row. Adair preferred to be in the back. Sometimes people looked for her at these things. They wanted to shake her hand, often only to prove they were willing to, and she could always tell because they were the ones who did not let go right away. Once, an audience member asked where his niece was buried, because she had gone to the cemetery here in Culleton to visit the graves of his brother and sister-in-law and saw that the little girl wasn't with them.

Hearing that made Kit wish she'd gotten a beer.

When the reading was over, he'd stayed outside and talked with a few people. After a while, Adair came out and asked when they were leaving. He told her soon, and asked her to finish picking out whatever books she wanted. Anyway, Adair hadn't found anything, and they'd left probably ten minutes later.

"She didn't mention seeing Rowan?" Kit asked.

"No," Michan said. "Not a word. And no, I didn't see her either."

They'd gone back to Moye House for the writers' celebration of the day, which meant wine and cheese in the front parlor and readings from *The Lost Girl.*

"Did Adair mention Rowan at all during the rest of the day?"

Michan drank from his beer. "I didn't see Adair much for the rest of the day."

He was busy with the other writers all afternoon. Adair, he assumed, was outside at the party. If he'd stopped to think about it, though as far as he could remember he hadn't, he would have assumed that Rowan was also at the party and that Adair was with her.

"You told the police the girls were acquaintances. Evelyn said something like that too. From what I've found, they were actually pretty good friends."

Michan didn't answer immediately. "Rowan's stepfather, David, didn't want Adair around his baby. Evelyn said as a first-time father he was being paranoid. She was sure once the baby got a little older, he would let up."

"You didn't think so?" Kit asked.

"I wanted to talk to him myself, but Adair—" He paused.

"She didn't want to make a scene," Kit said.

"I wouldn't have confronted him in public." Michan smiled thinly. "But, yes, she didn't want a scene."

"When did Adair find out that Rowan was missing?"

"The day after she disappeared. Sunday. I might not have told her yet, but I had to, because the police came to search the house."

"They asked to talk to Adair?"

"No. They were there because of the party. Evelyn thought Rowan had been there even though she hadn't seen her. They'd had a fight. She thought Rowan was avoiding her."

"You gave them permission to search?"

"Of course." Michan looked down at the table, frowning. "I was worried, but the way you are when you're in a fucked-up situation and you're sure you'll be laughing at how worried you were when it all turns out okay."

Kit nodded. "When did you first realize that it wasn't going to turn out okay?"

"When the police finished searching every inch of the house and grounds and hadn't found her," Michan said. "That's when

I had to admit to myself that she might have actually been grabbed. It was surreal."

"When did Adair tell you she saw Rowan in the bookstore?"

"Not until Monday afternoon." Michan shook his head grimly. "I was downstairs talking to some of the residents. It was during quiet hours, but most of them had given up and were sitting around the kitchen table, talking about what had happened. Adair came in. I guess she'd read a newspaper that someone left lying around, and that was when she realized that Rowan hadn't been seen in town all day Saturday. She said that she had. She saw Rowan in the bookstore, carrying an envelope."

"Did she say, 'It looked like an envelope,' or 'I thought it was an envelope'?"

"What does it matter?"

Kit took a deep breath through her nose and released it.

"I want to know who first used the word 'envelope,' that's all. Did Adair say 'she was carrying something but I couldn't really see it'? Did the detective questioning her then ask if it was the size of a purse or the size of an envelope? Adair says 'envelope' and that's what gets written down, and bam, Adair saw Rowan in the bookstore carrying an envelope."

"I don't goddamn remember," Michan said. "I don't think they pushed her on what Rowan was carrying. Most of their questions focused on whether or not Adair was confused about what fucking day it was."

"I'd very much like to talk to Adair," Kit said.

"No," Michan said, so pleasantly that Kit thought she'd misheard.

"No?" she repeated.

"I'm not criticizing either the police or you when I say this, but I don't think she's going to be found."

"Never?" Kit asked.

"By chance, if ever. A hiker. A hunter," Michan said. "Not by subjecting my niece to another round of questions that will only torment her because she can't answer them."

"I promise you, I'd be careful not to upset her."

"That's not a promise you can keep," he said.

Kit, stung, knew he was right. She was used to dealing with the shady and the desperate and with people who had been hurt, but nothing like what this kid had been through.

"My brother would say to leave her alone. My brother Cathal. Adair's father. Co-parenting with the dead isn't easy. But that's my best guess."

"A father might also say, as a parent I can't even imagine what Evelyn's going through, and Rowan's biological father, and I'll do anything to help."

Kit did not add, because it was too cruel, that when he lost his niece, at least he would know her fate. There would be a proper funeral.

"Can I show you something?" Michan drained his beer and stood up.

He didn't wait for her to leave the booth before he started walking. Kit hurried after him, catching up at the bar.

"Do you mind if I—" Michan pointed to the wall.

The bartender glanced curiously at Kit and then shrugged. "Sure. But close it behind you."

Michan stepped up to the wall and tugged. A door slid open. He stood to the side and gestured for Kit to go ahead of him.

He was not drunk, not even close, but she sensed that the alcohol was doing its work, loosening his caution. Without a word, Kit went through the door and found herself in the bookstore. There was a woman behind the counter, reading and smoking a cigarette, which she stubbed out as they came in. Michan shut the door.

"Hey, Gin, I need to show Ms. Sullivan something," he said. "It'll only take a second. Don't tell Charley I used the door."

"Sure," Gin said, looking from Kit to Michan.

"He doesn't want anybody making it a habit," Michan explained to Kit.

There were three bookshelves in the center of the store. Michan turned down one of the aisles between them. The shelves were high, over Kit's head, and slightly over Michan's, which would make them a bit over six feet. There wasn't much space between the opposing bookshelves. Kit could not have held her arms out straight. Someone claustrophobic could not have browsed for long.

"This is where Adair said she was standing," Michan said.

Charley had said he couldn't remember where she'd gone in the store. Kit did a quick assessment. There was no view of either the register or the front door. The side door that led to the alley, too, was out of sight.

"The girls would have been hidden here," Kit said.

"Rowan didn't come down the aisle and pass by Adair," Michan said. "According to Adair, she was looking at the books"—Michan pointed to the shelves to Kit's right—"and looked up and saw Rowan over there."

Michan pointed straight ahead, toward the front of the store.

"She was heading in the direction of the front door. That's why Adair thought she'd left."

Kit walked up the aisle. Books were piled haphazardly on the floor, and there were two cardboard boxes full of paperbacks between the two windows. She noted that the register was in the center of the store. Which meant Rowan would not have walked in front of it if she went out by the front door. It was at least possible that she'd left without Charley noticing her.

Kit walked back to Michan. She rubbed her eyes, itchy from the dust.

"This gives me a better picture," Kit said.

"Does it?" Michan asked. "Look at these books."

Obligingly, Kit skimmed the titles. *A Short History of World War II. The Day Lincoln Was Shot. FDR's America. The Tudor Queen.*

"Adair wouldn't have been interested in anything here. I asked her what she was looking for and she said she didn't remember."

"Didn't remember?" Kit paused. "Did she have a paper due at school?"

"She'd have gone to the library for that," Michan said. "She wouldn't buy a book for her homework, even if it was only a couple of bucks."

Kit rubbed her eyes again, trying to shape her thoughts, because he had a point.

"Would she have gotten in trouble for leaving the store alone?" Kit asked.

"No," Michan said. "This was before Rowan."

Before Rowan, Kit thought. How long before? Hours? Minutes?

"Why do you believe her?" Michan asked.

"I don't believe her. I don't disbelieve her. I haven't talked to her," Kit said. "But I think Evelyn's telling the truth. She last saw Rowan in the parking lot. Rowan was alive on Saturday morning. Your niece's statement dovetails with hers. Why don't you believe her?"

"I know Evelyn, and I don't think she had anything to do with it, if that's what you're asking.

"It isn't," Kit said.

Absently Michan pulled a book off the shelf and shoved it back.

"Last summer, Adair's health started going downhill. I want to say 'finally,' but that sounds like a good thing, and I only mean it's years later than the doctors predicted. She was in the hospital twice. Her doctor says it's ARC, AIDS-related complex. Do you know what that is?"

Though she'd heard the term, Kit couldn't coherently explain it. She shook her head.

"It's when your T-cell count drops and you start developing full-blown AIDS. It's the beginning of the immune system crashing."

"I am sorry. I really am. Maybe I'm not following, but I don't see what Adair's health has to do with me talking to her. She's okay, from what I understand. She's still in school—"

"She's not on her deathbed, no," Michan said.

"I didn't mean—"

"You did," Michan said. "And that's fine. I'm not afraid of the word. Adair is holding on, for now. But she has a disease that is one hundred percent fatal. If I let you talk to her, you're going to take her right back to the day the only friend she ever had walked out of her life. Adair knows she didn't go willingly, but Rowan is gone. You'll go at her with the same questions the police did."

Kit started to speak, but Michan interrupted.

"'Adair, if Rowan was your friend, why didn't she talk to you? Did you have a fight? Where might she have been going that she didn't want you to come? The post office was already closed. Why would she have been carrying an envelope? Are you sure you saw her at all? Are you thinking of a different day? Was it a dream? Do you get confused a lot?'"

"I would phrase the questions more carefully," Kit said. "I'm not a cop who's under pressure to make an arrest. I'm not stuck on one theory."

Michan shook his head. "When Adair was younger and ran a high fever, she would talk about seeing things that weren't there. Her father. Dogs. Birds. Whatever. I don't think she outgrew it. I think she just stopped saying it out loud. I told you, she didn't tell me she saw Rowan here until she'd been missing for two days."

Kit understood. "You think it was a dream."

"Yes. Maybe. A fever dream," Michan said. "The detectives took it further. They kept asking her if she gets confused. They asked her if she knew what year it was and who was president. Do you know why?"

Kit shook her head.

"People who don't know much about AIDS do usually know two things. That cancer with the purple sores, and people with AIDS lose their minds."

"Dementia," Kit said.

"She didn't have it. She doesn't. And I told them, as patiently as I fucking could, that's usually near the end. She's not at the end yet," Michan said. "I cannot make Adair feel guilty all over again for not following a figment of her imagination out the door. And I cannot have her wondering if what happened to her mother is already happening to her."

The cessation of Kit's voice was like closing the window on a storm.

Ciaran and I were both silent, considering what Kit had just told us. She waited patiently, her hands folded on the table.

Then Ciaran made a soft sound, like a person waking up.

"When did you stop working on the case?" he said.

"Officially, after about six months. But I've never really stopped. Rowan's mother forwards me emails that come in through Rowan's website. There aren't many, but sometimes there'll be something that sounds like a tip. I've followed up on things over the years," Kit said.

"Like what?" Ciaran asked.

Kit picked up her coffee mug and held it.

"Possible sightings. There haven't been many. I check on Jane Does that match Rowan's description. With most, it's been obvious right away it wasn't her, but twice I've passed the information on to the detective handling her case."

"They followed up?" Ciaran asked.

Kit was silent for a moment. "I hope so."

Ciaran turned to me. "What do you think?"

I didn't know if he wanted me to assess how helpful Kit's investigation had been or acknowledge how hard she'd worked.

"About—?" I asked.

"What your uncle said."

Listening to Kit, it had been easy to distance myself from the story, pretend it wasn't about me.

"They don't call it full-blown AIDS anymore," I said. "You're either asymptomatic or symptomatic."

Ciaran frowned, but Kit said, "I'm very glad that you're doing well."

I nearly asked if she would have sent flowers to my funeral. Janus would have laughed. *Leo* would have laughed.

"Those questions the police asked, I thought that's what

they asked everybody." After a brief silence, I added, "My mother was sick forever before she started . . . forgetting. I knew that. Michan should have let me talk to you."

"He was trying to protect you," Kit said. "Can't blame him for that."

"He should have let me decide," I said.

Outwardly I was calm, but I was angry at how illness had turned me into a bundle of rioting cells that had to be placated.

Ciaran cleared his throat. "What would you have asked Adair?"

"A lot of the same questions the police did. Michan was right about that."

"What else?" Ciaran asked.

Kit looked at me. "What were you looking for in the history section?"

It was like being addressed directly on the subway. After only a few weeks in Brooklyn, I'd learned to draw an invisible curtain around myself. When someone yanked it aside, a tourist asking for directions, a panhandler asking for change, I got a shock.

I turned to Ciaran. "The anthology of Moye House stories that your father was in. Rowan asked Charley if he had a copy of it. And he said yes, but damned if he knew where. Charley didn't pay much attention to shelving. I didn't believe him, or at least I thought he couldn't possibly know for sure. But I helped Rowan look. We'd spent most of the summer hunting for it," I said.

Ciaran looked pained. "You never found it?"

"No. By the time school started, Rowan had given up," I said. "One day we were in there, checking the books that were stacked on the floor, and Rowan jumps up and says maybe

Charley shoved it in with the children's books. But she didn't find it, and she was crushed."

"Crushed," Ciaran repeated quietly.

"We'd never looked in History either. That day, I was skimming titles, hoping to see it," I said. Because I looked for the book out of habit by then, the way I look for Rowan's face among the living now. "I thought how cool it would be if I found it and surprised her on her birthday."

But now that I've read it, I'm glad it stayed lost—I kept that thought to myself. This wasn't the time.

"What made you believe Evelyn?" Ciaran said abruptly, as if Rowan's being crushed were too much for him.

Kit drummed her fingers on the arm of her chair. "For the most part, I think a parent who accidentally causes their child's death, their instinct is going to be to lie about what the fuck happened. And by this I mean they caused the death directly, out of rage. First reaction is probably not going to be to get rid of the body and stage a kidnapping. I say this to a cop, I'm going to hear the exceptions," Kit said ruefully. "But in those cases, most of the time the story falls apart fast."

"What if Evelyn's story never fell apart," Ciaran said, "because Leo helped her? All he had to do was take Rowan into the woods and leave her somewhere hikers never went near. He'd have known where to go."

At the mention of his name, both of them might well have cast Leo as a nineteen-year-old enthralled with an older woman, willing to do whatever she asked. Whether or not they believed it had actually happened that way, they'd let the scenario play out in their minds, weighing it.

But I remembered him, Leo, shaking my hand, proving by his grip that he was not afraid of me.

Kit nodded slowly. "Maybe. But if he was involved, being told he's going to prison for ten years but maybe not, if he cooperates? Facing jail time does a very, very good job of persuading someone to act in their own best interest. That said, it's possible his lawyer got him to stop talking in time. It's possible he is that cold-blooded."

"He isn't cold-blooded. He was ordinary. An ordinary guy," I said.

"You were a child then yourself," Ciaran answered. "How could you know?"

Leo, who would only talk about prison in the dark, lying beside me, saying he understood why people confessed to crimes they didn't commit. All you want in the world is to get away from the police, and they're telling you all you have to do is say that you did it. The words the police want to hear start to feel like the opposite of a lie. Instead, they're magic words, what will set you free.

But it wouldn't have worked, I'd said to Leo, because you couldn't say where Rowan was—they'd realize you were lying to get away from them. And Leo had answered, very tiredly, They wouldn't have thought I was innocent, they'd have thought I was fucking with them. I looked away.

Kit's eyes flicked to the clock on the wall, a reminder that her investigation of Rowan's disappearance may have been painful for her, but it was still her work, not her life. Each time she checked in, spent an afternoon, or more likely a night, I thought, looking at pictures of Jane Does, she could get up from her chair, shut down the computer and close the office door.

* * *

Ciaran and I got back to Moye House during dinnertime. We paused in the hallway and listened to the conversation, which was lively, a blend of voices.

"Are you going in?" I asked.

"I suppose I should," he said. "I'm going to check my mail first. I made my mother promise to send a postcard, so I'd get something."

Residents' mail was set out on a side table in the library. Long ago, it had been a pre-dinner ritual. Writers forwarded their mail from home or had family send anything important. Each evening at the end of quiet hours, they'd go in to see if they'd gotten any acceptances or rejections, or postcards from the outside world. One writer learned she had sold her first story here. Another got a Dear John letter from his wife and later used it to begin his novel, without even changing the names. Some writers, aware of the stories, had their mail forwarded for the sake of tradition.

I followed Ciaran. There were two envelopes on the table.

"Nothing for me," he said. "I'd better get in there. I'm going to be here all day tomorrow, on lockdown."

He sounded almost apologetic, and it was embarrassing, as if he thought I'd expected to spend the day with him.

"An old friend of mine is coming to visit tomorrow," I said.

"From college?" Ciaran asked.

He had no context for me outside of tragedies, my parents, his sister, and though I understood this, it bothered me.

"No." I smiled. "He's literally my old friend. He's a little past my parents' age. The age they would be."

"You mean he knew them?"

"Them and hundreds of others," I said.

"Hundreds of others?"

"With AIDS," I said, though maybe it was thousands. Could it have been? Janus called himself a museum of the dead.

"His name is Janus. J-a-n-u-s."

"Looking to both the past and the future," Ciaran said. "Was he a doctor? Is that why—?"

"He's a doctor now. A therapist," I said. "He used to be a priest."

18
JANUS

The boy was raised on Long Island, post–World War II, those years that are remembered now as the upbeat chorus of a song. He was the son of a veteran and a housewife. Of their six children, he was the third. He played baseball (not well) and had a paper route that took him all over the neighborhood on his bike. He liked the solitude of being up at dawn.

Even in his earliest memories, the years when his parents were still bringing home new babies, he had a sense of being different. Everyone around him believed the sky was blue, and he agreed with them, despite knowing it wasn't. He wanted, just once, to stop and point and say to someone, anyone, Don't you see?

When he was fourteen years old, he confessed to the older of the two parish priests, deliberately choosing him over the younger one. Years later, he'd question this decision. He'd wonder if it was his fear that the younger priest would be compassionate and help him understand that some boys dream of other boys.

This was a fantasy. Nothing the younger priest said or did during his time at the parish suggested a renegade spirit. Nothing suggested compassion.

The boy knelt in the confessional, the old upright coffin,

and he buried himself alive. The old priest listened, his breath rattling, a distant train in his throat.

As an adult, Janus framed it as comedy. He imitated the priest's phlegmy voice, his wet words and his own relief at being told he was not a faggot. The priest didn't use that word. Janus did.

But the priest explained that his dreams were not erotic but apostolic. He, Peter, had been called by God, like the first Peter. The boy chose to believe it. His confusion would end in the simplest way, a life of celibacy. He would touch no one. At sixteen years old, he told his parents that he had a vocation to the priesthood, and they were proud, as parents were in those days. And he would be spared Vietnam.

One afternoon, his third term at the seminary, he was in church by himself, praying the rosary. He had climbed up into the choir loft, the better to look down on the sanctuary, which was decorated for Christmas. The smells of pine and incense filled the gabled roof. The crèche sat beside the altar. Mary and Joseph and the shepherds knelt before an empty manger.

He was dizzy with it. He bowed his head lower.

The Joyful Mysteries.

He didn't turn when he heard footsteps coming up the stairs, or when they approached him. There is voice in the breaths we take, from the first to the last. He knew it was Benno.

Benno, fellow seminarian, whose piety he claimed to envy —though it was really Benno's sense of humor and the easy charm with which he talked to everyone, from the senior priests who taught them to the housekeeper who did their laundry.

He didn't call him Ben, as the others did. Always Benno.

I believe in the Holy Spirit, the Holy Catholic Church, the communion of saints, the forgiveness of sins, the resurrection of the body and life everlasting.

Benno leaned over and kissed him between his shoulder blades, where his wings would be, were he an angel. Peter the seminarian didn't move, didn't respond. He continued with his prayers. After a moment, Benno went away.

Glory be to the Father,
the Son
and the Holy Spirit.
As it was in the beginning,
Is now, and ever shall be,
world without end.
Amen.

They never spoke of the choir loft, but simply continued on in their studies, friends through ordination, after which their lives diverged.

Father Benno went to Vietnam as a chaplain.

Father Peter was assigned a comfortable parish on Long Island, near his childhood home. His parents drove to his church to hear him say Mass, as did his two married sisters.

Father Peter became a favorite of his parishioners. He did his best to memorize the names of the children, but devised a trick for when he was stuck.

"And you are Bert, or are you Ernie?" he'd say to the boys.

"Are you Gertrude or Bertha?" he'd say to the girls.

The children believed he was only teasing. Their priest knew exactly who they were, but they still chimed out their names to him, in on the joke.

Jack! Jimmy! Joseph! Katie! Colleen! Kerry!

Father Peter loved them. He loved the high schoolers too, passionate and angry, brilliant and dumb. He cheered them on in basketball and baseball and softball and soccer. Some boys may have guessed. Father Peter was never slurred on bathroom walls, and he took it as a compliment, a sign of respect, though probably the ones astute enough to understand were the kind to write only in journals. Besides, there were no actual rumors to go on, nothing but instinct, since Father Peter did keep his vows, kindly turning aside the few subtle passes from married men of the parish he'd received over the years.

Father Peter knew all the words for what he was, though he never spoke them. He did not know if remaining celibate made him some lower order of saint or high order of hypocrite. His father had died and his mother was frail, and of all her children, she was proudest of him.

Father Peter decided he would wait until she had passed away before leaving the priesthood. This he would always count as his greatest sin, because it left him wondering daily, When? How much longer? He continued ministering to his parish of middle-class families, tending to their troubles, which were not inconsequential, for all their invisibility outside the home. Alcoholism, spousal abuse, drug use, teenage pregnancy.

He watched the news stories on AIDS with increasing alarm, as it became clearer and clearer the disease was no fluke afflicting a small number of men. He prayed for those who were suffering and thought once or twice about giving a homily about it, suggesting compassion and prayers for the dying, though it would certainly offend his older parishioners and not a few of the younger ones.

August 1985.

On a broiling summer afternoon, Father Peter had a rare few hours free, so he sat in the kitchen of the rectory reading a novel at the table. He had liked to do this as a child. The kitchen was where his mother was, cooking or ironing. Only the bedrooms of the rectory were air-conditioned. That's where his fellow priest was, taking a nap. In the kitchen, the fan was adequate, the whirring a comfort, like voices of a family from another room.

The doorbell rang and Father Peter closed his eyes, saying a brief prayer to Jude, patron saint of the impossible, that it would be a delivery or something else the housekeeper could handle.

When the dark-haired priest came into the room, in clericals, collar in place in spite of the heat, Father Peter knew two things at once: who he was, and that he had AIDS.

He had learned from pictures in the newspapers and on the news to recognize the razored cheekbones and, even more, a look in the eye. Wary and hunted.

"Benno," Father Peter said, getting to his feet. "Benno."

He hugged him, and it was a long embrace. Father Peter looked into the brown eyes of his old friend and then at his bare arms. The short sleeves spoke not of the weather but that Benno didn't care who saw the marks, the Kaposi lesions.

Father Benno said, "Will you help us?"

"Yes," Father Peter said.

Father Benno had laughed then, in relief, he later said, because he had not been at all sure. He laughed, touched Peter's cheek and said, "You are the rock upon which I build my church."

Almost from the beginning, the Catholic Church had mounted a response to the crisis through Catholic Charities and hospitals, like St. Vincent's in the Village, where the sick and dying were cared for. A paradox, Benno said, that the Church should minister to the gay men who were victims of the disease while proclaiming them "disordered," and while the pope stands up and says condoms are a mortal sin.

Don't protect your bodies. Pay for your pleasure, your comfort, the particular expression of love that is sex. Pay for it with your lives. Your lives are worth nothing.

Father Peter worked with Father Benno, as long as Father Benno was still able, making sick calls to the hospital to hear the confessions of men long estranged from the Church. He didn't quite understand why they wanted the comfort of an institution that turned them away, but Benno said it had to do with their past, not their future. They had no future. The two priests called mothers and fathers in faraway midwestern towns to tell them their sons were dying in New York.

He wants to see you. Will you come?

Quaking, elderly couples found their way to the bedside, as frightened of the subway system as they were of the disease killing their sons. Others said in cold voices, "He is already dead." More mothers than fathers came alone. About an equal number, from what Father Peter could see, of brothers and sisters. The grown children of men arrived as well, to say hello and goodbye, sometimes in a single breath.

Father Peter and Father Benno, and a cobbled-together network of volunteers that included men and women, family members of the dead, nuns, nurses and doctors, worked both within the confines of Church-led organizations and outside of them.

Priests were sick.

Father Benno, removed from his own parish against his wishes—for "health reasons," his flock was cryptically informed—told Father Peter about one priest, in the suburb of a city he would not name, who had infected at least five other priests.

Father Peter and Father Benno ministered to priests in hospice, many of whom had come from other states to die in hiding. Some said they had sinned only once. Some claimed they had caught the virus (somehow) from a drug user or prison inmate they had prayed with. Their death certificates listed the cause of death as pneumonia, brain tumor, emphysema, heart failure.

A friend of Father Benno's died and left Father Benno his brownstone in the Village. Father Peter assumed they had been lovers, but he did not ask.

Father Benno started a support group for men with AIDS that met in the living room, something he had long been trying to do. But he'd not wanted it to be held in a hospital conference room or some other such sterile space.

Father Benno asked Father Peter to take it over when he couldn't any longer, which would be soon. He didn't have to be a licensed counselor. He didn't have to have AIDS. All he had to do was find men who wanted to talk and invite them in. Answer the doorbell. Still, afraid of the responsibility, Father Peter suggested that one of the men already in the group take over.

"We need someone who isn't going to die," Father Benno said simply. Then he smiled. "Be careful crossing streets, Pietro."

Father Benno died on December 31, 1986, the date he'd been hoping for when it was clear he was at the end.

"If I live past midnight," he'd said that morning in the scrap of voice he had left, "I'll be trapped another year."

Father Peter spoke at the funeral, in Benno's church. He did what Benno had asked. He told the people what killed Benno, both ending his own life as a priest and winning him the respect of Benno's group. Brave, funny, bitter, angry men, all of them grieving, so it was almost possible to believe that what was killing them was grief.

The funeral Mass was the last time he wore the Roman collar.

Sometime during that first blurred year, Peter changed his

name, because he was no longer the rock but fluid, a protean man. He understood where he had been and where he had to go.

Janus did as Benno had asked, aware that he would probably be in the same place as these men had he not allowed himself to be led into the priesthood, sick with the fiercest denial possible. Yet his refusal to accept who he was had saved his life.

Lissa McCrohan was the first woman with HIV that Janus met who had not contracted the disease through needles or sex work. There are no groups for women, Lissa said. And she needed to talk.

Some of the men were angrily opposed to her. Lissa was an "innocent" victim, as was her hemophiliac husband, whom society would not blame but pity. To many, she was a victim of the homosexual community. Her life, her husband's and her child's would be a loss; the men's were not.

Others agreed that this was true, but hardly her fault. If she wanted to become an activist, then she should. If it took a dying young family to get the government to act, then so be it.

A few men did leave the group. Others gradually took their place. Lissa began bringing her daughter and her camera to meetings.

No one ever resented Adair. These men, cut off from their own children, nieces and nephews, either for being gay or having AIDS or both, reveled in a child they were allowed to be near. They braided her hair and bought her clothes.

"I am going to spend my last dime before I die," one man said.

Another taught Adair some phrases in French. Another had her sit with him at the piano. He put her small hand on the keys. Like this, he said. Like this.

The attention could be too much. Sometimes Adair hid under Janus's bed. Janus had moved into the brownstone not long after Benno's funeral. The rectory had been his home. He had no place else to go.

Janus would watch Adair as her mother talked and wept and took photographs in the next room and spoke about the book she was going to write.

For Adair's sake, Janus found more children, which was a sadly easy task. Foster care was filling with HIV-positive children, many of whom had already been orphaned by AIDS and abandoned by what family they had left.

There was one four-year-old boy Janus had first seen on the news. At his aunt's apartment in the Bronx, he'd fallen three stories from a window that had had no safety guard. Because he'd broken his collarbone and not his skull, the nurses nicknamed him Lucky. It stuck, even after blood work revealed he had HIV. Both his parents had already taken off. They may well have been dead of AIDS by the time the boy went into the system. Janus sought out his foster mother, and she brought Lucky to some of the meetings.

There was one child, a six-year-old named Hayley, whose mother brought her out of desperation, hoping she might find some answers. Doctors had no idea how the little girl, who was eight, had contracted HIV. Her mother and father, who were her birth parents, were negative. Hayley had never had a blood transfusion. There was no known history of sexual abuse, and she'd never displayed any signs of it in her behavior. But her father raged. He wanted to compel the men in their family to be tested, also the fathers of his daughter's friends, men who worked at her school, even neighbors. Some uncles and cousins had, but no one outside the family would comply. Nor should they, his wife said. She worried that a positive test would turn up and that her husband would murder the man with no other proof.

She put her own faith in some long-forgotten accident on a beach or in a park. Could her toddler have stepped on a needle? Or were the doctors wrong about how AIDS was transmitted? She feared Hayley might be a terrible harbinger of the future, a doomsday child, her name a curse.

Janus suggested something had happened in the hospital when Hayley was born. Had she been brought to the wrong mother and breastfed, the mistake discreetly corrected to avoid a lawsuit?

Her mother had seized on this, and Janus was glad to have brought her some relief, though he thought her husband's nightmare was more likely.

When the widowed Lissa got too sick to travel to Manhattan, Janus went to see her, and so did some of the men she was closest to. Many more stayed away, unable to bear it.

Janus had spoken to Lissa about Adair. He had suggested not leaving her with family at all. Not her own mother or sister or father-in-law, who would probably drink himself to death before long. Not her brother-in-law, who Janus suspected was lying about his status to spare his family a modicum of pain.

Give her to a foster family, he'd said. One that's taken kids with HIV before. But Lissa trusted the uncle. At Lissa's funeral, Janus told Michan to stay in touch. Bring her by to see us. Even as he said it, he thought the young man would not follow through.

But Michan surprised him. He called when he had questions. He put Adair on the phone. He brought her into Manhattan at Christmastime. Lucky died, and so did his foster brothers, and so did Hayley, but Adair, she lived.

* * *

Though he hadn't said so, I knew Janus would take the train to Culleton. He didn't own a car and wouldn't bother renting one.

I spent the morning in North Light, straightening the shelves, and by noon I'd settled on the balcony, where I idly sketched the trees that lined the drive, not as they looked in autumn but in winter, stripped, their branches stocked with snow.

I was listening for the sound of a cab coming up the drive, so when I saw the man with unkempt gray hair appear around the curve, I briefly saw a Civil War soldier coming slowly toward the house. I stood and blinked and he became Janus, the strap of a messenger bag across his chest. When he traveled, even on short trips, he always brought at least three books.

He waved and I waved back. My grip loosened and I was able to feel the pencil in my hand again.

Nearly twenty minutes passed before I heard a tap at the door, and I opened it to find Janus standing there with a coffee mug in each hand.

I'd seen pictures of him when he was Peter, the young priest, his dark hair short and perfectly parted, his somber blue eyes searching. I would not have known they were the same person.

After antiretrovirals became available, Janus returned to school to get a master's in psychology. In his therapy practice, he had many patients who'd lived through the crisis years. He said they bore the same wounds as those who had survived a war. You, he once told me, are a baby born during the Blitz, but it made me uncomfortable. I had done nothing heroic.

"Can I hug you?" he asked.

"Please don't," I said. "Just the coffee."

He handed me the mug. "For a dog person, you are awfully like a cat."

Janus sat on the loveseat in the corner, and I perched on the chair that I used at my easel.

"I'm starting a new support group," he said.

"For the newly diagnosed?"

Janus smiled. "The opposite. Long-term survivors. Positive seniors. Another forty years and you can join."

"Can't wait," I said.

"If you're alive, that is," he said.

"Did you come all this way to lecture me?"

But whatever Janus had in mind, I'd withstand it. He brought my mother with him. I caught her scent, a blend of tart perfume and darkroom chemicals. My father's living person, I believed, had been his father, Darragh.

"I came all this way because you asked me to come visit. It's my professional assumption that you want me to lecture you because Uncle Michan has not. Or not much. Probably because he spent a lifetime on medication himself, and he knows what it's like to be told to take it."

"Why isn't it the opposite?" I asked, genuinely curious.

Janus leaned back, settling in. This was the kind of question he liked.

"When he was a child, he took factor VIII when he was bleeding, and it made the pain stop. You, on the other hand, are quite well but still have to take meds. Different mindset! But Michan has also been told his whole life that the medication is for his own good and that he might die without it. He knows what it's like to want to be like everybody else. Striking any chords?"

"Nope," I said.

"Why did you stop?" he asked.

"Why don't you tell me."

He laughed. "I'd love to hear your version first."

But it was like trying to remember a movie I'd seen long ago.

"I moved," I said. "When I had to refill, the pharmacy wasn't close to my new apartment, and I kept meaning to get over there to pick up the prescription, but . . . it was never on the way home from wherever I was working."

Janus nodded. "An extra couple of stops on the subway or having to switch trains. That's worth risking your life for." He sighed.

"I didn't think of it as risking my life."

"You wouldn't jump off a bridge to see if you'd survive the fall, would you?"

I didn't answer, and we sat in silence. He would wait for me to speak, I knew, for as long as it took. When I finally did, my question surprised him.

"Rowan," I said. "Do you remember who she was?"

"Rowan . . ." I saw that he was going through the catalog in his mind, the names of the dead.

"The girl who was my friend."

"My God, yes," Janus said. He raised his eyebrows. "Don't tell me there are new developments?"

I shook my head and then explained who Ciaran Riordan was.

"He's here now?" He glanced at the closed door as if he could see through it, down the hallway.

"He's in his room, working."

"He's her brother? Sad business," Janus said cautiously.

I had always changed the subject if he tried to mention Rowan to me, and he never pushed.

"Rowan wasn't afraid of me," I said. "And she never believed I would die."

"Kids have a hard time understanding death."

"She understood it perfectly," I said, frustrated. "She knew what AIDS meant. But she didn't think *I'd* die of it." I nearly whispered the last part.

Janus didn't try to tell me that in the fall of 1995. No twelve-year-old girl could have predicted 1996, the Lazarus year. He waited for me to go on, so I did.

"Sometimes I think she found a way to trade her life for mine."

Janus didn't laugh. For a moment I thought he might ask me how I thought she'd done it. But he chose a different question, a harder one.

"Why?"

"Why?"

"Why would she have done that?" He sounded puzzled, and curious.

Because we were friends, I wanted to say, yet I knew he was right. It wasn't quite enough. We had not been sisters, after all. We had not loved the same mother, the same father. Then, perhaps, she might have done such a thing, to spare them grief.

So I only stared down at the coffee, growing cold in the mug.

"Tell me about when Benno visited," I said.

Benno, I didn't remember. Many others I did. Some of the men Janus mentioned from time to time. Others he never spoke of, and long ago I decided not to ask if they were still alive, assuming they were not. But I could talk about Benno, who to me was like a movie star from the silent film era.

Janus was quiet for a long time. I knew he was trying to decide if he should press me more about Rowan or let it go for now. Benno won.

It happened shortly after midnight, New Year's Eve. Benno had been dead for one year. Apartments packed with partygoers had their windows open to let the guests breathe the cold night air. People were singing up on the rooftops. Janus opened his own window to let some of the noise in, so he would feel less alone, though solitude this night had been his choice. Out in the city, friends were toasting Benno and so many others.

Janus looked up from his book because the letters were running all over the page, the *p*'s, *q*'s and *g*'s turning into one another, *m*'s and *n*'s switching places. Because the words would not behave themselves, he could not read. Yet he kept the book open on his lap, the way he did on a train or a plane when he didn't want to risk conversation with a seatmate.

When he looked up, he saw Benno standing on the fire escape, casually leaning against the railing, grinning. He was quite young, eighteen or so, and dressed in jeans and a tight white T-shirt. His hair was shaggy. It was the Benno of summer. The Benno before seminary. The sky was bright behind him.

"How do you know it wasn't your imagination?" I asked. "Wishful thinking?"

Janus smiled. Because it was so brief. A respite. In the space of a blink, Benno vanished.

It was like drinking a glass of water when you are very thirsty. It heals. But then you are soon thirsty again.

"If he were visiting from my imagination, I would have had him stay much longer."

Janus had a soothing voice, a gift that had served him well as an AIDS activist. He must have been a good priest, I'd often thought.

"Have you ever seen anyone who's still alive?" I asked.

"No," Janus said. "It's a trick only the dead can perform."

I set my mug down on the floor. It had grown heavy as an anchor.

"I think Rowan was in the bookstore that day." I twisted my fingers together. "I've let everybody tell me I had the wrong day. I was mistaken. I mistook a dream for reality. But it doesn't feel like a dream. It never has, and I can say it now."

"Memory does play tricks," Janus said gently. "Even when you're not traumatized. I remember this beautiful day I spent at the beach. It wasn't too hot. The sky was cloudless and the water was not too cold. It wasn't crowded. Nobody else sitting too close. Some days I can see Benno beside me, though it was before the seminary. We hadn't even met."

"Isn't that a daydream, then, and not a memory?" I asked. "If you sometimes think he was there but you know he couldn't have been."

Janus raised his gray eyebrows and nodded once. "Well argued."

"My parents didn't think I was going to be okay."

"No, they certainly did not."

"They tried to kill me," I said.

I'd startled him, I could see, as practiced as he was in hiding his emotions, staying neutral.

"Adair, I don't know. Good God."

I got up and went into a small alcove that I had not shown Ciaran. Canvases. Sketchbooks. Stacks of photographs. Cameras. Paintbrushes. My parents' work, their instruments. Their fingerprints on all of it.

My father wrote his name on the cover of all his sketchbooks, and I wondered if he'd thought of it as autographing them, picturing the day when they might be worth something. The pre-1984 books are full of my mother. There are many nudes. I've tried to look at them critically, one artist studying another's work, but I can't for long. It isn't her actual nudity that's difficult for me to look at; it's that I know how it ends for them, artist and subject.

The postdiagnosis ones are immeasurably darker. There is

the self-portrait, my father's face marked by Kaposi. There are the sketches of me, always serious. There are plenty of photos of me where I am happy, shots my mother took. But my father always drew me as if I'd understood from the very beginning. As if, perhaps, I knew before they did.

I opened the book to my favorite one, drawn when I was three years old. My father's projection of what I would look like, grown.

"Have you ever seen this?" I asked.

Janus took it, shaking his head. He smiled. "My God, he got pretty close."

Cathal didn't always title his work, but this one he had. *Adair, Never,* he'd called it.

I took the book back and turned a few more pages until I came to a much less polished sketch. It was an aerial view of a garage, the roof gone. A parked car, also without a roof. A man and woman sit in the front seats. There is a child in the back. All you can see are the tops of the heads. The garage door is closed. Somehow it's clear that this family isn't going anywhere.

"This happened," I said.

"What?" Janus asked.

We were still living in the small house they rented when I was a baby, in what would become known as The Year Before (diagnosis). It is Christmastime. The tree is up and colored lights surround the windows.

My father can still walk, but his vision is failing and he is so thin that his smile takes up his whole face. My mother looks fine, and at five years old, I do as well, though I have already had pneumonia twice, the second time so recently, the long hospital stay is still my primary nightmare. The slick touch of gloved hands. The strange eyes, kind or cold, peering down at me above the masks. I memorized the cuts of furrows. Only my parents showed their faces.

The family comes to us for Christmas—my grandparents Darragh and Cecilia, and Michan as well. I run to him. Uncle Michan, I say. Niece Adair, he answers, and I laugh. There is a big dinner on Christmas Eve. My father is not at the table.

That night, I wake in the back seat of our car, which is parked in the garage. My father is in the driver's seat with my mother beside him. I am in the seat directly behind her, unbuckled. I'm wearing my winter coat over my nightgown. The car is cold and silent. I ask where we are going, worried about Santa Claus. My mother turns around in the seat. Go back to sleep, she whispers.

And I do. I wake the next morning, Christmas morning, in my bed.

Janus listened wordlessly and still said nothing when I'd finished.

I had to prompt him. "Well?"

"Ask Michan, not me," Janus said. "I wasn't there."

"Please," I said. "My mother would have told you."

Janus sighed. "Lissa talked about it, but almost everyone in the group talked about taking matters into their own hands and not waiting until they were helpless."

"Don't judge the plague years by the HAART years," I said.

But Janus didn't smile as he usually did when I recited his own words at him.

"You survived. Be grateful." He spoke gently.

"But why did they change their minds?" I asked, unable to ask out loud why my parents had decided that I should live.

"Hope?" Janus said. "It was a death sentence, yes. But there were constantly rumors that a breakthrough was coming. Constantly."

He rested his hand on top of mine. "Maybe they decided that however bad it was going to get, all three of you had to stay until you each reached the end. Just in case."

I took the sketchbook back and closed it.

"I'm going to send you the name of a few therapists and I want you to think seriously about seeing one of them." Janus held up a hand to cut off my protest. "Promise me you'll consider it. You didn't stop taking your medication because going to the pharmacy was an inconvenience. But for now, I will say try not to live in the past so much, Adair. Whatever this memory is of the garage, let it go. Don't dwell."

Don't dwell in the past, he meant. But my parents were there, and Rowan as well.

Later that afternoon, as Janus was getting ready to leave, he asked if I'd ever considered curating my parents' work.

"Curating?" I repeated.

"You have your mother's photographs too?"

"I have everything."

"Think about organizing all of it. A book. An exhibit. Off the top of my head, I can think of four friends of mine who'd be willing to help."

"That would be . . . public," I said.

"It would be telling, you mean," he said. "Yes, everyone who sees it will know. You'd be disclosed, and not just to Michan's readers and the writers who come here. Think about it."

Lissa McCrohan, undressed, lying on a bed, her long brown hair spread over the pillow. One knee raised, her arms crossed over her breasts. She is smiling slightly, her gaze forthright, her eyes clearly on the artist.

To show this, what was lost? To show that before dying there was art, and beauty.

I promised Janus I would think about it.

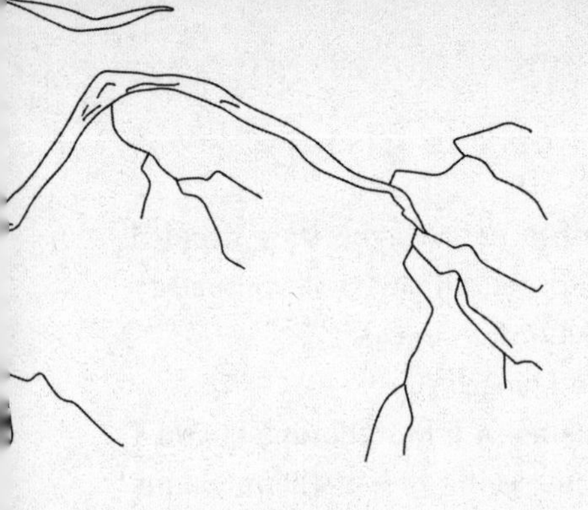

19
ADAIR
2010

For Columbus Day weekend, Shannon was going away with her husband and children, and I had agreed to fill in for her on Friday, answering the phones, talking to couples who'd come to see the grounds and decided impulsively to ask about getting married there.

Friday was gray and wet, and I was glad. There wouldn't be too many people visiting, so I would be mostly alone in the office, which was warm and inviting. Shannon had a green thumb, and she kept several plants around the room in vases she'd made in pottery class.

I picked up the *Culleton Beacon* and sat down at her desk.

> On October 28, a candlelight vigil will be held at Maple Street Park in memory of Rowan Kinnane on the fifteenth anniversary of her disappearance.

A woman identified as a Culleton resident was quoted: "You think of the Moye story, 'The Lost Girl,' and how she comes back after fifteen years, and you can't help but wonder, what if?"

I set the paper down. What if *what?* What if Rowan appeared at her own vigil, perfectly fine but refusing to say where she'd spent the last fifteen years?

Then I thought, almost laughing, that she would do exactly that if such a thing were possible.

The phone rang a few times, easy calls that I handled quickly. I skimmed the emails that had come into the general account, but they were specific questions that Shannon would have to handle, and I left them alone.

Shannon had told me I could leave at four o'clock instead of five. With no more than a half hour to go, the door opened, and I reluctantly looked away from the computer.

"Leo," I said as he closed the door behind him.

He stayed on the welcome mat.

"I got you something," he said. "My boots are muddy. You're going to have to come a little closer."

Slowly, I came from behind the desk, and when I was near enough he held out a pale wooden box that looked almost like an eyeglass case, except it was flat. The lid was engraved with Celtic knotwork.

I held it in both hands.

"Open it," he said.

I slid back the lid to see seven small compartments, and above each, in cursive script, the days of the week. I looked up at him questioningly.

"It's a pill organizer," he said. "You don't have one, do you?"

I laughed and shook my head. Shyly, Leo shoved his hands in his jacket pockets.

"I was reading about HIV and not taking medication. This is supposed to help, because you can leave it out on your dresser or the counter."

I had also read those articles: How to Combat Pill Fatigue.

Take your medication with a vitamin. Take it before/after brushing your teeth. Take with the meal you eat every day. And yes, use a pill organizer.

"Thank you." I closed the lid and traced the knotwork with my finger. "It's beautiful."

"It's made of oak," he said.

I laughed again. "You have a good memory."

Once, one night when we were together, I'd told him how I'd gotten my name from Edward Adair, the artist. Adair meant oak. Neither my mother nor my father had known that Darragh meant oak as well, and so I had been named, accidentally, after my grandfather.

"Fuck my memory. I felt like shit about what I said." Leo would not meet my eyes.

"What did you say?"

"When you were at my place, what I said about how I'd take a pill a day if it would fix my life."

"Oh, that, yes." I nodded, unable and unwilling to pretend it hadn't hurt.

"Use it, okay?"

"I will, I promise."

He smiled and then turned as if to go. I was about to tell him to wait when I saw a woman in a gray jacket heading straight for the office.

"Looks like I have a customer. Can I find you later?" I asked.

Leo looked out the window reflexively, nodded and stepped aside.

The door opened and a teenager came in and closed the door behind her. She leaned against it as though she were being pursued.

"Hi," I said, mystified. "How can I help you?"

She was far too young to be a bride. Perhaps she was the

daughter of one of the writers, killing time before 4 p.m., when visiting hours started.

She pushed off her hood and I looked more closely at her face. A moment before she gave her name, I realized who she was. I looked at Leo and saw that he already understood.

It's easy to say fifteen years and to understand that it's a long time, but seeing Libby Brayton was a visible measure of how very much time had passed since Rowan had last been with us.

Libby was three when her father took her away to live on Long Island, while Evelyn remained in the house where she'd lived with Rowan. Did David Brayton believe his wife was guilty? Some said yes, and this was proof. Another year passed before Evelyn moved away herself. Whenever I'd thought of Libby, I pictured her as a baby, as though her life had also paused on October 28, 1995.

I couldn't quite remember what David had looked like, except that he'd been a big, imposing man, graying at the temples. This tall, slender girl resembled Evelyn so strongly, it was hard to believe there was any trace of her father in her.

She said her name and added, "The lady in the kitchen told me you were here." She glanced at Leo without a hint of recognition. But that was not surprising. Surely, if she'd seen him at all, it was only in photos taken when he was nineteen.

He tilted his head toward the door. I understood that he was asking if he should stay or go.

"It's okay," I said.

We exchanged a look over her head—his pained, mine panicked. What to say to her? What did she want?

Leo closed the door and walked away. I fought the urge to throw the door open and call for him not to leave me alone with her, though I knew he would not want to be seen around her and risk whatever rumors might arise from *that*, on the off chance someone who knew them both stumbled upon the scene. Sister of Missing Girl Confronts Suspected Killer.

When he'd gone, Libby began to speak. Most weekends, she said, she visited her mother, and she'd heard from a friend in Culleton that I'd come back to Moye House.

"I've always wanted to meet you," Libby said.

"Sit, please." I gestured to the couch, but she sat in the chair in front of the desk, leaving me behind it as if I were the principal at her school. But I'm not the grown-up, I wanted to say. Not me.

"I always wanted to talk to someone who knew her. My mother says to leave it alone."

"Well, that's—understandable," I said, lacing my fingers together to keep from fidgeting.

Libby shrugged. "You've met Rowan's brother?"

"Yes, he's doing a residency here."

"I know," she said impatiently. "I read in the paper that he's writing a book about Rowan. I want to tell him something. I mean, I want to meet him because he's Rowan's brother, but also I have something to say." She unzipped her jacket and then yanked the zipper back up.

"Ciaran's working right now," I said slowly. "A lot of the writers don't check their email or phones during the day. But I can try and reach him."

As I thought it would, his phone went right to voicemail, so I texted him.

"I can't say when he'll see that," I said.

"Can I wait for a while?" Libby asked.

I nodded and she sat back, tucking her hands beneath her thighs.

"Is this where my mother worked?" Libby asked, looking around.

"No. Back then, the office was in the house itself, in one of the downstairs rooms."

"Oh." Libby jiggled her leg. "I stay with my mom over the summer. She doesn't live too far away. Do they ever hire you here if you're in high school?"

The answer was yes, actually—not Moye House itself but the company that handled the catering. Summer was a busy time for events. But I said I didn't know. Libby narrowed her eyes as though she knew I was lying.

"Did Rowan like school? Was she smart?"

"She was smart, but she didn't like school much," I said.

Libby leaned forward. "How come?"

I wondered if it was the first time anyone had said anything about Rowan that didn't make her sound like a saint. I explained that Rowan had not been happy at the Catholic school. She'd wanted to go to Culleton Elementary.

"Yeah, my mother said once she should have let Rowan do what she wanted."

"Does Evelyn know you're here?" I asked hesitantly.

"God, no." Libby made a noise that was part sigh, part laugh, a familiar sound. Rowan had made it almost every time she mentioned her stepfather.

"I told you, she's all *leave it alone.* The past is the past. Except it isn't! That's stupid, since we still don't know what happened."

Libby was right, of course.

We lapsed into silence. I glanced at my phone, willing it to ring or buzz with a text. I didn't really know how to talk to teenagers. The years I was one were mostly a blur, probably a deliberate trick of memory.

"What was she like?" Libby asked.

I wanted to say that she'd been a cross between Harriet the Spy and Claudia Kincaid, but I doubted Libby would have read those books.

"Smart, like I said. But unless she was interested in a subject, she didn't exactly try too hard. She had a good memory," I said. "She didn't like to sit still."

"Did Rowan hate me?" she asked, not meeting my eyes.

"Hate you?" I said, startled. "No, no, of course not."

"I've read a bunch of stuff about Rowan online. There was a posting on this website, this true-crime forum thing where people post theories about cases." Libby spoke with her eyes on the floor. "This one person said they thought she'd tried to hurt me, and so my mother . . . did something. Maybe not on purpose, but then she had to cover it up."

If you believed Brian Kelly was right, that scenario was indeed more plausible than Evelyn, who had no history of abuse, lashing out at Rowan during a fight between the two of them. But Evelyn protecting Libby from a jealous Rowan? A rough shove, the back of Rowan's head connecting with a sharp corner of the walnut table in the hallway.

I pressed my palms to my eyes, willing the image away. Behind Libby, near the window, Rowan, her arms crossed over her chest.

She's pretty. I always knew she would be. That would have been my whole life.

I turned my head, banished her to my peripheral vision.

"Being the stepdaughter was hard for her," I said, "but she never would have hurt you."

I didn't dare tell Libby that of Rowan's two half siblings, Ciaran was the one who had truly interested her. Libby belonged to David.

Libby gathered her hair in a ponytail and then released it.

"I wasn't allowed over your house," I said. "I don't know if you know that."

"The AIDS thing? Yeah, I know," she said, looking bored.

"I have HIV, not AIDS," I told her reflexively.

"Huh?"

I wondered if her high school—or any high school—covered HIV in health ed or sex ed, or whatever it was called.

"Never mind."

She caught something in my tone and her mouth thinned. I saw Evelyn, aggravated at Rowan.

"Dad said they didn't know as much about it then as they do now. That's why."

I could have told her precisely what "they" knew in 1995, and how her father was not only misinformed but cruel, but I decided it wasn't worth it. It didn't matter anymore.

It matters. It will always matter.

Rowan perched on the wide windowsill.

Libby's frown cleared. "Well, anyway, there's this guy online who says he can hypnotize people and retrieve memories from before they were two."

I stared at her. "Libby, no. You can't. That wouldn't work. It's impossible."

Rowan laughed. *She should do it.*

"I was there. It would solve everything if I tell what happened. It would clear my mom. You should read the things they say about her online. She's a murderer. She's a bitch. My dad was going to leave her because of Rowan being a brat, and so she—none of it is true."

"If anyone believed what you said, but most wouldn't." I leaned forward. "They'd say the memories were planted, or that you made them up, maybe not even on purpose."

Libby made the noise again, a laugh that was not a laugh.

"Yeah, well, he won't do it until I'm eighteen anyway."

"He shouldn't be doing it at all. Because it's not real." I tried to sound stern, but I had to admit that if I were in her position, I might be tempted too.

"If I remember something, and then it leads to actual proof, then we'd know," she said.

But all Libby could hope for was to recall driving away from the house with Rowan in the car, and then Rowan taking off across the parking lot, their mother calling after her. Memories did not leave DNA behind. They were not stains sunk into fabric, waiting for technology to catch up and name them.

Libby stood up. "Come someplace with me?"

"Where?" I asked, but I was already on my feet. I would follow Libby as I had not followed her sister.

"Into the woods," Libby said, tilting her head as though she'd explained it a dozen times already.

I placed my hands flat on the desk. "Why?"

"I have to get home soon. I'll tell you what I want to tell Rowan's brother, and if I don't get to see him today, you can tell him. He can call me if he wants to. What's your phone number?" Libby pulled out her phone.

I recited my number, and she entered it into her phone, barely glancing down, pressing buttons with an ease I'd never quite have.

Rowan grinned. *You're so old, Adair.*

Be quiet, I thought. My God, be quiet, unless it's to tell me where you are.

* * *

The chilly air smelled of smoke and rain. I let Libby lead. We walked mostly in silence, except for an occasional question she asked about the house or gardens.

Soon we reached Chapel Road, which was marked by a brass sign installed for tourists that explained the history of the Rosary Chapel. Libby started walking and I followed.

In the woods, afternoon darkened to twilight. Libby stopped when the chapel came into sight, and I stood beside her.

"We're cousins, you know," she said without looking at me.

"Yes," I said, briefly closing my eyes. "I know."

Libby walked until she reached the quicken tree.

"Do girls in town still come here on Quicken Day?" Libby asked.

"They haven't in a long time," I said, "as far as I know."

"Because of Rowan?" she asked.

"No, before."

Maybe long ago, the ritual had belonged to the popular, the kind who always led the way, but by the time Rowan and I were of age, it had become the province of the bookish girls who knew the history. Like Rowan.

Libby asked me if I knew the story of Elspeth and Bevin, and what they reported happened to them in the woods.

I did, I told her.

"Everyone thinks it was ghosts of the foundry workers and the maids, going to Mass one morning."

"That's what people have said," I agreed.

"They're wrong."

I moved closer to her. It was as if she were the feverish one and I could feel the heat radiating from her.

"Are they?" I asked.

Her voice quivered. "Elspeth was my mother's grandmother. My mom always says she'd never believe anybody else if they told the story Elspeth did. But Elspeth and Bevin got it wrong. They didn't understand what was really happening."

"What was really happening?"

Libby picked up a red leaf from the ground near her foot and twirled it by the stem.

"Do you know what a time-slip is?" she asked.

I shook my head, though I guessed, and dreaded, what she was about to say.

In a time-slip, she said, the past and the present merge. There were plenty of stories about people it had happened to.

Two women tourists who were walking in the gardens of the Palace of Versailles in 1901 were suddenly surrounded by men and women in powdered wigs. They saw Marie Antoinette. In the 1970s, two men were driving down a highway when a car from the fifties appeared next to them from out of nowhere. The woman driving was frantic, looking from side to side so dramatically the car was swerving. Her hairdo was the way they wore it back then. The men signaled her to pull over so they could help her. Then the car disappeared.

Most time-slip accounts were about people falling into the past. But some were glimpses of the future. A pilot was flying over an airport, getting ready to land. This was during World War I, and he looked down and saw that the airport was different. He didn't recognize the kinds of planes there. He never saw anything like them before, and didn't again, for another twenty years.

Elspeth and Bevin had not heard the parish ghosts that night, but the search for Rowan, eighty-four years in the future.

"Libby," I said weakly. "No."

She lifted her chin, another Rowan gesture. "What do you remember about the weather the day Rowan disappeared?"

That morning, the weather had been the talk of Moye House. Such a perfect autumn day. But winter arrived with the night.

Elspeth and Bevin had described an ordinary October night. And then it began to snow.

If there was something in these woods that allowed that to happen then, a portal of some kind, then maybe something similar had happened to Rowan. Only she had gotten trapped. She couldn't get back.

"Libby, I don't—"

"Look!"

Libby reached into the back pocket of her jeans and took out what I could see was a sepia photograph.

"It's getting dark," she said fretfully as she handed it to me. "I should have shown it to you inside."

I took it. The photograph was creased, as though it had once been folded and the edges were yellow. Of the five women in the picture, three of them appeared to be in their twenties or early thirties, and the two on either end of the group were younger, girls between sixteen and eighteen, I'd guess.

"This was taken here," I said, surprised.

The women were standing in front of the chapel, the door open behind them.

I wondered for a moment if it might be a portrait of Moye House's maids and kitchen girls. The solemn expressions, the way they had their hands folded demurely in front of them, made me consider it. But though they were dressed similarly, tight bodices and full, long skirts, their dresses were different shades of light and dark. Nor were they wearing aprons. Not in uniform, then. Still, it might have been taken on a Sunday, after Mass.

"Do any of them look familiar?"

I moved the picture closer to my face. Round faces, thin faces. Homely, average. Only the woman in the center could be called pretty. I studied her, trying to decide if that was objectively true or if I only thought so, because of her position in the photo and because of all of them, she was the only one with even a hint of a smile. Yes, I decided, she was the beauty of the group, but certainly not familiar to me.

I paused at the girl on the far left, touched her with the tip of my pinkie. She was the only one whose hair was not gathered in a bun. Rather, it was pulled back from her face (tied back with a ribbon? some old-fashioned version of a barrette?). She was slightly in profile, the only one who had not been looking directly at the camera. A small white dog sat at her feet, also gazing off, looking at the same thing the girl had been, I guessed.

I looked up at Libby, fidgeting beside me.

"Her," she said almost gleeful. "Yes, that one."

"What about her?"

"It's Rowan," Libby said.

Although we were outside, I felt suddenly claustrophobic, as if the trees had leaned in to listen, collectively drawing their breath.

"No, it isn't," I said, shaking my head. "Libby, no."

"She looks like Rowan's age progression," she said.

I looked again and saw that yes, there was a slight resemblance in the shape of the face, the eyebrows.

"Helen Dunleavy—" I said, though I had no idea if it was possible there could still be a resemblance, so many generations removed.

But Libby was shaking her head. "I asked at the historical society if they could tell when it was taken, and the woman said probably around the 1880s, based on the clothes and the type of photo. That's too late to be Helen. And it's not either of her daughters. We have their pictures."

"People look like other people out of nowhere all the time," I said. "Total strangers. They just do."

But Libby was shaking her head. "Rowan thought it looked like her. That's why she kept it. I know it."

I handed the photo to Libby and she put it back in her jacket pocket.

"Where did you find it?" I asked.

"In a book. Mom gave away Rowan's clothes a long time ago, but she kept things like her hairbrush, her pillow, her books. It's proof," she said.

"Proof of what? Time travel?" I said it gently, afraid she would think I was mocking her.

"It was in a book about magic. I found the picture in between two pages that have spells on them. I think Rowan found the picture, and no, I don't know how or where, but she knew it was her and she put it in the book. She knew there was something weird in these woods. And she came out here and—something happened."

A book of magic. I closed my eyes briefly, trying to remember. *This spell will make you think you're beautiful.* Rowan, laughing.

"*A Charm for Lasting Love*," I said.

"Yes," Libby said, surprised. "That's it."

"She took that from Moye House," I said. "It belonged to our library."

"I don't care. I'm not giving it back."

"I'm not asking you to," I said. "But it's an old book. Rowan probably found the picture stuck in it."

"So? She still could have figured it looked like her."

Yet Rowan had never seen the projection of herself as a grown-up.

"Maybe," I said, to appease Libby. "But you don't know that would have meant anything to her."

"Fine, think I'm crazy. But where is she, then?"

"I don't think you're crazy. And I don't know where she is."

"The past is the best answer," Libby said. "What I've figured out is better than what the police think. You know what it means, then? If I'm right?"

"It means that she died a very long time ago," I said.

Because a Rowan who had traveled back in time to the nineteenth century was just as out of reach as a Rowan who had been killed in this one.

"Sure, technically," Libby said. "But what it really means is that she might come home someday, if she can find her way back."

I looked down at the ground, littered with leaves whose edges were beginning to brown and curl. Libby's theory, I knew, wasn't entirely about inventing an adventure for Rowan instead of accepting her death. Libby must have wanted the last fifteen years of her own life erased and redrawn. And I could hardly argue.

I drove Libby to the train station. She had taken the train one stop from Onohedo, where her mother lived, and walked from there to Moye House. I offered to take her all the way home, but she vehemently refused, and I guessed she did not want to risk her mother seeing her get out of my car. Whatever lie she had told about how she was spending her afternoon clearly could not include a ride home.

By the time I got back to Moye House, it was dark.

I went in the servants' door and began climbing the stairs,

the pill organizer from Leo in my hand. The stairwell smelled of smoke, and though there was nowhere to go but up, it seemed that I was following the scent. Right before the bend, I stopped. I didn't move until he called my name.

Leo was sitting on the step beside the window, hunched over, his clasped hands dangling between his knees. He straightened when he saw me, and I sat beside him so our shoulders touched. His clothes, his skin, smelled of smoke. The crew had been burning leaves, I guessed.

Leo listened as I told him what Libby believed.

"Should I call Evelyn and tell her?"

"Why the hell would you do that?" Leo asked.

"Because it's crazy," I said.

"If it makes her feel better, let her think it. She's a kid. She'll outgrow it."

I decided he was right. I was not Libby's sister. To shred her fantasy was not my responsibility. Better that I leave her be, let her nurture it, trusting that she would set it aside someday when she realized it was time to accept the probable truth.

I showed him the pill organizer. "Thank you again."

He smiled tiredly. "It's not jewelry."

"When do I ever wear jewelry?"

He shifted so he could see me, as if to check.

"You cut your hair."

"A long time ago," I said. "It was much shorter, to my chin. It was supposed to be a bob, but it's so straight it looked stupid. I'm growing it again."

He laughed. "I liked how it was."

My hair had been very long then, halfway down my back.

Then. When we were together. As together as we dared to be. Never going out in public in Culleton, not willing to face the heads turning.

How could she?

How could he?

This was what we'd told each other would happen, but I wondered now if it would have been as bad as that.

"Last time I saw you, you were talking about leaving town," I said.

"I was asking you to leave with me," he said. "You don't remember?"

"I was already gone."

"To college. I was talking about never coming back. Crazy talk."

"Why is it crazy?"

"Nothing would change," Leo said. "Walking down the street, nobody would know me. But all somebody's got to do is Google my name and they find out the rest. Might as well be here, where at least some people don't believe the worst."

I turned and rested my forehead on Leo's shoulder.

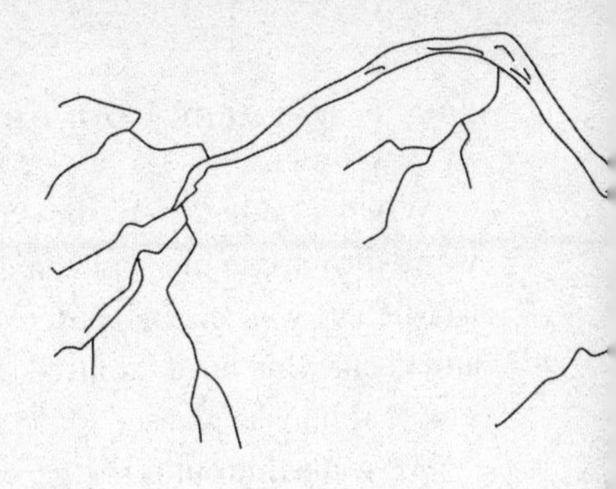

20

ADAIR

September 1995

Rose Day was for the members of the board and donors to Moye House, a cocktail party timed for the September bloom of the rose garden.

My dress was ivory with rosebuds on the sash. It was the prettiest thing I owned. Only the thought of not ever getting a chance to wear it propelled me to put it on and go outside. Michan never insisted I go to these events, but I knew that he liked me to come.

I'd look forward to the party until I actually took the two stone steps up into the rose garden and walked the gauntlet of appraising eyes. The collective gaze consumed me, kind and curious, and I retreated, afraid of being a disappointment, of failing to inspire.

I had circulated a few times, answering the dull questions about school put to me because no one knew what else to talk about. Rowan came through the white gate. She was wearing a blue dress with a flouncy skirt that was slightly too big for her. Her hair had been released from its ponytail for the day, and she had her bangs clipped back with two pink barrettes that were so small they might have been Libby's. She was wearing her glasses, though, and they alone kept her familiar.

When I joined her, she said, "You should have said you wanted to invite me, so I came anyway."

Michan was in the center of a cluster. He spotted Rowan and cocked his head, amused. Party crashing at twelve? But I saw that he was pleased.

We walked around the garden, me trailing Rowan. Rowan, whose mother had helped plan the event, pointed out the good food and the famous writers.

When the party had been under way for an hour, thunder rolled across the sky. The sound seemed to come from Degare, as though the mountain had arched its back. The staff, who had been instructed what to do if the forecasted storm came to pass, immediately began the work of moving the party indoors.

As they gathered bottles of wine, gripping the necks between their fingers and scooping the glasses with their other hands, the rain came in heavy drops, sending up theatrical shrieks from the guests. Some people decided to leave, but most simply followed the caterers and waitstaff into the house, many doing their part by carrying platters of crackers and cheese, glad to be seen as helpful, to continue the festivities with all the comradery of people bonded by adverse weather. Now they could talk and drink on the first floor of Moye House, out of the humidity and away from the bees.

Rowan and I tagged along, until Rowan tugged my elbow and we diverged from the throng heading up the back terrace. She led me around the side of the house and through the servants' door.

We sidestepped the laughing guests clustering in the kitchen. I opened the door that hid the servants' staircase and we stepped through it, Rowan first and then me. I closed it and we stood in the near dark.

Rowan started walking up the stairs and I followed without even trying to argue.

Years ago, on Wednesday afternoons during the school year, students used to come for tours. They'd come in the servants' door and take these stairs all the way up to the attic, where the servants' quarters were restored to how they'd looked in the mid-1800s. Four women had slept in the attic room: the parlor maid, the cook's assistant, the laundress and the maid of all work.

But the tours were too disruptive, Jorie decided. Moye House could not be both a writers' colony and a museum. One or the other. Yet the exhibit had never been dismantled.

After the third floor, the staircase pitched sharply and the light from the window on the second-floor landing disappeared.

"It's like being blind," Rowan said in wonder. "They would have carried lanterns, I guess, or maybe plain candles?"

"Candles, probably," I said. Lanterns or lamps seemed too rich for servant girls.

There was no door at the top of the stairs. We stepped directly into the room. One window faced north, the other south. Two narrow beds were on either side of each window, covered with one thin blanket. There was a small table with a basin and pitcher on it.

Rowan approached the wardrobe and ran a hand over the door.

"This looks like the one in *The Lion, the Witch and the Wardrobe.*" She turned the key in the lock and back again.

Rowan opened the wardrobe and, with a brief exclamation, turned, holding a white apron on a hanger.

"This isn't real, is it?" she asked.

I knew if I laughed, Rowan would be annoyed. "No. It's from a costume shop. If it were real, it'd be a hundred years old."

"So? Clothes can last a hundred years."

Rowan put it on and tied it in the back. The hem was at her ankles. She walked around the room while I lay on one of the beds.

Two sets of servants' bells hung on the wall, near the door. One was attached to a bell pull in the master bedroom and the other ran all the way down to the kitchen. The rain was incessant on the roof.

"Whoever rang the bell that night of the sleepover wanted us to come up here," Rowan said matter-of-factly.

I could have asked who she thought would be calling to us, or why, but I didn't like to think about that night. With daylight, the fright had been replaced by a sense of foolishness. We had heard some sound and assigned it to the servants' bells.

"I bet this was the nicest place they ever lived," I said, to change the subject.

My head ached, as it often did. I knew if I closed my eyes, I'd fall directly into a deep sleep.

"The summers would have sucked, though," Rowan said. "It doesn't get hot in Ireland, not like here."

I closed my eyes, and Rowan laughed.

"Are you falling asleep for real?"

"I'm tired."

Rowan lay down on the opposite bed, taking off her glasses.

"You'll be at school on Monday?"

"Maybe," I said.

"You look fine," Rowan said.

She sounded angry and I opened my eyes, with anger of my own rising.

"They want me to try medication again."

It's time to take steps, the doctor had said somberly at my last appointment.

I could have supplied Rowan with a T-cell count and explained the difference between good and bad, high and low, falling, falling, falling. But that was too much work, and I thought she wouldn't even try to understand.

"Okay. So you'll take medication," Rowan said.

"Maybe," I said, rolling over on my side.

"Michan won't let you not take it," Rowan said. "No way."

I said nothing. *He's a fighter!* The McCrohan brothers had heard this their whole lives. Michan told me that my father, especially, had hated how this was said of the sick, as if they'd contracted their disease for the very purpose of proving they could beat it.

I liked to imagine some Grim Reaper arriving to pick me up with a box of candy in hand, only to find himself jilted because I'd gone ahead alone.

"It prolongs the inevitable," I said, repeating words I'd often overheard back in the days of Janus's support group. Those on the other side of the debate argued that it bought time and that was what they needed: time for the cure to be discovered. And the counterargument went that the cure was probably decades away. Diseases don't arrive out of nowhere and then get vanquished within a generation.

My mother had ignored the advice of doctors and the psychologists and even Janus, early on. Let your daughter grow up in peace. Don't tell her unless she reaches an age when she must know. She may never need to know. But my mother had been too afraid that she would die before me. She wanted me to hear from her that my life would be brief, and though I might get very sick, at the end I would find both her and my father waiting for me. Where, she couldn't quite say, and I'd always pictured something like the doctor's office, with pale furniture and a tough carpet. There they would be sitting, thumbing through magazines and watching the door, waiting for me to arrive and release us all.

It won't be long, she'd once promised. It won't be long at all.

The doctor was uneasy with how much I understood. He glanced disapprovingly at Michan over the tops of his glasses when I asked for my counts. Michan only gazed back. He would neither accept responsibility nor criticize my mother.

"But you don't know, not for sure." Rowan paused. "What if your parents decided you should all die together?"

"My father died first and my mother second."

"I know that's what happened," Rowan said impatiently. "You're here. But what if you died when you were in kindergarten? You wouldn't have had all these years. Seven whole years."

"Seven," I repeated, but I was thinking not of the years behind me, but the ones to come, the way you might start to ponder snow just as autumn begins.

I closed my eyes, and it was a long time before Rowan spoke again.

"The rowan tree was magic," she said, and now she sounded drowsy too. "The wood of a rowan tree was only supposed to be used for spells. Not firewood or building stuff. The wood keeps the dead from wandering. That's why in Ireland they plant rowan trees in cemeteries."

"They do?" I asked without opening my eyes. "How do you know that?"

"My father told me."

I let my eyes close as Rowan continued with one of her monologues that I knew could go on and on. She recited:

"The hags returned
To the queen in a sorrowful mood,
Crying that witches have no power,
Where there is rowan-tree wood."

We lay on the beds in our colorful dresses, two wildflowers, taking naps.

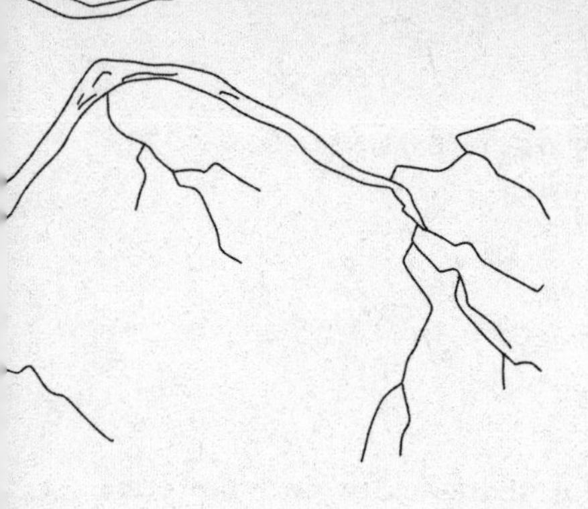

21
ADAIR
2010

Ciaran and I went to talk to Evelyn on October 13.

Libby had told her mother about her trip to Moye House, and about Ciaran's book, and Evelyn called me. I told her that he was sincere and that I thought he would be fair.

Evelyn lived on a tranquil street in Onohedo lined with trees, hers the only apartment building. The rest were modest private houses, surely filled with families. Ciaran and I had passed a school on our walk from the train station. I couldn't help but think of the huge house that Evelyn was supposed to have moved into with David and Rowan and Libby, with its rambling yard and spacious front porch, a room for each daughter.

It was three o'clock when Ciaran and I took the elevator to the top floor of the building, the fifth.

He rang the bell. We waited so long that Ciaran lifted his hand to ring the bell again, but hesitated. We looked at each other. I was sure Ciaran was also picturing Evelyn standing on the other side of the door, trying to work up the courage to answer, or otherwise willing us to go away.

Ciaran was about to press the bell again when the door opened.

Evelyn was wearing a red sweater and gray pants.

"Come in," she said.

She closed the door behind us, then introduced herself to Ciaran. They shook hands, staring at each other frankly.

"Ciaran," she said. "I'd know you anywhere. You look like Jamie."

Before he could answer, she turned to me.

"Adair. Don't you look well," she said.

Typically, my response to this, when it was someone who knew me as a child, was to say, Yes, I am alive. It often made people laugh and then relax. But here, that would be cruel.

"I'm good," I said. "Thanks."

"Rowan used to bombard me with questions about you," Evelyn said. "Your health. I kept telling her that you could have years left. She kept asking, as if she thought one day I'd have a different answer. And see? I would have."

I nodded. Evelyn saved me from responding by abruptly saying she'd worked that morning and would change and be right back.

We could see the kitchen from the living room. It was so small there wasn't room for a table. There was a counter, though, with two stools, and I guessed that was where Evelyn ate. It struck me as incredibly lonely, and I went still for a moment, imagining her sitting there eating a sandwich by herself.

But for all I knew, Evelyn might have had a dozen friends and maybe a boyfriend. Yet I noticed how stark the place looked, not so much as a pair of shoes kicked off casually or an open book left on a table.

Evelyn emerged from the bedroom wearing jeans and a loose, long-sleeved black shirt. She was in her stocking feet and she'd taken her hair down. It was much shorter than she used to wear it, barely skimming her shoulders. There was no gray at all, and I felt better, guessing that she colored it. It mattered somehow that she took the time.

Her face was bare of makeup. The lines around her eyes were from aging, not grief, I thought. She did not appear ravaged, as she had in the photos published right after Rowan vanished, when it was clear she had barely slept for days.

We sat on the couch and she settled in the armchair beside it.

She asked Ciaran questions about his father, coolly, with no particular inflection, and Ciaran followed her lead, updating Evelyn on Jamie Riordan's life since they'd last been in touch, over five years ago. He taught. He wrote book reviews, articles about literature, things like that. No fiction, not anymore. Ciaran said he believed it was Jamie's way of punishing himself, for Rowan.

Evelyn's only response was a tilt of the head.

She thinks he deserves it, I thought.

She asked Ciaran about himself as well; a stranger walking in might have thought she was interviewing him.

I realized Evelyn was probably used to people being awkward in her presence and had learned how to make them feel at ease. It was a skill that took practice, and patience.

Finally, when a silence fell, I sensed Evelyn steeling herself. Go ahead.

Ciaran reached into his backpack, which he'd set at his feet. He took out his tape recorder and held it up. Evelyn nodded indifferently.

"As I've explained to you, I'm writing a book about several cases. Not just Rowan's."

"Why?" she asked.

"Why? These are other cases I've read about, and there are no answers there either."

Though he hadn't quite answered her, Evelyn nodded.

"What are the other cases? Don't go into all of them, pick the one, besides Rowan's, besides your *sister's*"—a faint smile—"that haunts you the most."

Ciaran stared down at his hands for a moment and nodded once.

"In Brooklyn, New York, about four o'clock in the afternoon of November 22, 1963, a twelve-year-old girl went to her church, a few blocks from her house, to light a candle for President Kennedy. A few people there were saying the rosary. The priest himself was there. He was to say a special Mass that evening. The girl lit her candle and she left. She never made it home. The family called the police, and by the next day they'd gone to the press, but one girl against a presidential assassination, they didn't have a chance."

"Did they ever find her?" Evelyn asked.

"No," Ciaran said. "Not a trace."

"Did they ever develop a suspect?" Evelyn stopped. "Listen to me, falling right back into it. Following all leads. Person of interest."

"They didn't," Ciaran said. "Nobody ever emerged."

A blank canvas and not a single drop of paint nearby. No brush. No way even to begin.

"Her parents can't still be alive," Evelyn said.

"No, they're both gone a long time," Ciaran said. "But there are brothers and sisters still. Nieces and nephews as well."

"And they're still looking," Evelyn said flatly.

In those first few months, I'd chosen milestones and decided that the answer would have to be known by then. Forty years was as unimaginable as one year had been, in the beginning. Rowan would be fifty-two. Would she bother coming back if she found a way?

"I don't know if I'd say that, exactly. No work's been done

on the case in decades. But the family wants to know what happened."

Evelyn rubbed both hands against her knees and then got up and went into the kitchen.

Ciaran and I looked at each other. The alarm on his face surely reflected my own. So she was not as composed, as resigned, as she seemed.

The refrigerator opened and then a cabinet. She came back with a wine bottle in one hand and three glasses in the other, expertly held by the stems.

"I'm going to make the bad joke of all functional alcoholics and say it's happy hour somewhere." She poured one glass and looked at us, eyebrows raised.

I nodded, then Ciaran did too.

Evelyn poured wine for us and sat back down. She sipped hers and closed her eyes.

"What was the girl's name?" Evelyn asked.

"Caroline Kennedy," he said.

I thought I'd heard him wrong.

Evelyn lowered her glass. "Is that supposed to be funny?"

"God, no. That was her name," he said. "When I was first planning the book, I scrolled through this site online that's dedicated to missing kids. The name along with that date got my attention. A girl with the same name as President Kennedy's daughter goes missing on the same day he's killed?"

"What did the police think? There has to be a connection," I said.

"The police were baffled. The girl wasn't called Caroline. It was always Callie. Her sister told me they're not sure how many people even knew her given name. She wouldn't have introduced herself as Caroline."

"That day she might have," I said.

"Some of the family believe she did just that, though how and why it might've led to whatever happened to her, they haven't a clue," Ciaran said. "Others say no. It still wouldn't have entered her head."

"Coincidence." Evelyn pursed her lips as though the word tasted bitter. "The detectives who investigated Rowan's disappearance didn't know the meaning of the word."

"You mean there are things they should have put down as coincidence and didn't?" Ciaran asked.

"That's exactly what I mean. Very good," Evelyn said.

Ciaran said calmly, "Like what?"

"Leo being at the house the night before. David being away on business. David and Rowan not getting along," Evelyn said. "He was a decent man, but I married him for the wrong reasons, and he married me for different wrong reasons."

"What were those reasons?"

"Security, for me and Rowan. I wanted another child, too. I didn't realize until we were living together how set in his ways he was. He and Rowan were like oil and water." Evelyn looked at me. "He was being ridiculous not letting you around Libby. I told him that. That's why I never stopped Rowan from seeing you."

"Rowan liked the challenge," I said.

Evelyn smiled. "I let her think she was fooling us."

"What were his reasons for marrying you?" Ciaran asked.

"Children," she said. "He and his ex-wife hadn't had any kids and he regretted it. I wasn't so young that I looked like a walking midlife crisis, but I could still have a baby. I'm not saying we were both thinking all of these things then. But time, you know—you see things.

"David would probably tell you that what happened to Rowan broke up our marriage, but I knew when Libby was an infant that we weren't going to make it. After, David thought Libby deserved to grow up without stigma. He figured she'd be pointed at in school. The sister of the missing girl."

"She would have been," I said.

"I know. He was right, but I couldn't leave."

"Did you try and stop him?" Ciaran asked.

"I didn't know how." Evelyn shook her head. "I didn't want to stop him. When he'd take Libby places like the zoo or the park or the movies, he'd try and get me to go with them, but I wouldn't. The house was so quiet when they were out. When he told me he was leaving with her, I thought: It'll be like that all day. I can think. Finally. Back then, I thought I could answer the question if only I tried hard enough."

"The question?" I asked.

"Where is she?" Evelyn said.

"Did you really believe you could answer it?" Ciaran asked.

"I did for a while. But a therapist told me I gave Libby up to punish myself. I don't know if that's true, but she was very pleased with her theory. I drove to Long Island on the weekends for visits. The trip filled up the hours. Now she comes to me. It works, as well as it can."

"Can you tell me about the day Rowan disappeared?" Ciaran asked.

"It's the only day of my life," she said.

Evelyn had no strong sense of the morning and early afternoon. The three of them were in their little backyard at one point. Rowan had played with Libby, rolling a ball to her. Evelyn had been glad to see it but hadn't commented, lest Rowan get self-conscious. None of the neighbors saw them, or at least nobody came forward and said they had.

The fight had begun at one o'clock, when Evelyn started

getting Libby ready to leave and called to Rowan, who was in her room, that she'd better get her costume on. Rowan yelled back that she wasn't wearing that stupid dress. It was an old-fashioned calico dress, *Little House on the Prairie* style. After the disappearance, it had been found in a heap on the floor in front of Rowan's full-length mirror.

Evelyn leaned forward and refilled her glass. She looked from Ciaran to me.

"And this is the part of the story where I kill my daughter." She sat back.

Evelyn supposed the police had pictured them screaming at each other at the top of the stairs, but Rowan had been in her room, where the damn dress was found, and she'd been in the living room, dressing the baby.

It was really an argument that never developed into a fight, because Evelyn had quickly caved, for the sake of peace. But then Rowan had decided she didn't want to go at all.

Every parent of a missing child has a cache of "if onlys." Evelyn's biggest one? If only she hadn't been afraid of being a doormat. Her family had a fine tradition of mothers and daughters not ever recovering from the turmoil of adolescence. Her own mother had also given in over stupid things time and time again because she didn't want to fight. It only encouraged her, Evelyn, to push harder. She was trying to avoid that pattern with Rowan by remaining firmly in charge.

No costume, fine. But you are coming with us, Evelyn had told Rowan. That's that.

"Brian Kelly?" Ciaran asked.

"Oh, yes, Brian." Evelyn twisted her mouth. "He didn't fucking see her. That's all."

"Do you think he's lying?"

"I'd like to say yes because he was such an obnoxious kid. He used to play basketball in his driveway for hours. Thump, thump, thump. But no, I think he's probably not lying," Evelyn said.

"He just wasn't looking at the exact moment Rowan came outside?" I said.

Evelyn stared into her glass. "I was getting Libby into her car seat. If you've ever had to deal with one of those things, God. I always had trouble with the buckle. I looked up and Rowan was climbing in the front seat. I didn't hear the front door open. I think Rowan was probably in the backyard and then came up the driveway. The car door, the back-seat door, was open. It would have blocked his view."

I swallowed a gulp of wine as if it were water, realizing she must have said this to the police a hundred times. It had not been enough to take her off the list of suspects.

"What about her sneakers? She wasn't wearing them," Ciaran said.

"Her sneakers," Evelyn said impatiently. "Yes, I told the police she was wearing her new sneakers, but they were by the back door. Which made me a murderer because none of her other shoes were missing and she sure as hell wouldn't have left the house barefoot. Her school shoes and her Easter shoes and her snow boots were all in her closet. So were her old sneakers that she wouldn't throw away even though there was a hole in the toe."

"She wore those all summer." I smiled. "She wore them without socks and would stick her big toe out the hole."

Evelyn turned to me. "That's right," she said. "I haven't thought about that in years. There are so many things I've forgotten."

I thought fleetingly of my own parents, and I knew what she meant. It was unfair how much memory let go.

"When I told the police all of her shoes were in the house, they thought I'd slipped up with my cover story," Evelyn said. "The detective made me repeat it three, four times—no shoes missing—before he asked, 'Then what the hell was your daughter wearing on her feet when she left the house that day?'"

She mimicked an accusatory tone and I flinched at the sound.

"What do you think she *was* wearing, then?" Ciaran asked.

"She had an allowance. Back then, I figured she bought a pair of shoes with her own money, for some reason. There was one shoe store in Culleton that sold kids' shoes she liked. But all the clerks said no, she'd hadn't bought anything. They'd have remembered a kid coming in alone."

I shook my head. "I don't think she would have spent her money on shoes."

"Neither do I, but it was my only explanation until they did the first age progression. I never looked at her Missing posters. I couldn't. But the age progression I did. It gave her height at the time she disappeared as five feet. It sounds crazy, but I thought, She couldn't have been that tall. That's when I realized she might have been wearing a pair of my shoes. They would have fit."

"Did you check?" I asked.

"I'd already moved by then. I'd gotten rid of almost everything of mine. I don't remember any shoes being missing, but I wasn't really paying that much attention."

Evelyn began to speak more hesitantly when Ciaran led her into the earliest hours of Rowan's disappearance.

When she did not find Rowan at their house, Evelyn had

genuinely expected to find her at the movie theater. When the teenager selling tickets said he hadn't seen her, Evelyn should have made the boy call the police. In the age of cell phones, she would have done it herself. But out of pure denial, she started looking for Rowan in other places.

"What made you think to look for Leo at the bar?" Ciaran asked. "He wasn't twenty-one."

Evelyn's smile flickered. "I was *not* looking for Leo. I was not sleeping with Leo either, by the way. I thought Rowan might be there."

"In a bar?" Ciaran said.

"There were Irish musicians there, for Quicken Day. She liked Irish music. She had some idea that her father did too. I don't know why. I told her Jamie couldn't have cared less. I didn't really think I'd find her, but it was getting so late. I hadn't seen her in so long . . ." Her voice trailed off.

"But you saw Leo," Ciaran said.

"Yes. And I called him over to ask if he'd seen Rowan at all that day," Evelyn said. "He hadn't. Coincidence! I ran in there thinking, God, let Rowan be there, just let her be there, I won't be mad. But there's Leo, the handsome young handyman who was always at my house. And so I end up being there to make sure he's gotten rid of my daughter's body before I pull the trigger on our big conspiracy and call the police to report her missing." She took a sip of wine, then another, and said, "I've always felt bad about Leo."

"Bad? What do you mean?" I asked.

Evelyn turned her head so she was speaking to us in profile.

"He only got dragged into it because of me," she said. "The police didn't have a way to make their theory work otherwise. They needed to explain why Rowan was never found. David wasn't there. Somebody had to have taken Rowan away. A lone woman with a baby? Leo—he was their only option."

I traced my finger around the top of the wine glass.

"Do you think she's dead?" Ciaran asked.

"Yes," Evelyn said.

Back when she still sat for interviews with the press, in the hope of drumming up a lead, and was asked about the worst part of the whole ordeal, she was expected to say: Not knowing. Missing Rowan. Being under suspicion herself.

And yes, to all of these things. But in truth the worst part came before the ordeal began. When she learned Rowan hadn't bought a ticket at the movie theater, Evelyn had known—even given the very real possibility that the boy selling tickets just hadn't noticed Rowan, or that another person had been behind the counter then.

Evelyn couldn't quite describe it. It was a shot of pure cold up her spine. A separation of mind and body. Trouble is here. For all the talk of hope over the next few weeks, months, years, she'd known then that Rowan was gone.

My throat hurt from the effort not to cry.

"I think she left the parking lot and started walking to Moye House," Evelyn said. "Somebody she wasn't afraid of pulled over and offered her a ride. She got in the car."

"You don't think there's any chance she's still alive?" Ciaran asked.

"Oh, God, no," Evelyn said. "I don't think she survived the night."

Ciaran and I sat silently. Evelyn gazed at us both.

"She wanted to go back to Ireland. I was planning on taking her for summer vacation. Eventually. Someday." Then she turned to me. "This is awful and I shouldn't say it. I used to think it wasn't fair that this had to happen to Rowan. I used to wish it were you."

Ciaran said, "Listen, Evelyn—"

"I understand," I said.

"Good," Evelyn said. "I liked you. I felt sorry for you. I was glad Rowan finally had a real friend. But that's what I used to think."

Ciaran started to speak, but I put my hand on his arm.

I told Evelyn that I'd lain awake many nights thinking the same thoughts. It would never be fair. She smiled sadly.

"Ciaran," Evelyn said. "Jamie's *son.* This has been going on too long. Write your book. Pretend it's your tragedy too. I don't care. It's been fifteen years. End this, will you?"

Ciaran was breathing rapidly as we left the apartment building, and I had to walk fast to keep up with him.

"She'd been drinking," I said. "I bet she was drinking before we got there. That bottle was already open."

"I understand what she said to me. She's got a history with my father. I went in there sort of expecting it. I'm the reason he left the States."

"She can hardly blame you because your father missed you."

"Adair, he called for my birthday and I wouldn't come to the phone. 'What do you expect?' my mother tells him. A month later he was back in Ireland."

"That's not your fault."

"Most days, I know that. Other days, it's 'what if.' What if he were still in the States and Rowan had been visiting him that Saturday?"

"What if, on a weekend visit, there was a car accident and both she and your father were killed? What if a woman met a man who needed medicine to live a normal life, and that medicine gave him a deadly virus that killed them both?"

"Point taken," Ciaran said, his words clipped. "But she shouldn't have said that to you. It was cruel."

"It isn't," I said.

We were keeping our voices normal for the sake of passersby.

"It is."

I stopped walking, and he stopped too.

"If one girl has a life expectancy of eighty and another is already past hers, who should be killed?" I asked.

"Neither," he said quietly. "Neither."

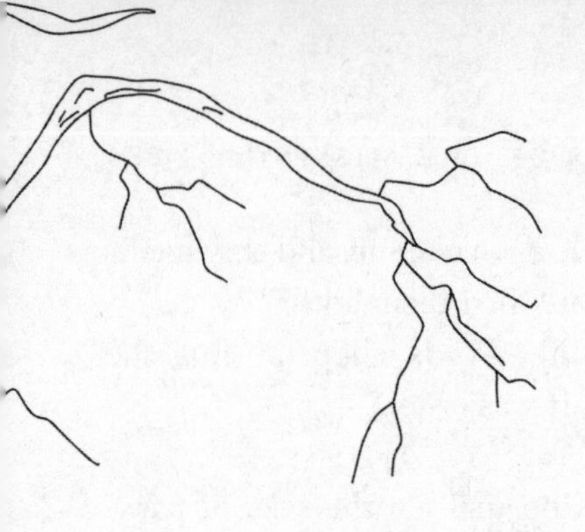

22
ADAIR
2010

For the first two years after Rowan disappeared, there were no Quicken Day celebrations held at all. But by 1998 the tradition was restarted, made permissible by the fact that the last Saturday in October was Halloween itself. The children would be dressed for trick-or-treating anyway. It would be a Halloween parade. The following year, Quicken Day was back to what it used to be, though the town's police force and parents were vigilant.

For several years, a group of fathers appointed themselves as an undercover neighborhood watch. If Rowan had been abducted and the man returned for a second victim, he'd avoid the uniformed police, but dads in jeans and windbreakers would hardly be feared. They might catch him unawares.

There was no party at Moye House after 1995. Michan was not asked; it was understood he would refuse, for my sake.

Moye House continued to host a reading of "The Lost Girl," but only on October 27. The writers' residence and the town's celebration have never merged again.

At seven o'clock, at evening drinks, Michan read "The Lost Girl" in the front parlor. I slipped in as he was giving a brief introduction to the story. He glanced up but kept speaking, too well practiced to be bothered by any interruption. I sat beside Ciaran on the small couch in the corner of the room.

Michan held a copy of the book, but he probably could have recited it by heart.

When he finished reading, the writers talked about the story. Sometimes it ended up sounding more like a classroom discussion, Michan once said, but this group kept it informal. I knew he would be pleased.

"Could this story be written today?" Ciaran asked. "A DNA test would answer the question in hours. Identity is no longer a riddle, as long as there are family members to compare a sample to."

Michan was intrigued by the question. Cassius would have to work around that problem. He could have made the sisters only friends, but she also would have to have been an orphan whose parents were unknown, to avoid inconvenient grandparents, aunts, uncles and cousins.

One of the women asked another question, and the discussion went a different way.

I slipped out and went to the kitchen and then outside, where I picked ivy from the gate around the kitchen garden.

The woods were dark, but I knew the way well enough. There was no one at the chapel, but I hadn't expected there would be any other girls celebrating Quicken Day as it was supposed to be celebrated.

I twined the stems of the ivy leaves together to make a small wreath and set it at the foot of the tree. Walk around the tree once and make a wish. The answer will come in a dream in nine days' time.

I walked slowly around the tree and whispered my wish. I leaned back against the trunk.

I took a small bell out of my pocket. It was called a keepsake bell, used for weddings or Christmas ornaments. Gin sold them in the bookstore. I had tied a piece of red thread through the top. I stood on tiptoe and tied the bell to a branch. Then I rang it, and as I did, I closed my eyes and saw Rowan, pulling the mask over her face and handing me my own. Fox and hare.

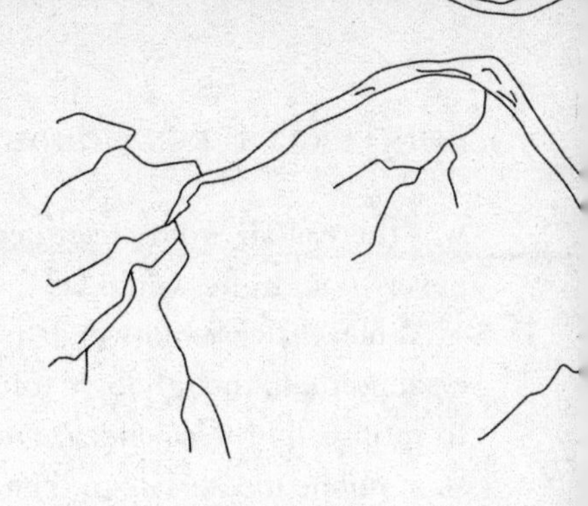

23

ADAIR

2010

Ciaran and I stayed at the back of the crowd in the Maple Street playground. I had accepted a small candle, fitted through a small paper plate to catch the wax. Preparing the candles for the vigil probably had been the project of a Girl Scout troop.

Rowan had been a Brownie, but she'd dropped out. It was boring, she'd said. I thought she'd roll her eyes at all of the earnest townspeople come to mark this anniversary, many of whom had not known her.

The mayor spoke about the power of community and said he had faith that there would be answers someday.

Ciaran's gaze was continually shifting, and I was doing the same, looking, I suppose, for a man alone. An older man. Not, in other words, men who had been children fifteen years ago. It was a dizzying thought: kindergartners of 1995 were now twenty years old.

Ciaran touched my elbow, and when I looked up at him, he jerked his chin. I followed his gaze and saw Libby with a man I initially thought must be her grandfather. I realized it was David Brayton. Libby's head was bowed over her candle. David had his hand on her back. Evelyn was not with them. If she was there at all, I didn't see her. Leo, too, was not there, but I'd never thought he would be.

When the ceremony ended, I blew out my candle, strangely disappointed, though logic told me murderers were not moved to confess by the calendar. They certainly didn't choose to do so at public memorials to their victims.

Ciaran and I let the crowd disperse around us. Libby came over and hugged him. After a startled moment, he hugged her back. She pulled away and turned to me and handed me a small gift bag. *Happy Birthday*, it said on it.

"This is that book I told you about, the one you said belongs at Moye House. I still want it back, but I wanted you to see it."

"Thank you."

She walked back to her father, head down. He was watching, but only nodded his head at Ciaran and, after a pause, at me.

The writers were in the parlor at evening drinks, all of them. Time was short now, and they were no doubt thinking about how they would be separating soon.

I went up to the third floor and down the hall to Michan's room. The door was closed, which meant he was working. I sat on the floor and tilted my head back against the wall. I closed my eyes and even dozed off before the door opened.

Michan was shrugging on his jacket.

"My very own foundling," he said.

"Very funny."

"What's up?"

I sat up straighter. "You're going out. It can wait."

"It's okay. Gin's patient."

Michan sat down opposite me, so we could see each other. There was just enough room for him.

"The anthology of stories written here, the one Ciaran's father is in? Ciaran had a copy," I said. "I read most of the stories."

"Most of them?"

"I read Ciaran's father's. And yours. 'The Last Night' by Michan McCrohan."

"I only wrote it because Jorie asked me to contribute a story to the anthology. You were I guess about seven or so when it was published. I'd decided long ago to stick to poetry."

"'The Last Night' is good," I said.

There's a blood transfusion after an accident years before the child is born. When the story opens, the mother is already dead.

"Did you think I'd never read it?" I asked. Live long enough to read it, I meant.

"Never." Michan closed his eyes briefly.

"Once you found out who Ciaran was, you must have thought that he might mention it. Why didn't you tell me?" I asked.

"Because I'm a coward."

"Don't say that."

"I came here when your father died and never left." Michan moved his hand, a gesture meant to encompass the entire house.

"It's not like you're a hermit."

Michan smiled. "What if Jorie had been in a monastery? A St. Brigid's monastery that allows men and women. Then I would be a monk and not a poet."

As if it were Moye House that had granted him his talent, his drive. As if, wherever he had taken refuge, he would have simply become part of the place. I started to say as much, but instead I smiled.

"Men and women both, but children?" I said. "I probably couldn't have lived in a monastery."

He laughed, as I meant him to, and then grew serious. "You remember that night?" he asked hesitantly. "Lissa was glad when you stopped talking about it. We thought you'd forgotten."

But I hadn't. I'd only lost the whole picture. Imagine zigzagging an eraser through a sketch done in pencil.

"I remember bits and pieces," I said. "Was it Christmas Eve? God, Michan, why would they have done that to their parents?"

Michan took so long to answer, I started to think he would not.

"Cathal tried to tell us not to come, but my mother knew —not that she said it out loud—but she knew it would be his last Christmas. She didn't tell my dad and me that we weren't invited."

"Why didn't they wait until you left?"

Again, a long silence.

"Someone in Janus's group told your mother there was an old Irish saying: the gates of heaven are open on Christmas Eve. Whoever dies that night will go straight in. All sins forgiven."

"We didn't even go to church. They couldn't have really *believed* that?" I asked, not sure if I meant in heaven, Catholicism in general, or that it allowed for that kind of loophole.

"Adair, I can't—" Michan said. "Listen to me, please. With AIDS nobody knew exactly what they'd die of or how long they had. But there were a few certainties. Your father was going first. Then Lissa would watch you die, or she would go first and you'd be without both of them. Cathal knew Lissa couldn't do it. He felt it was the last thing he could do, as a father."

"Kill me."

"Spare you." Michan's voice took on an edge that served to remind me that I'd been a child, and shielded as such.

In Michan's story, the ending is ambiguous. The father never actually turns the engine on. You don't know what happened. You don't know what to hope happened.

"What made them change their minds?" I asked.

"They didn't," Michan said. "My father woke up and went to look in on you, and you were gone. He went to Lissa and Cathal's room to see if you were there, but they were gone too. His first thought was the hospital, so he went to the garage to look for the car. Cathal had put a note on the door saying not to come in, call an ambulance. He was afraid if anybody opened the door, the fumes would knock them out."

"Did he leave the number for a funeral home that would touch us?" I asked. When I came to that part of Michan's story, I'd had to close the book.

Michan nodded. "He did. Dad went in the garage anyway. Cathal hadn't turned the engine on yet, thank God. Dad took you out of the car and put you back in bed."

The car. My parents in cold silhouette, not speaking. Arms lifting me up. Arms far stronger than my father's were by then. My cheek against a solid chest. Not a dream but a memory.

"Why did Darragh do it?" I asked.

"I don't know. It may have just been his generation. You play the hand you're dealt. You don't take the easy way out. You don't cheat. Or it might've had to do with factor VIII coming along the way it did. Miracle treatment. And it was. Before it killed us, it saved us."

You're still alive, I nearly said, but let it be. "They didn't try again."

"No. It was Christmas Eve or never."

Sins forgiven. As in suicide. As in murder.

It was my turn to close my eyes. When I opened them again, I said, “So they stayed.”

“They wouldn’t leave without you.” Michan got to his feet and held out a hand. I took it and he pulled me up.

24

ADAIR

2010

The fall residency ended on Saturday, October 30, the same day as the Quicken Day celebration, a fluke of the calendar that year. Moye House was not a hotel. Residents didn't have to be out of their rooms by eleven o'clock, but there were no extensions, even by a day. There had been writers who weren't ready to go, who asked to stay one more night, and then two. Just until I finish this part. I'll never be able to write it anywhere else.

Michan doubted it would happen anymore, given the pace of the world today, but he kept to the policy. Even if planes were canceled or trains delayed, they had to go. There was the hotel in town and a number of bed-and-breakfasts.

Ciaran and I went into town that final residency day, not to participate in the Quicken Day festivities but to observe them.

We walked around Culleton, which was crowded because the weather was good. Most of the shops had tables set up out front with items for sale. We spoke little. There were couples heading for a daytime drink, parents ushering their children, holding bits of their costumes.

The air smelled of apples and of cinnamon from the bakery, which was selling doughnuts two for a dollar. Ciaran and I sat on the bench outside Wild Books and watched the parade's uneven takeoff. The costumes were store bought. Plastic masks and capes. Disney princess dresses and cowboy hats.

When the last of the children were out of sight, having turned the corner a block away, Ciaran stood up and said he had to go. He had to pick up the keys to the studio he'd rented in Brooklyn, sight unseen.

I felt something close to panic, and then disappointment as I looked up and down the street. Had I expected, as Libby dreamed, we would turn around to see Rowan coming up the street, still a girl of twelve, grinning at us both?

Ciaran thanked me for my help. When he had Rowan's chapter written, there were bound to be questions. He would probably be back on some weekends, he thought.

"If your place is uninhabitable, come back," I said.

Ciaran laughed, and then he left for the train station, a ten-minute walk, and I went back to Moye House alone.

The next morning, returning to the house after walking Poe, I saw Ciaran coming up the path from the parking lot. I thought he'd come back because he had no place to go. The sublet he'd arranged had been a scam.

Ciaran came closer, and when he was near enough for me to see the grim set of his mouth, I understood.

"Adair—"

I wanted to run. "They found her."

"They have a place to look."

The old foundry. Two outbuildings, one a garage, one a toolshed. Fifteen years ago, both had had dirt floors. In the course of renovations done in the late 1990s, both floors had been covered with cement.

The tip had come by letter to Ciaran, mailed to his apartment in Brooklyn, unobtrusive in the stack of mail his tenant handed him.

Undated, it was typewritten on plain white paper. He'd read it and called the police

I didn't ask Michan if Ciaran could stay. I told him myself that he was welcome, as my friend. But Michan didn't object —I hadn't thought he would, particularly when Ciaran explained in detail what the letter had said.

Later, after a dinner of leftovers that both Ciaran and I barely touched, we went up to the third floor, to the small balcony off my bedroom.

We sat in two chairs we'd brought outside. The cold air felt good.

"How long will it take?" I asked, though he'd already told me more than once.

"A few days at least. They're going to bring in dogs, I think, and if they hit, then they'll dig."

"Bloodhounds?"

"Not bloodhounds, no. These are dogs specifically trained to find remains."

"Bones," I said.

Ciaran nodded.

"Tell me again what it said."

The letter writer had referred to her only as Rowan. The use of her first name suggested that the person might have known her. She was not, in other words, "the missing girl" or "Rowan Kinnane."

He (assuming it was a man) claimed to have heard the story from someone who was actually there. Late that afternoon, as it was starting to get dark, Rowan was walking alone on the road.

Two teenage boys went by in a car. They stopped beside

her and said some things. She picked up a rock and threw it at the car. It bounced off the hood. They were in front of the old foundry. Abandoned. No one around for miles. Falling-down buildings. They got out of the car and she ran into one of them. They followed. If she hadn't run, they would probably have driven off. But she ran. They chased.

They cornered her. What exactly happened doesn't matter, only that she died. They'd been drinking and they were high. Scared, they'd left the scene. Later, they went back to hide the body, afraid their car had been spotted by the side of the road. Too freaked out to put her in their car, they'd brought a shovel.

Ciaran returned to his room on the second floor. I didn't see much of him during the day. He said he was working. It was the only thing he could do. Evelyn had been told by the police detective working the case. Ciaran left her a message, but she didn't call back. I was glad Libby was with her father. Were she nearby, I had no doubt she would have gone to the foundry. She would have seen the cars parked on the road outside, the police and dog handlers and lab techs and gawkers.

One of the dogs hit on a corner of what had once been the toolshed. The police weren't releasing the information, but it was obvious when the shed was roped off with yellow Crime Scene tape and a crew was demolishing the cement floor.

On Wednesday, the day they began ripping up the floor, Ciaran and I went there, but we didn't leave the car. We watched a young reporter speaking into a camera.

"I hope to God they've told Libby," Ciaran said.

"I'm sure they have," I said.

"Her dad's an old man, Adair. I don't know that he's going to realize she'll see it online even if she's not looking. I wouldn't be surprised if she's got a Google Alert for Rowan's name."

"Evelyn will tell her."

"I don't know that she will. Evelyn might still think of her as a little girl, if she thinks of her at all."

Ciaran was right, of course. Both he and I got an angry email from Libby later that day, asking us to let her know what was going on. Ciaran answered, telling her he didn't know anything more than what was being reported.

Michan, tense, clenching his jaw so tightly that I was afraid he would crack a tooth, had been asking me every morning, "Did you take your meds?"

Yes, yes, yes.

I had carefully filled the pill organizer with a week's worth and left it on my nightstand. Every morning, I slid back the lid.

Yet I almost wished I could come down with one of the old fevers that came out of nowhere and spiked in the night while I slept, bringing the dreams of my parents and of Rowan that I thought might be more than dreams.

There was some evidence for it, I explained to Ciaran when I told him this during the long afternoon of checking our phones and trying not to check our phones. We had walked together to the residents' library and were sitting on the couches in front of the fireplace. Me on one, Ciaran on the other. It felt like we were stranded together in a beautiful train station with nothing to do but wait. Wait for someone to arrive. Wait for a train to call us to board.

Fevers did alter the brain. Children who couldn't speak sometimes did when they were sick. Some believed fevers gave a window to the dead.

"I don't know if I believe any of that," Ciaran said. "But I will tell you, as badly as you want an answer, for yourself or Evelyn or Libby—"

"For you," I said.

"For me. In the end, Rowan will still be gone. There's no point in your ruining your health for it."

I lay down on the couch, tucking a pillow beneath my head. Illness would hardly be instantaneous, but I was too tired to explain. Sometimes I could picture the scenario from the letter very vividly. Other times, it felt off. Wrong. There was something I should realize. Something lurking just out of my sight. Not Rowan herself. She had retreated, disappeared again.

Late in the afternoon on Friday, I came in from a walk on the grounds, which I'd told myself was not a search for Leo, who would be out there working. I didn't see him and I didn't have his cell phone number. But I reasoned that if he wanted to talk to me, he certainly knew where to find me.

I entered the kitchen to find Ciaran there, not reading or typing on his laptop, just sitting at the kitchen table. The lights were not on, but the room was still bright enough for me to see how red his eyes were.

"They found bones," he said.

For a minute I couldn't breathe. Then I said, "They're not Rowan's. They can't be."

"They aren't. They're animal bones," Ciaran said. "Not human. They think now that the letter is from a crank. They're done. I should have been prepared, I know that, but some part of me really thought this was it."

"I didn't," I said.

Ciaran looked at me. "Why not?"

I went over and opened the door to the servants' stairs. "Come with me?"

Ciaran followed me to the second floor, then down the hallway past my room. All the way to the loft that overlooked the library. He asked no questions, made docile by grief and disappointment. And, I thought, possibly guilt as well. Certainly, now he could continue with his book, as he'd planned it. There was no need to place Rowan in a prologue or afterword.

In the loft I asked him to sit down on one of the loveseats, and then I sat, too, on the one opposite, facing him.

Friday, October 27, 1995

I stayed home from school, the last bout with bronchitis lingering but slowly leaving.

Michan taught me how to play gin rummy and then I made him watch *Days of Our Lives* with me. He said it was the stupidest thing he'd ever seen and went and got me a book.

Lightning by Dean R. Koontz.

A better use of your time, he said.

I lay on my bed to read but soon fell asleep. It was still afternoon, light out, so I didn't turn on my lamp.

When I woke up, the room was dark. I sat up groggily, my throat so dry I could barely swallow. My fever was back. I always kept a cup of water on my nightstand, and I gulped half of it. I had just set the cup down when she appeared. I jumped and the water spilled over my hand and trickled down my arm.

Rowan was standing at the foot of my bed. She grinned and put a finger to her lips.

She had a mask on top of her head and she was holding another one.

"What are you doing?"

She said it was Quicken Day, the one that counted, not the parade one. She pulled two ribboned bells out of her pocket and showed them to me before tucking them away again.

"I'm sick," I said.

She lost her grin and came over to the bed and pressed her hand to my forehead.

"You're fine," she said.

"I've never been fine," I answered.

"We have to go."

Rowan pulled down her mask. Hare. She handed me mine. Fox.

Rowan walked quickly in the dark woods, glancing back to make sure I was keeping up.

When we reached the chapel, she pulled her mask up. I'd already done so with mine, the better to breathe. I didn't ask where she'd gotten them.

"Quiet, in case somebody's already there."

We stayed close together, walking slowly.

But nobody was at the tree. We were alone. She had a bag over her shoulder and from it she withdrew an ivy wreath, which she set beneath the tree. She walked around the tree, and then I did. We tied the bells to one of the branches.

This quicken tree was good enough for the bells, she said.

This quicken tree? I thought it, but didn't ask what she meant.

Rowan reached into her bag and took out a pair of scissors. We couldn't be blood sisters but we could exchange locks of hair, and that was almost as good.

I was tired and the world was tipping. I wanted to go back to bed. I didn't argue. I didn't ask questions. I let her snip a bit of my hair and she did the same to her own. She put her hair in a baggie and gave it to me and then put mine in a separate one.

I asked shouldn't we be mixing the hair together? That's what you were supposed to do with blood, but she said no, this was right.

Rowan pulled her mask down and pulled mine down and we walked back to Moye House together.

Ciaran listened without interrupting.

"I got back in bed, and when I woke up in the middle of the night, Michan was asleep in a chair beside the bed. I was trying to drink water, and I dropped the cup and woke him. My fever was about 102. He gave me something for it and I went back to sleep. I was never sure whether or not it really happened, or if it, and the bookstore, were all part of some dream."

"I don't know what this means," Ciaran said.

"You've asked everyone you spoke to what they think happened to her. Except for me," I said. "It's okay, though, because I wouldn't have had an answer before."

He smiled wearily. Fine. I'll play.

"What do you think happened to her?"

"The Moye House anthology. She found it."

"I never sent it to her."

Possibly she had found a copy in Byrd's Books on a day I wasn't with her. Stumbled upon it. Or maybe in those pre-Amazon days she'd called up some bookstore and had them order it, but I wasn't sure she'd have thought to do that. Maybe her mother did have a copy hidden away in their house somewhere.

I reached down and picked it up. For an anthology, it was a slender book. But then some of the stories were no more than two pages. I slipped off the book jacket to reveal the red cover beneath it.

Ciaran looked at the book and then at me.

"It might be mistaken for an envelope," I said, "if you only see it for a minute."

"You can't know for sure if she had it, Adair."

"She read it," I told him. "Because she read Michan's story, 'The Last Night.'"

Ciaran shook his head, confused. "'The Last Night'?"

The dying father and daughter. The garage.

I told him about that day in the servants' quarters when Rowan asked me to imagine the years I wouldn't have had if I'd died when my father did. Then, I hadn't thought much more about it. I was always being told I was lucky.

"She was in town the day she vanished," Ciaran said.

I nodded. "I think so. Yes."

"She was in the bookstore. She went outside. And then where does she go?"

"Anywhere," I said. "But she was probably on her way to Moye House," I said. "I think that's why she was carrying the book. Maybe she was going to put it where she thought it belonged, on our shelves with the other residents' books. She would have walked. Some man might have asked her directions. She might have gone up to the car. Somebody she knew might have pulled over to offer her a ride. She got in."

"Nobody saw her," Ciaran said.

"Nobody was looking," I said. "Not yet. Not for hours."

After a moment, Ciaran asked, "What now?"

"Write your book," I said.

He nodded, gazing past me, and I could tell he was already measuring this information, trying to frame it, trying to decide how to present it in prose.

I told him then that since we'd talked to Kit, I'd been imagining Rowan as some town's Jane Doe. In some place we'd never guess because it was so big or so small or too far away to contemplate. Perhaps she'd been mistaken for a boy and was buried as a John Doe. The remains of young girls were sometimes misread. Today, with DNA testing, it wouldn't happen. But back then, it may have. Whatever the reason, she was buried anonymously, but properly, in a cemetery with a headstone. On the anniversary of when she was found, the locals brought her flowers and tried to guess her name. They never would. Maybe Ciaran's book would find its way to one such citizen, or maybe some of the police officers who'd worked the case and had never let it go. They'd look up from the the photos of Rowan Kinnane, breath catching, knowing where they have seen her face before.

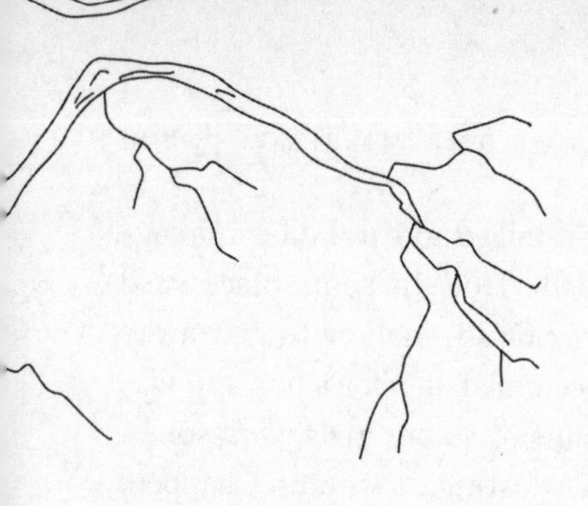

25
ADAIR
2010

Again, in the dark, I climbed Leo's porch. It was cold for early November. I'd pulled a black winter coat out of my closet that I hadn't worn in years. My next-season clothes were still packed in the boxes I'd brought back from Brooklyn.

Wearing it, I'd gone to Michan's rooms and knocked, not sure if he'd be there. But when he answered, I told him where I was going. He didn't tell me, as he had before, that I must find a way to tell new people. It was no good to seek friends and boyfriends only among those who already knew. But that advice was part of the reason I'd left Leo years ago, because I thought I had to at least try, no matter what I really wanted. This time, Michan only hesitated, and told me to be careful.

This time when I knocked, Leo opened the door. He didn't say anything as I followed him down the hall.

At the kitchen he paused, then asked, "Can you drink on whatever you're taking?"

I laughed. "I'm supposed to drink in moderation."

He rolled his eyes. "Me too."

I sat down on the couch and watched him pour two beers. He handed me one and sat down beside me.

"The brother's gone?" Leo said.

I nodded. "He's finished. He only stayed longer because of the search. He left yesterday."

"With no answers."

"He doesn't want answers. He wants questions," I said. "He does think they should have searched the foundry longer. But she's not there."

"How do you know that?" Leo asked. "It was abandoned then. It's possible." I explained Rowan's search for the Moye House anthology with her father's story in it, and why I believed the book was what I saw in her hand the day she disappeared.

Leo listened, very still, waiting for the moment when all of this began to mean something.

There was one children's story in the anthology. It was written by a woman named Winifred Coen. Edward Adair illustrated many of her books, which took place in the gardens of Moye House. He drew the rose garden, the kitchen garden, the wildflower garden. She also wrote about Degare Mountain and the surrounding woods.

For the anthology story, Edward drew the quicken tree—the rowan tree—by the chapel, and another one, a flying rowan, deeper in the woods, up the mountain, beneath an outcrop.

The story is about a bird that takes a berry from the rowan tree by the chapel and drops it into an old oak tree that's split in two. From there, the second tree begins to grow. The bird flies back and forth between the mother tree and the daughter, telling each about the other.

I reached into my bag and took out the book. I touched the title, the letters in gold against the red cover, and opened it to the drawing of the flying rowan.

Leo studied it, then looked up at me with a shake of his head, puzzled.

Then I showed him the book Libby had given me, *A Charm for Lasting Love: Spells and Cures from Ireland.*

"It was written by Lucy, Helen's daughter. I think these were her mother's remedies. Edward Adair did these drawings too. He was her husband. I assume it was among his books and papers donated to Moye House when he died. Rowan took it."

I handed it to Leo. "Page fifty-two," I said.

The heading said, "A Cure for the Chronically Ill."

Cut a lock of hair from the head of the ill person. Go to the flying rowan and slice the bark of the tree. Put the hair inside the cut. The bark will heal over the hair. Pick three berries from the tree and plant them. The ill person will become well.

Leo closed the book and silently handed it back to me.

Then he leaned forward, and I knew that he understood what I did, that Rowan had seen and read these things and they had led her to believe she alone could save my life.

"Have you seen the flying rowan?" I asked. "Did she ever ask you where it was?"

"I know where it is," Leo said. "It's called an epiphyte. A tree that grows from another tree. One of the rangers I worked with at Degare showed it to me when I was training for the job. It's off the regular hiking trails. Rowan never asked me about it. To go off and try to find it, that's literally looking for one tree out of thousands. She wasn't stupid, Adair."

"But she was stubborn," I said. "The sketch in the book shows the surrounding area. The ledge right above it? She might have thought it'd be easy to spot."

"I bet she thought if she asked me, I'd have told her not to go off into the woods by herself." Leo smiled sadly. "And I would have. But maybe I would've taken her there."

"Tomorrow we can find it together. You'll take me there."

Leo spoke so softly that I had to lean in to hear him. "If she got lost out there looking for this tree, this flying rowan, there's no telling where she is, Adair."

I closed my eyes. Rowan, sitting still for the night, knees to her chest in the dark, moving again in the morning. How long? How many days? There may have been an accident. She may indeed have been gone before Evelyn began to look for her.

"Can I still root for Libby's theory?" Leo smiled. "Rowan did go back in time. Maybe we can find a way to get there too. Nobody would know us."

Imagine a life in the past. Imagine turning this life's whole history into the future, safely distant. But the comfort in that was not for me.

"I couldn't go with you," I said, and felt the loss as if he'd really found a way to go. I'd never told him that I picked him the day he shook my hand.

I leaned over and touched his cheek. He turned to my palm, and I saw he realized why. Thinking, maybe, of the pill organizer, empty, the medication a century out of reach.

"I have to look. I have to try," I said. "I owe her that."

"It could take forever," Leo said.

"I have forever."

Rowan could not have known the virus that was supposed to be the cause of my death would soon be tamed, if not cured. She was my cousin, a cousin so distant it perhaps shouldn't have counted, but it did. Still, set aside whatever blood we shared. She was my friend. She died for me.

ACKNOWLEDGMENTS

Ghosts of the Missing sold on the basis of a single sentence and never would have become an entire novel without the guidance of my agent, Caryn Karmatz Rudy. Thank you, as ever, for your advocacy and for your friendship.

To my editors, Lauren Wein and Pilar Garcia-Brown, thank you both for the insights that made this book better with each draft.

Thank you to masterly manuscript editor Larry Cooper as well as the entire team at Houghton Mifflin Harcourt for all their hard work.

My parents have always been supportive, and for this I will always be grateful, as I am to my sister Elizabeth, my brother-in-law Alex, and my nieces and nephews: Eddie, Megan, Nicky, Lily, Kristen, Michael, and Luke.

In the acknowledgments of my first novel, I thanked my sisters, "the two people who have always been on either side of me." Though Jennifer is gone and we are now two, this will always be so.

As my writing desk is in a corner of my living room, I am indebted to both the Brooklyn Writers Space and Park Slope Desk for providing me with an affordable place to work outside my apartment.

To my husband, Travis, and my son, Liam, who said goodbye and good night for countless evenings as I left to "go writing": when it was time to come home, it meant everything to know that you would both be there.